Landscape by Design

LANDSCAPE BY DESIGN

Tony Aldous with Brian Clouston

Research by Rosemary Alexander

HEINEMANN:LONDON

William Heinemann Ltd.

10 Upper Grosvenor Street,
London W1X 9PA

LONDON MELBOURNE TORONTO

JOHANNESBURG AUCKLAND

© Landscape Institute 1979

ISBN 434 01805 8

Printed in Great Britain by
Butler & Tanner Ltd., Frome and London

Published on the occasion of the Golden Jubilee of
the Landscape Institute

FOREWORD

KENSINGTON PALACE
LONDON W8 4PU

A client will only use the services of a professional when he has accepted the concept, that a trained and experienced brain is more likely to achieve an effective plan, than that of a well intentioned amateur, hoping that common sense will solve all problems.

Professions consequently are dependent on their tradition for providing a service, in order to advance. There is therefore the greatest difficulty in creating a new profession that has to work twice as well to provide both its tradition of service and find its clients at the same time.

This book traces the story of how the profession of Landscape Architects developed its skills and at the same time convinced a sceptical public of the need for its services.

It is a story of how personalities managed to show, through their skill, that their work was not just a form of rural decoration for the affluent and leisured, but a vital necessity for the survival of an environment, threatened by ever bigger machines and more ambitious projects, whose scale was beyond the experience of most architects and designers.

Inevitably it was a battle to show that it was right to spend large sums of money on landscaping, even if there was no return on this money to those who spent it but 'only' to the community in general. The successes and failures to get this concept accepted are all too obvious to see.

Any history will lack drama when we know the final outcome; but a 50th Anniversary is a suitable occasion to record the work of the pioneers and at a time, when the Profession thrives, it is salutary for all concerned to read of the early struggle and to appreciate the foundations on which the professional traditions are most firmly planted.

vii

In offering my congratulations for the 50th Anniversary of the Institute, I know that they are all the more sincere for having read this book and the story it tells. Your next 50 years should be easier as your collective reputation should mature along with the many schemes you have designed even if inevitably nature gets most of the credit which should be yours!

As a member of the public I would like to thank you for what you have achieved as a whole for the community, and hope that the knowledge that what you have done was worth doing is sufficient recompense in view of the lack of public acknowledgement of the effect you have had on the environment.

Richard.

Introduction

This book sketches the story of the landscape profession in the United Kingdom during the five decades since the foundation of the Landscape Institute in 1929. The story is subdivided according to the type of client who has commissioned substantial landscape work during this period. If the book had been written by a landscape architect, it is likely that its framework would have been based on the land or on the use to which the land is put, for the interaction of these two lies at the heart of professional landscape work.

However the structure adopted reveals that a large number of land-using interests now see landscape design and the proper care of the landscape as an important adjunct to their activities. In recent years these organizations have also started to employ ecologists and other land scientists; their investment must lead them on to more frequent employment of landscape managers in future.

The book also shows how many active landscape architects there now are. Understandably, the work discussed is by senior members of the Institute, but there is now also a large body of younger members, who have experience behind them and are gaining in stature and skill all the time. The situation presented is more encouraging than is usually apparent.

As the Institute grows in size and its members grow both in experience and in breadth of outlook – a trend particularly encouraged by the recent addition of science and management decision makers to the original membership of landscape architects – there is growing pressure to improve technical knowledge. This must partly be achieved through formal research of which much more is needed. But much could also be achieved simply by bringing together analytically the knowledge already available to individual members. Many members have created successful landscapes, shaping land, restoring dereliction, designing pavings and terraces, establishing vegetation of many sorts in town and country, on coast and mountainside, in hostile and gentle environments. I have seen many design and written theses by students, which explore the

INTRODUCTION

borders of knowledge, illuminating a new aspect of landscape work. But all this knowledge remains unavailable, like alluvial gold buried in the bed of the river of our members' enthusiastic involvement in day to day life. We need to expose this information, sift the sands of everyone's experience in the sure knowledge that many precious grains and nuggets are there. Until this is achieved, it will be necessary to tolerate patiently calls for proof that there is a unique discipline or a distinctive academic core of landscape architecture justifying academic and professional recognition. Our own faith in the seriousness of our activity will need to be backed up by demonstrable information before it comes to be shared by everyone else.

At the same time members of the Institute must sometimes ask why so few others know that they can help to solve landscape problems. The architectural press, for instance, sometimes propounds as a new sort of problem a subject which many landscape architects have been solving for years.

Behind the difficulty encountered in gaining recognition for practical performance as a major contribution to society, there lies an attitude to priorities which starts in the values of many leading thinkers. Historians, for instance, rarely see history in a way which can properly value creativity as a widespread human activity of the highest value. In his generally delightful book *The Imperial Age of Venice 1380–1580*, Dr. D. S. Chambers of the University of London writes of education in that city in the early sixteenth century: 'It is not at all clear how much an adequate primary, to say nothing of an elementary education, was available to the majority of those inhabiting Venice ... Some of the ample funds of the *scuole grandi* or the *procuratas* of St. Mark might have been better spent on providing education.' Education for what? At that moment the majority of those inhabiting Venice were in the middle of creating the most marvellous city in Europe, in which every paving stone, bridge detail, street light, humble alleyway or important piazza sings out a sophisticated education in tactile creativity. Dr. Chambers might have questioned what sort of educational values achieved this result. Whatever they were they are needed in Britain now, more perhaps than those referred to by Dr. Chambers.

The Landscape Institute exists to promote and conserve fine landscape. For this purpose technical and professional skill alone, though essential, are not enough. A mood which includes the landscape as part of the process of thinking about everything must also

INTRODUCTION

underlie the ideals of the whole population, in particular those who govern.

The craftsmanship exists already. In this country tnere is a marvellous horticultural tradition with numerous growers of impeccable skill. Landscape contractors tend to like doing a good job and to do it honestly. There are many machine drivers as skilful as any craftsman from older traditions. I have seen a JCB operator use the spikes on his bucket to create a fine tilth, caressing the soil with his great machine as delicately as a swallow shaping its nest with its beak; a master drag line operator can throw his ten ton bucket to cut away spoil a few inches from precious flowers to be conserved. To call upon such skill is part of the pleasure of our task. To inculcate delicacy towards the landscape into society has become an obligation for the landscape professions. It needs to be common knowledge that understanding of the land and vegetation should precede policy making, that change in the landscape requires art to design it properly, and that the whole landscape needs continuing care since it is a living thing.

We do not need to be too shy of our little size. Bacon pointed out three hundred and fifty years ago in his description 'Of the True Greatness of Kingdoms and Estates' that 'the Kingdom of Heaven is compared, not to any kernel or nut, but to a grain of mustard seed; which is one of the least grains, but hath in it a property and spirit hastily to get up and spread'. Of Gardens he wrote: 'God Almighty first planted a garden. And indeed it is the purest of human pleasures. It is the greatest refreshment to the spirits of man; without which buildings and palaces are but gross handyworks; and a man shall ever see that when ages grow to civility and elegancy, men come to build stately sooner than to garden finely; as if gardening were the greater perfection.'

HAL MOGGRIDGE

Contents

Photographic Credits

Sylvia Crowe, CEGB, Maurice Lee, James Riddell, Geoffrey Collens, David Atkins, Colin Westwood, Will Pulling, Mary Mitchell, Richard Bryant, John Dewar, John Maltby, Derek Lovejoy & Partners, Machinary, Susan Jellicoe, Architectural Press.

List of Plates

Preface

The Landscape Institute commissioned me to write this book for a number of reasons. The first and most obvious was that 1979 marks the fiftieth anniversary of the Institute of Landscape Architects, the foundation on which the new Institute – which includes also land scientists and landscape managers – has been formed. But a second reason implicit in the commission was the tremendous change that has taken place in the nature of the profession and its work during the last thirty of those fifty years.

From the Institute's foundation until the Second World War, landscape architects in Britain worked almost exclusively on the design of gardens. In the postwar period they were called upon to design much wider landscapes – for large power stations, whole new towns, industrial complexes, motorways, North Sea oil terminals and other large developments. Today in Britain, few large-scale developments can sensibly be embarked upon without the early involvement of the landscape profession in their design. Its clients, and the public at large, are belatedly realizing that good landscape design and management can transform people's living and working environments, and their attitudes towards them; and that the earlier the landscape designer is involved the more satisfactory the result is likely to be. For landscape is not a cosmetic, to be applied after the main stage of development is settled; it is – or should be – a major factor right from the start in the overall design.

The landscape profession today is, then, not a collection of long-haired aesthetes designing gardens for other, richer aesthetes. It is a collection of highly professional men and women involved in creating the best settings for large-scale developments, ranging from inner city renewal in Britain to new towns and other large projects in the Middle East and the developing countries; from major industrial complexes to prestige speculative housing schemes. The profession, though small in numbers as compared with architects or engineers, now has a workload valued in tens and hundreds of millions of pounds. All this a wider public now

PREFACE

dimly discerns, but the full picture has never really been shown to them.

Neither the Institute nor I realized, when agreeing that I should write this book, quite how big a task it would turn out to be. The volume of information and advice showered upon me was all but overwhelming. The task of turning it into a book – as well as the chance to visit designed landscapes both classic and modern – has proved both fascinating and rewarding; and I should like to express my thanks to the Institute for giving me those opportunities.

In the forefront of other acknowledgements I must place my warm thanks to Rosemary Alexander, an indefatigable and most effective research assistant, without whose efforts the book could never have been written; also to Brian Clouston who put Mrs. Alexander's services at my disposal, set the book project up, and was a most hospitable host when showing me landscape schemes in the northeast of England. I thank warmly Geoffrey Collens for his valuable advice and assistance in the selection of illustrations. Finally I thank most sincerely all the landscape architects who gave their time and effort for the interviews on which this book is in large measure based, and state that any errors or omissions arising from those extracts are the responsibility of the author alone.

TONY ALDOUS

Chapter 1
NATURE'S WAY AND
MAN'S WAY

As applied to most parts of Britain, the term 'natural landscape'
is a misnomer. Almost all British landscape is manmade in some
degree. Our lowland countryside of fields, hedgerows and woods
results from man's deliberate intervention in the past – from a
series of enclosures of unfenced and unhedged open land which
took place from medieval times up to the 'parliamentary enclosures' of the eighteenth century. Those eighteenth-century enclosures, with their characteristic regularity of field shape, were (as
Professor W. G. Hoskins has pointed out) only the most thoroughgoing and systematic version of a process that had been going on
for many centuries. But even the fells of the English Lake District
are in some sense manmade. The lower fells at least are what they
are because man put sheep and highland cattle to graze on them.
Take those animals away and, within a very few years, you have
in place of the smooth green grass-covered hills first bracken, then
an increasingly wild and impenetrable tangle of scrub.

Two factors governed what man could do to landscape: climate
and his numbers and technical resources. Before man came on the
scene Britain had a tundra-like landscape, with mosses and lichens
its only vegetation. By about 5500 B.C., with a warmer climate,
Middle Stone Age man's landscape included Scots pines, oaks,
elms and the small-leaved lime, with birch on the hills and alders
and willows in wetter places. At about this time Britain's land
bridge with Continental Europe disappeared, fixing the range of
our native flora. By 2500 B.C. Stone Age man had become a
farmer: he grew corn, grazed animals, cleared the forest. He had
begun making the landscape. But – despite the direct and ecological
effects of these activities – for the next 3,000 years his numbers and
impact were tiny. The English landscape as we know it today, said
Hoskins in 1955 in his pioneering *The Making of the English Land-*

scape, is almost entirely the product of the last 1,500 years. In that book and the county studies which followed, he and his collaborators showed again and again that landscape features which country dwellers as well as visitors take for granted as 'natural', in reality have their origins in the social and economic needs and practices of earlier centuries.

Hoskins regards 500–450 B.C. as a turning point, after which man's impact increasingly altered the face of the English (and to a lesser extent Scots, Welsh and Irish) landscapes. Invasions and migrations transformed Britain from a country whose population, numbered in tens or hundreds of thousands, merely scratched at its surface, into one with a population numbered in millions, steadily clearing and cultivating a large part of its total land area. Monastic communities had a particularly potent effect on surrounding landscapes. Visitors to such sites as Fountains Abbey in Yorkshire often remark: 'The monks knew how to pick their sites.' In reality the monks *made* those landscapes: clearing, planting, damming streams, altering the microclimate; building stone walls to contain and shelter their flocks, thus changing the landscape directly and – for instance, through more intensive grazing – indirectly. But, quantitatively, peasant farmers played a much bigger role than monks in making the landscape: many of its idiosyncrasies and attractions stem from the practical and social exigencies of the medieval 'frontiersmen'.

All this, however, was utilitarian. A sweet and seemly landscape grew almost entirely from functional activities. Only in Tudor times did this to any great degree change. The Dissolution of the Monasteries and sequestration of their lands helped to create a new order of lay proprietors with a sense of style and pretensions not previously found in Britain, just at a time when internal stability and peace decreased the need for fortified dwellings. Instead of tiny, walled gardens within castle walls (cultivated for herbs as well as beauty), the Tudor magnate could push his garden outwards into a park. This, perhaps, marks the beginning of consciously designed landscape.

And yet in truth consciously designed gardens did exist in this island fourteen centuries earlier, under the Romans. Miles Hadfield tells us that the earliest known garden in Britain – that of the famous Fishbourne villa in Sussex – dates from around 75 A.D. It was a regular, geometric affair some 75,000 sq. ft. in size: a place of straight paths, pergolas, and fountains. After the Romans, in the

Dark Ages, 'designed' gardens, like so much else, went by the board. Then, from the fifteenth century onwards, with the spread of Renaissance ideas, the concept of gardens as works of art came to England from Mediterranean lands; and in such early examples as Montacute (c. 1590) and Wolsey's Hampton Court, we find an altogether geometric formality – straight gravelled paths, rectangular 'canals' – almost as if garden design in England had picked up where the Romans of Fishbourne left off.

This formal, geometric approach persisted into the seventeenth century, with great landowners like 'Planter John' Montague laying out straight, long, tree-lined avenues (at Boughton in Northants, Montague could boast seventy miles of formal avenues). At least in the later seventeenth century, the great inspiration was the French landscape architect André Le Nôtre (1613–1700) who laid out Versailles for Louis XIV. The scale of his work was immense. At Vaux-le-Vicomte, laid out for the young Louis's finance minister Fouquet, the landscape took five years and the equivalent in today's money of £5 million to create; it involved demolition of three villages and two churches, and employed 18,000 men. It also contributed to Fouquet's fall. Louis took over the design team: Le Vau the architect, Le Brun the interior designer and Le Nôtre the landscape architect. It may be noted that the landscape architect had at least equal status, the design of the gardens being considered an integral part of the ensemble of chateau and grounds. Landscape was *not* a cosmetic extra to be added on cheaply once the building's design was already settled.

In England gardens followed this formal fashion, though on a markedly more modest scale, right into the eighteenth century. George London and Henry Wise, with their 100-acre nursery at Brompton, then west of the metropolis, often provided both designs and plant materials; they had been pupils of Charles II's garden designer, John Rose, who it seems had studied under Le Nôtre in France. But already when London and Wise were at the height of their influence, radical new ideas on garden design were beginning to influence some potential patrons – ideas which would eventually end not only in formal garden landscapes becoming unfashionable in England, but in all but a handful being destroyed in the face of a new and studiedly informal style which the world came to think of as essentially the English Garden.

Two strands of ideas seem to have intertwined to bring this about: one aesthetic, one political. The first had much to do with the Grand Tour and greater travel abroad. We find Addison as early as 1703 poo-pooing the Italian gardens which were the original source of English formal styles. He believed that 'nature is at her happiest when she comes nearest to art'; that is to say, instead of a laboured and obvious symmetry, he wanted the appearance of nature subtly contrived as a painter might seek to do, to maximum aesthetic and dramatic effect. And indeed painters as well as writers had a profound influence on changing taste. As Edward Hyams has put it, 'landscape painters showed the gardeners how to make great works of art out of the elements of landscape'. Claude Lorraine, Poussin and Salvator Rosa were among the key figures here.

As for political ideas, it is clear that the antipathy of the rising Whig aristocracy in Britain towards the kind of centralist, autocratic rule exercised by Louis XIV, extended also to the absolutist fashions in architecture and landscape design associated with the French monarchy. There was so much ostentatious display, so many trees in serried ranks, not valued individually but for their disciplined adherence to a centrally imposed order. Georgian gentlemen, unlike their French contemporaries, were politically emancipated and fiercely independent. Their monarchy was constitutional and limited; their monarchs lived relatively modestly. They were, nonetheless, much concerned with appearances – with 'taste', with good design and handsome proportion. But, in garden design as in architecture or furniture, subtlety and classical understatement were the order of the day. The English approach to landscape design, as enunciated by Horace Walpole, asked the designer to 'consult the *genius loci*' – to build his landscape round the individual character of a particular site, taking its topographical features and using them to maximum effect.

'Capability' Brown carried forward this approach not by developing these 'picturesque' theories, but by applying them on a larger scale. His strength lay in a superb grasp of scale in landscape. Surprise, variety, concealment, the serpentine line of beauty; looped drives, belts of trees to conceal, clump planting, and the lake in the valley, visible from the house – all these he took and used, but bigger and more boldly. After Capability came Humphry Repton, merchant and watercolourist, who took up landscape architecture in the late 1780s, deliberately filling the vacuum left by Brown's death. He continued his approach, defending it against the attacks of a new picturesque school that sought 'rugged gran-

4

deur' and found Capability's calm, rounded contours too bland; but he provided more small-scale landscape features closer to the house – walks for the household among shrubberies and flowers. His approach was akin to the modern practitioner's 'survey, analysis, design'; and in his famous *Red Books*, of which he produced more than 400 to show clients what he proposed for their properties, he customarily employed the 'slide' rather as in children's 'pop-up' books today; the reader pulled a paper tab, and the picture changed magically from the existing to the intended landscape.

The nineteenth century introduced many new species brought by plant collectors from distant lands, and a new eclecticism. A rising middle class with money but often without much taste drove design out of gardens. Joseph Paxton, best known for his Crystal Palace building for the 1851 Great Exhibition, rose from the position of head gardener to the Duke of Devonshire to become architect, landscape architect, MP, businessman and the Duke's chief adviser and friend, creating for him at Chatsworth a prodigious landscape set-piece and having a profound and pioneering influence in public landscape design. But despite his eminence, he often fought in vain – even in the Royal Parks – for garden *design* as distinct from indiscriminate flower bedding. Other important influences in the nineteenth and twentieth centuries included William Robinson's *The English Flower Garden* of 1883; Gertrude Jekyll, a painter who carried the Impressionist approach into garden design; J. C. Loudon and his wife Jane; the Garden City movement of the early twentieth century; civic and highway landscape design as practised by Olmsted in the United States; and the work of Scandinavian architects such as Alvar Aalto and Arne Jacobsen, who designed their buildings into the landscape in a way then unknown here.

During the last thirty years three major developments have changed the scope and impact of landscape design in Britain. The first – a huge and rapid expansion from garden design to the much wider and larger-scale field of landscape for big public and industrial or commercial developments – is the thread which runs through Chapters Two to Twelve of this book. The second – a broadening of the skills and concerns of landscape practice, more especially by an awareness of the ecological implications of landscape design – is also a constant counterpoint in particular projects described in these later chapters. The third development – change in, and conservation of, Britain's rural landscapes – perhaps demands some further mention in this opening chapter. The appearance of our countryside, we have seen, is largely the product of functional needs and activities rather than conscious aesthetic decisions. Sheep and hill cattle keep the uplands in grass rather than bracken and scrub; traditional lowland husbandry until fairly recently preserved the familiar 'enclosure' landscape of field and hedge and coppice. But new agricultural technology and the nation's demand for cheap food changed that. Agricultural efficiency meant big fields suitable for mechanized agriculture; fewer hedgerows and ditches, fewer woods and spinneys.

Subsidies offered primarily on social grounds have kept hill farming alive and thus, indirectly, familiar upland landscapes. Greater recreational use, though it brings welcome fresh sources of income, tends to put pressure on hill farmers and therefore on the landscapes they maintain. The Countryside Commission's Upland Management Experiment (UMEX), by making available extra resources in a flexible way, has helped to maintain a balance in many areas; though conflict between farming economics and landscape conservation in Exmoor recently convinced government that it must intervene to protect valued wild landscapes.

In the lowlands, a combination of mechanized efficiency and Dutch elm disease has transformed many areas from the ecologically and visually rich pattern of traditional enclosure landscapes to an almost prairie nakedness. Here the Countryside Commission, after lengthy studies, is seeking to show how these new agricultural landscapes can be given visual interest and incident, a new kind of beauty, and a reasonably healthy wildlife. Its Demonstration Farms Project, presided over by Ralph Cobham of Clouston, Cobham & Partners, is already showing how skilful planting and conservation measures, economically carried out and generously grant-aided, can strengthen and restore farm landscapes without impeding farm efficiency. Most encouragingly, the scheme (like the Commission's Urban Fringe experiments) has produced many more takers than its experimental stage can handle. It will take many, many decades to repair farm landscapes denuded in the first full flush of productivity-at-all-costs farming; but at least now farmers, landowners and the Ministry of Agriculture all publicly accept that landscape and wildlife conservation are important; and the Commission and its consultants are busily showing them how to reconcile these with farm productivity.

The rise in conservationist thinking has also made people more aware of threats to the great historic *manmade* landscapes of past centuries. Sometimes, as at Stourhead (the National Trust) or Fountains Abbey (North Yorkshire County Council), an enlightened owner possesses the resources, skill and will, not only to preserve but to restore what are, indeed, major works of art – though by their nature of a most vulnerable kind. Elsewhere ignorance, lack of concern, and lack of resources are all too common. It was this state of affairs that led a past president of the Institute of Landscape Architects, J. St. Bodfan Gruffydd, to undertake a study into the feasibility of protecting such historic landscapes by law, rather in the same way as statute protects historic buildings. This notion is a radical and controversial one; but Mr. Gruffydd's report, *Protecting Historic Landscapes: Gardens and Parks*, demonstrated both an acute need for some kind of protection and, by reference to selected sites in Oxfordshire, the feasibility of scheduling for protection the essential and conservable elements of landscape design as distinct from their more ephemeral aspects. They need protection at least as much from outsiders as from wanton or unthinking owners. The road engineer who tried (unsuccessfully) to thrust a high speed road through the historic avenue of oaks at Levens Park, Cumbria, would not have taken a knife to a Turner painting. He knew not what he did. Scheduling might at least divert people from unthinking vandalism. The climate of official and public opinion is now more favourable than ever before to landscape conservation – if only we can get the machinery and the economics right.

Chapter 2
THE PRIVATE CLIENT

Eighteenth Century to the Present Day

The relationship between client and landscape designer is the key
to many of the most inspiring or delightful garden landscapes, both
in the eighteenth-century 'golden age' of the English garden and
down to the present day. Perhaps it is partly that an owner feels
more able to intervene and influence the development of landscape
than he would with a house and its architect. Growth is more
gradual and organic; there is very little finality about a garden,
and there may be a sense too of mistakes being less irrevocable.
Sometimes, the owner is the 'designer'; sometimes his enthusiastic
and understanding patron; sometimes his essential partner in the
design process.

Thus what perhaps launched the great age of eighteenth-century
English landscape design was the arrival back in England from Italy
in 1719 of the Earl of Burlington *and* his protégé William Kent,
full of enthusiasm for Palladian architecture to be recreated here
not in an authentic Italian garden setting, but in an idealized pastoral landscape made to match. Kent's work as seen at Chiswick
and at Mereworth Castle shows something that to today's eyes looks
remarkably formal, and yet it did mark a substantial step away
from the geometrical approach of Le Nôtre and towards nature as art
or art in nature. These landscapes are in essence a series of vignettes;
and as has often been said Kent showed himself a markedly better
painter in landscape than on canvas. Moreover he was able to
share Burlington's enthusiasms. Thus at Chiswick the finished
set-piece of pool reflecting obelisk and rising terraces designed to
display orange trees in tubs, so entranced him that he stayed all
night 'as if enchanted ... until released by the morning sun'.

The relationship between individual client and landscape designer, and the personal interest and knowledge shown over a

period of years by the client, have often been crucial and also creative in a way which collective clients, whether public bodies or large corporations, find it difficult to achieve. For instance at Stourhead the banker Henry Hoare as individual client was, in very considerable measure, creator of the scene which the National Trust now conserves for posterity. Henry 'the Magnificent' took an immense pride in the way in which, over more than half a century, he caused that landscape to be developed and embellished. The detailed ideas seem to have been generally his rather than any outsider's, as the following passage of a letter from him to Harriet Dungarvan written in 1770 shows.

I am building a Hermitage above the Rock, & when you are about a quarter part up the Walk from the Rock to the Temple of Apollo you turn short to the right and so zig-zag up to it as Mr Hamilton advised. And we stop or plant up in Clumps the old walk up the Hill to that Temple. It is to be lined inside and out with old Gouty nobbly oakes, the Bark on.... I believe I shall put in to be myself the Hermit.

At Castle Howard, too, we have clear evidence of the creative role of the owner/client, in this case the Earl of Carlisle. His professional landscaper was George London but, in one respect at least, he rejected the consultant's plans. Stephen Switzer (1682–1745) records in his *Ichnographia Rustica* that London 'prescribed within Wray Wood a star which would have spoiled the wood but that his Lordship's superlative genius prevented it and to the great advancement of the design has given it that labyrinth diverting model we now see it ...'; and Miles Hadfield tells us that documents in the possession of Castle Howard's present owner, Mr. George Howard, suggest that this 'was not servile flattery but a genuine tribute'.

It may be argued that the real distinction in the eighteenth century was not between landscape designer and client, but between professional and 'amateur'. But the word amateur is for many readers misleading and the distinction is, I suspect, otiose. For the important difference here is not between the man who earns his living by designing landscape and the man who (though he may have studied the subject as thoroughly) neither needs nor considers it fitting to 'act professionally'. It is rather between the designer called in, seeing the landscape with new eyes, to advise on implementation, and the owner who has lived with that landscape and will continue to live with it; who not only will regularly test how vistas and surprises work in practice, but will be aware how

9

weather and climate and the changing lights and seasons colour
for those who experience them the results of that detailed design.

Moreover the eighteenth-century client/landowner generally
had posterity very much in mind, and could take a long view of
the results of planting, even if like Viscount Cobham at Stowe he
also wanted to make an impressive show for present consumption
and (as Vanbrugh put it) 'spends all he has to spare ... on the improvement of his house and gardens' – Elysian Fields, Palladian
Bridge, Temple of the British Worthies and so on and so on. The
professionals at Stowe were Vanbrugh, Bridgeman, Kent and (to
a doubtful extent) Capability Brown; but from 1733 when he
ceased to hold political office Cobham devoted much time and
attention to the development of the estate.

Cobham was also important as a patron of the young Capability,
for though Brown's contribution to actual design at Stowe seems
to have been limited, he did progress there from merely a worker
in the kitchen garden to the role of head gardener, not only trusted
with *some* design for Cobham's landscapes but permitted and perhaps encouraged to draw up designs for other landowners. Paxton,
by contrast, went to Chatsworth in 1826 in the role of head gardener, (having been spotted by the 6th Duke of Devonshire working
in the Gardens of the Horticultural Society at Chiswick) and graduated to the status of trusted adviser, business manager and friend.
His own account of his arrival at Chatsworth is charming enough
to bear repetition. He arrived at Chatsworth at 4.30 am, climbed
the park wall and explored the garden, set the men to work at
6 am and then went to have breakfast with the housekeeper Mrs.
Gregory and her niece Sarah Bown. After 'the latter fell in love
with me and I with her, and thus completed my first morning's
work at Chatsworth before 9 o'clock', he and Sarah Bown
married the following year.

A very close relationship grew up over the next thirty years
between Paxton and the Duke, who wrote of him that he was 'to
me a friend, if ever a man had one'. He took Paxton on extensive
tours of Europe, and entrusted him with his personal financial
affairs as well as estate matters at Bolton Abbey and Lismore as
well as Chatsworth. Paxton put the garden there, which he found
in a neglected state, quickly to rights. He introduced and accom-
modated exotics in a new greenhouse of his own design, laid out
the arboretum, and built the Wellington Rock, which visitors may
easily think occurred there naturally; and he designed in 1843 the

Emperor Fountain, still the highest gravity-fed fountain in the world, with the eight-acre Emperor Lake to feed it.

In contrast to Paxton and Brown, both self-made and patron-made men, who became the friends and confidants of those for whom they worked, and increasingly more sophisticated in their tastes and methods, Repton was sophisticated and well connected before, propelled by financial loss and the gap left by Capability's death, he set up as landscape consultant by writing round to rich and influential friends canvassing his services.

Has the twentieth century no equivalent of the Carlisles, Cobhams, Hoares and Devonshires of yesteryear? Not many, it seems. If we look for counterparts to Henry Hoare, the owner who is in large measure his own designer, there are however two twentieth-century instances that spring to mind: Clough Williams-Ellis at Portmeirion, and Pochin or Aberconway at Bodnant. Portmeirion is pre-eminently landscape of the townscape kind rather than landscape garden; but its creation underlines the truth that most of our most attractive townscapes are of gradual, organic growth, though in this case consciously created over the years by one man's artistic eye. It is an Italian hill town scene painted in bricks and stone and stucco and tiles, generally (though not quite everywhere!) three dimensionally. And, like many a great garden, the picture has depended not only on that one man's overall vision, but on his attention to detail – so that some would say that, since Sir Clough's death, the loss of that eye for detail and one-man owner/designer control has already resulted in small changes carried out in a way that he would never have sanctioned.

Bodnant – that is to say, the gardens, not the house – is of course now a National Trust property. But the controlling mind is still that of Lord Aberconway, who, following in his father's footsteps, has known that garden all his life, and for the past twenty-five years guided and ruled its development. It was his father, the second Lord Aberconway, Bodnant's master for half a century, who saved, transported there and restored the beautiful Pin Mill whose façade makes such a striking set-piece at the end of a terrace of formal gardens flanking a canal – a coup which may be dubbed 'opportunist' in the best sense of the word. The present Lord Aberconway adopts the same gradualist approach to Bodnant's development. If a tree falls to the gale, there may well, for example, be a chance to open a new vista down into the Dell or across the valley, to engage in judicious new planting, or bend a path and add a vantage point seat. The National Trust appreciates that a resident tenant, if he has an eye for these things, is a landscape's best designer and manager. Lord Aberconway acts in its name through the head gardener, Charles Puddle, one of a veritable dynasty of Puddles who have had charge at Bodnant for nearly sixty years.

Two other notable English gardens which reinforce the importance of a resident owner/designer are Sissinghurst, where Vita Sackville-West, painter with words and painter with plants, created from the wilderness round a half ruined castle a garden that is essentially a series of contrasting 'garden rooms' divided by high stone and brick walls; and Hidcote Manor, where artist and architect Lawrence Johnston created a garden in which lavish planting softens a formal, classical layout, and colour and interest are maintained from early spring through to late autumn.

Sissinghurst, now a National Trust property, has had a considerable influence on the humbler gardens in town and country of the many thousands who visit it, because what is done in its 'garden rooms' appears relevant to the garden of villa or semi-detached suburban house. Another great influence, horticulturally, on small gardens was undoubtedly the work of RHS horticulturalist E. A. Bowles in promoting the idea that plants should 'earn their keep' by providing all-the-year-round interest, not just a flash-in-the-pan display of summer colour.

But what has so grand a concept as landscape architecture to do with the poor man in his 'semi' as distinct from the rich man in his hall? Increasingly it seems that the more successful landscape practices are geared to large-scale work, whether for public agencies or corporate clients wanting to soften the environmental impact of major developments. The kind of client for whom Jekyll and Lutyens worked has all but disappeared, except perhaps among the legendary oil-rich sheiks of the Middle East! It is true that a few of the stalwarts, like Kate Hawkins, Brenda Colvin's sometime assistant, still dub themselves 'garden architects' and concentrate on work at this scale; but the profession as a whole appears to address itself primarily to a much bigger kind of workload.

And yet is this healthy? Plenty of landscape architects can be heard to lament the increasingly poor taste and design quality of most garden exhibits at the Chelsea Flower Show. One solution to this problem came from landscape designer John Brookes, who provided a service via the magazine *Good Housekeeping*. Its readers received outline designs and planting schemes for their small gardens through the post for a £10 fee. The fee covered only a minimal amount of Brookes's time; the profit margin was slender, and the objection could be raised that he was designing without visiting the site. Yet for all that the scheme clearly answered a valuable need, supplementing the more general advice and influence of magazine articles. Brookes's book, *Room Outside*, has also exercised considerable influence in this way. For some – not the man in the 'semi', but the solicitor or merchant banker wanting a garden designed for him at the back of his Georgian terrace house, for example – the profession may be able to help more directly if large and medium-sized practices can gear themselves to this scale of work – can, to put it bluntly, run low-budget small works divisions alongside their larger and more lucrative projects. If they do not, then those less qualified will undoubtedly move in and provide the same service, usually less well.

A final coda to this chapter on the designer and the private client is provided by the award of the French Academy of Architecture's first medal for landscape architecture to the Englishman, Russell Page. One of the most prolific and respected landscape designers in Europe, Page was the partner before the Second World War of ILA past president Sir Geoffrey Jellicoe, but later cut his formal links with the Institute when he went to work as staff designer for a leading French firm of seedsmen, designing all their gardens and exhibitions. Among many penetrating comments made in an interview with the magazine *Building Design*, two may be quoted here. 'The only way to learn about plants is by handling them,' and (in the words of his interviewer, Sutherland Lyall). 'He won't work for municipal committees.' The reasoning is clear: no-one thinks of asking a committee to write a poem, and even if a committee commissioned one, they would generally have the sense not to interfere in its composition. But most committee members at heart believe they could design a garden. If there is to be intervention by the client, then it is better if the client is an individual, or at least is represented by an individual, with whom he can build up a rapport.

Chapter 3
THE PUBLIC CLIENT

Nash to Reith

'... Faultless, on the other hand, is the landscape gardening part of the park, which also originates with Mr. Nash, especially in the disposition of water. Art has here completely solved the difficult problem of concealing her operations under an appearance of un-restrained nature.' So in 1826 a discriminating visitor to London, Prince Pückler-Muskau, wrote to his wife of John Nash's grand and by then almost complete design for Regent's Park. At that time his was not a fashionable view. For at least nine years from 1812 onwards Marylebone Park, as it was then known, was in vari-ous parts a scene of turmoil and desolation: excavation of the lake seemed to the public to take an inordinate time; the young trees that Nash caused to be planted made as yet little favourable impact; and all round about stood scaffolding for unfinished houses con-nected by rutted, muddy tracks and a despoiled landscape. The London public could not share in Nash's and the Prince Regent's confident vision of *rus in urbe* and *urbs in rus*. Indeed, only two or three years after the start of the project, the landscape designer's clients, the Commissioners of Woods and Forests, complained that they had spent £53,650. 4s. 2d. on planting and landscaping the area – five times the amount estimated by Nash – without seeing any appreciable return.

Nash's grand design for a new park at Marylebone and a grand processional thoroughfare connecting it to the existing St. James's Park arose from the falling in of Crown leases in 1811 and their reversion to the Crown. It finds a place here because it seems to constitute the first major project of landscape design carried out for a truly public client and not a private one. For though Nash was able to fill the Prince Regent with enthusiasm for his plans as against the more pedestrian proposals of rival architects, it was a public committee – the Commissioners of Woods and Forests – who gave him the job and whom he had to haggle with, cajole and persuade. A private client may, at best, trust to the vision and professional competence of his designer; a government committee, be it ever so enlightened, must have an eye and an ear to the tax-paying public.

Although public scepticism dogged Nash's plans, and in particular dogged their apparently 'unproductive' landscape aspects, by 1821 when the first terraces were completed, the vision had become sufficient of a reality for the commissioners to be able to let the houses immediately.

Nash's notion that park settings could enhance and promote property values ran like a continual counterpoint through the history of nineteenth-century urban and suburban development. One early example was at St. Leonards. There James Burton (who had been involved with Nash at Regent's Park) and his architect son Decimus hung the success of their speculative seaside resort quite deliberately on the appeal of a romantically landscaped setting. St. Leonards, it may be noted, used a worked out quarry as part of the raw material of that landscape, and so ranks as an early example of derelict land reclamation by a commercial entrepreneur. But the most significant name in this field is Joseph Paxton, whose first essay in park design, Prince's Park, Liverpool, also bore the name of James Pennethorne, Nash's assistant on Regent's Park and his successor in the practice. Much influenced in its design by Regent's and St. James's Park in London, Prince's Park, whose plans date from 1842, was the vanguard of a whole series of public parks serving as a focus and adornment for private suburban housing speculations. More significant in the emergence of the public client is Birkenhead Park, for which Paxton drew up plans in the following year. Birkenhead was a deliberately planned nineteenth-century town, and Paxton's clients a board of sixty Improvement Commissioners charged with 'Paving, lighting, watching, cleansing and otherwise improving the Township or Chapelry of Birkenhead'. Half a mile or so back from the waterfront lay a stretch of swampy, low-lying land backed by the now suburban ridge of Claughton. It was, observes Paxton's biographer Chadwick, 'characteristic of the aspirations of the improvement commissioners that this un-attractive between-land was to be developed as a public park, at once adding an amenity to the town which as yet neither Liverpool nor Manchester had, and separating the close development of the town itself from the suburbs of villas which were confidently expected to spring up on higher land'. The Birkenhead Commissioners were in 1842 the first to seek powers to provide a public park out of public funds.

Essentially a suburban park, Birkenhead eschewed the formality of Nash's layout – except for the rather overblown main gate and somewhat truncated vista added by Birkenhead's architect Gillespie Graham in its northeast corner to provide a formal approach to the town centre. Paths are serpentine, as are the internal carriage drives; the two halves of the park, separated by a public link road to Claughton, each have their distinctive characters; and in excavating the lakes Paxton shaped them and their islands so as to give the illusion that what we see is only part of a much more extensive body of water. Another departure, even more radical in its day, was the setting aside of a large section of each half of the park as open grassland for recreational use.

At Birkenhead the Victorian town dweller was at last being invited and encouraged to do rather more than stroll sedately – to engage, in fact, in such rumbustious pastimes as archery and cricket! In the years following Birkenhead, Paxton found himself frequently in demand to supply designs for public parks as well as layouts for speculative housing developments in parklike surroundings. But he was never afforded the opportunity – which he must, like countless landscape designers since, have hankered after – to design and carry through an integrated housing and landscape development.

Birkenhead Park, which today presents a sadly run-down appearance, exercised great influence even beyond the shores of this country. An American designer, Frederick Law Olmsted, applied what he had seen at Birkenhead, laced with a certain French formality, in the designs he did with Calvert Vaux for Central Park, New York. Paradoxically, while landscape design as distinct from horticulture was by the mid-nineteenth century disintegrating in Britain, in the United States it went from strength to strength, with Olmsted and Vaux commissioned to design not only more parks, but landscaped settings for colleges and universities, for new towns and suburbs, and for highways themselves – landscaped 'parkways'. In England, by contrast, the low ebb to which design generally was shown to have sunk by the time of the Great Exhibition, and the poor visual taste of both the new industrial middle classes and the urban proletariat, provide one reason why landscape design went out of fashion. Another reason can be found in the great importation of exotic species and the resultant public interest in flowers and plants to the exclusion of wider concepts of arrangement and composition. Paxton himself, as an MP, fought fierce battles with the authorities responsible for the royal parks and Kew Gardens. In 1859 he was complaining that Kew now had 400 flower beds, requiring annually some 40,000 bedding plants. These had their place, no doubt, but he thought it a mistake to convert that landscape into a 'gaudy flower garden'. He also objected to the 'gardenizing' of Hyde Park. That approach has, at least until recently, dominated the parks world – remaining, as Chadwick puts it, 'in an antrophic state of mid-Victorian gardening'. It still survives, as witness the beds recently cut in 1977 in honour of the Queen's Jubilee, into the greenswards of Hyde Park.

The public client for the landscape designer, as distinct from the landscape gardener, remained largely in eclipse for the remainder of the nineteenth century. Some mature and now much admired landscapes date from this period, including many which we would now regard as 'public' landscapes – but they were generally commissioned either by private clients in the sense applied in Chapter Two, or by speculative developers like Bedford Park's Jonathan Carr who saw spacious, winding, tree-lined roads as much a part of his garden-suburb-for-the-artistic-middle-classes as its Tabard Inn, its shops or Norman Shaw's house designs.

The distinction between public and private client is, however, an ambiguous one; and for the present purposes it is proposed to treat individuals like Dame Henrietta Barnett, who saw themselves as acting for the public good, as public clients. Dame Henrietta's Hampstead Garden Suburb, begun in 1906, is important because one of its prime purposes was to safeguard a rural landscape. The original option on building land for the healthy, mixed community Mrs. Barnett strove after was linked to success in raising funds to buy the eighty acres of Hampstead Heath extension, for presentation to the London County Council. But even before the Hampstead site was in prospect, Mrs. Barnett had set out clearly, in an article in the *Contemporary Review* in 1905, her concepts of what such a new suburb should be, not only socially but physically. This included 'that the part should not spoil the whole … hence that houses should not spoil each other's outlook'; 'that the estate be planned not piecemeal, but as whole'; 'that each house be surrounded by its own garden; and that there be agencies for fostering interest in gardens and allotments ...'; and 'that every road be planted with trees and be not more than 40 feet wide'.

Formally speaking the client was Hampstead Garden Suburb Trust Limited, but it is clear that Henrietta Barnett dominated its six-member board. Colonel Thompson, for thirty years the Trust's chief official, has recalled that 'in vision and perception of method Mrs. Barnett was the leader. No opposition turned her aside from a policy on which she had decided.' The Trust's chief planners and architects were, of course, Parker & Unwin, with Raymond Unwin surveying and designing the layout of the estate and – thought an outrageous interference at that time – vetting and approving the plans of individual builders. A copy of Unwin's first layout for the suburb, dated 1905 and with Henrietta Barnett's handwritten comments, shows that she was very much concerned both for the wider landscape ('This is the high ridge from whence some of the most distant views are to be obtained') and for the closer landscape texture. Here, as in the two pioneer garden cities, Letchworth (1903 onwards) and Welwyn (1920 onwards) the designers were architect-planners, but architect-planners with a very clear appreciation of landscape qualities and possibilities. At Hampstead Barry Parker and Raymond Unwin were determined to conserve and exploit existing natural features in a positive way to produce an attractive and exhilarating new landscape. Unwin made a very thorough survey of the site in 1905, carefully plotting the position and spread of existing trees, with the aim that, in execution of the final plan, not a single tree need be lost.

Equally important was Parker & Unwin's central thesis: Nothing Gained by Overcrowding. They argued consistently for careful housing layouts, minimizing the space taken by roads, which under the mechanical application of bye-law standards had become wastefully large and visually destructive. At Hampstead Garden Suburb, the typical residential road is a short cul-de-sac with relatively narrow carriageway; elsewhere the roads wind with the contours or to avoid mature trees. This gives a double benefit. Visually the roads do not dominate; the land released by economical road layouts permits both larger gardens for individual houses and more generous areas of public landscape.

At Welwyn, the master planner was a young French-Canadian architect, Louis de Soissons, part of whose design education had been at the Ecole des Beaux Arts – and beaux arts formality it certainly had. Yet its major landscape feature, the $1\frac{1}{4}$-mile long central axis, Parkway, spacious and tree-lined with fountains, looks today – in spite of the cars – better than it ever did. It refreshes the mind and lifts the spirit in a way that less obtrusive landscape work somehow fails to do in an urban situation. Not that de Soissons landscapes are all formal, by any means. His road and housing layouts did what new town landscape designers and planners have frequently taken pains to do since – they preserved mature hedgerows and allowed minor roads to follow 'a rolling English drunkard's' path which is far more agreeable than the gridiron layouts adopted elsewhere at that time.

For the most part, however, the inter-war years were a dismal time for anyone who hoped to design landscapes for a public client as distinct from gardens for private clients. Only after the Second World War did the public client as we know him today begin to emerge. For this we must thank the polemicists of the 1930s, and certain key figures and reports in Churchill's wartime Whitehall. Lord Reith, as Minister of Works and Planning, busied himself with blueprints for the peace; and the 1942 Scott Report put forward the principle, incorporated into the 1947 Town and Country Planning Act, that landscape factors ought to be an aspect considered in granting or refusing planning consents. Reith, incidentally, had as his senior research officer at the Ministry Thomas Sharp, whose book *Town and Countryside* (1932) had already driven home the message that the English countryside, being manmade, required man's deliberate and careful maintenance.

It remains a matter of wonder that, during those dark years when all seemed subordinated to the war effort, ministers, civil servants and expert committees could be drawing up plans for the peace. But they were, and during that period Reith's ministry changed its name significantly from Works and Planning to Town and Country Planning. The Institute of Landscape Architects, though its active ranks had been much thinned by the needs of war, took full advantage (as Chapter Thirteen records) of the opportunities this process of 'Planning for the Peace' offered; though Sir Geoffrey Jellicoe, called in as president to brief a junior minister on landscape possibilities, was in some difficulty when asked about numbers of landscape architects practising. 'I had to tell him,' he recalls, 'that the profession hardly then existed.' From 1942 and Scott onwards, however, behind the scenes in Whitehall men like Lord (then plain William) Holford were laying the foundations for the profession's future growth by writing a landscape element into the proposed

statutory guidelines for future public clients. The need for landscape design in public developments was now appreciated; and
when Lewis Silkin, Minister of Town and Country Planning in
the 1945 Labour Government, asked Reith to chair a New Towns
committee, he was appointing a man determined to ensure that the
planning and building of Britain's new towns included an adequate
landscape ingredient. Dame Sylvia Crowe recalls that Reith,
whom the Institute had made an honorary fellow in 1943, asked
the ILA to submit evidence on this point. 'He included it verbatim
in the report,' she remembers. So right from the start consultant
planners and architects, and the new town development corporations themselves, learned to look on professional landscape advice
as mandatory.

Chapter 4

FRESH PASTURES, NEW TOWNS

Sir Frederick Gibberd, consultant architect-planner for Harlow, based his whole design for the town on the form of the existing landscape in the designated area. The valley of the River Stort, Sir Frederick has explained, with the railway and the motorway, forms the base line of the town on its north side; the bulk of the town is a rough semi-circle to the south of that base.

Agricultural wedges on the east and west are linked together by a natural valley with the town centre as the focus. Other valleys are left in their natural state and linked with the open spaces required for recreation to form a continuous landscape pattern that both defines and contrasts with the zones of buildings. The landscape and the built-up areas are designed to react on each other: thus the placing of the town centre on high ground is a focus of the views from the approach roads and would have presented a spectacular silhouette from the motorway – had this not subsequently been moved to the other side of the town.

Still, the completed reality of Harlow is pretty good. Sometimes the buildings are individually tawdry, particularly in shopping areas; but the overall structure, which is largely a landscape structure, holds it together. From the centre, those wedges of green separating the individual neighbourhoods do give long views out into the country, particularly towards the high ground to the south and west. It is significant that Gibberd regards town planning as an organic process, quite unlike the finite process, architecture and more akin to the gradual development – with careful thought at each stage and occasional flashes of creative intuition – of a great garden like Bodnant. We can indeed find a striking analogy between his town, Harlow, gradually developing to a flexible plan on the gentle terrain to the south of the Stort, and Gibberd's own garden, also on a much smaller scale running down to that river, and developing over the years as new opportunities and needs led

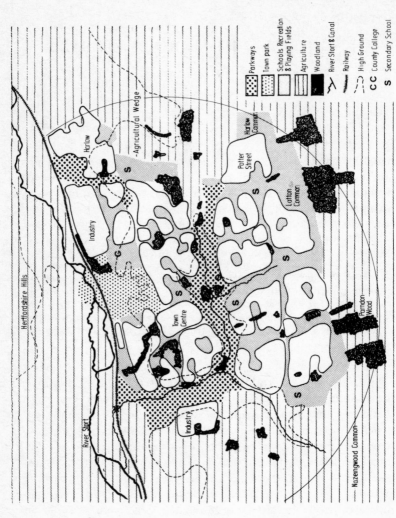

Harlow New Town. Frederick Gibberd & Partners.

Key (as shown in legend):
- Parkways
- Town park
- Schools Recreation & Playing Fields
- Agriculture
- Woodland
- River Stort & Canal
- Railway
- High Ground
- **C C** County College
- **S** Secondary School

Labels on map: Hertfordshire Hills, River Stort, Industry, Harlow, Agricultural Wedge, Town Centre, Potter Street, Latton Common, Harlow Common, Parndon Wood, Nazengwood Common him to fashion it. Frederick Gibberd was responsible to the Corporation for the overall design of the landscape. Bodfan Gruffydd as head of the landscape department made an important contribution to the design of individual areas as did Dame Sylvia Crowe who was appointed landscape consultant. Right from the start they worked closely together so that it is often difficult to say whether a particular solution came from Crowe, Gruffydd, Gibberd or more than one of them.

Other Mark I new towns followed the same nuclear plan of free-standing neighbourhoods arranged round a town centre, and there were critics who stigmatized them as 'standardised arcadia'; yet, as an agreeable and fruitful environment for people to live and raise families in, the formula has been very successful. Those landscapes are now a mature and lush setting, sometimes enhancing pleasing and original architecture, sometimes compensating for uninspired or unsympathetic buildings; yet scarcely anywhere save Harlow, and perhaps Stevenage with its grid of maples, did so firm and clear a landscape plan survive the vagaries of implementation. That might have been the case at Hemel Hempstead where Sir Geoffrey Jellicoe drew up the landscape master plan; but circumstances changed; the plan was superseded; detailed landscape design there, as in most other Mark I new towns, is like the curate's egg, excellent in parts; and the only element Jellicoe was able to implement was his water gardens just west of the town centre (see Plate 2).

As a leading consultant, Sylvia Crowe also advised other new towns, notably Basildon; while Bodfan Gruffydd advised another 'Mark I' new town, Crawley; but development corporations also began to employ staff landscape designers, as for instance Gordon Patterson at Stevenage, where the consultant was Frank Clark. It is perhaps a reasonable assessment of landscape design in these early new towns that the profession, whether on payroll or on contract, did a good job within the limits of manœuvre left them by the planners. When these new towns fail to hang together visually, the reason is often that town planners took the key decisions on the basis of land *use* and with rather less than half an eye to land*scape*.

The so-called Mark II new towns were a different kettle of fish. The first of them, Cumbernauld, showed two important characteristics: a much tighter urban layout (no green wedges between neighbourhoods here; indeed, originally, scarcely any visually distinct neighbourhoods); and much more lavish provision for the motor car. The tendency, says Professor Peter Youngman who was landscape consultant under Sir Hugh Wilson as chief planner, was to 'look for landscape effect round the edge of the town and in the surrounding hills rather than in garden city greenery'. Youngman as consultant was later joined by a staff landscape architect, William Gillespie.

With Runcorn (1964 onwards) new town landscape design began to change in its nature. Its pattern of expressways and re-served busways has been fitted into a landscape fashioned by large-scale moving and mounding of earth; and the existence of a rather run-down urban community and of considerable industrial derelic-tion within the designated area both posed new challenges and pre-saged the nature of landscape problems in such later, larger towns as Telford, Milton Keynes and the 'partnership' expansion exercises at Peterborough and Northampton.

At Telford, in industrial east Shropshire, a prime motive for designation of the new town was to repair a landscape ravaged by several centuries of industrial exploitation. The designated area contains something between 3,000 and 4,000 mine shafts and large areas of it consist of pitheaps of varying ages, often overgrown by scrub and small trees, but overall constituting a despoiled, almost lunar landscape associated in people's minds with a century and a half of industrial decline. Telford itself was designated a new town in 1968, but this followed the earlier designation of the much smaller Dawley area; and initially land reclamation tended to be seen as an engineering exercise to which a cosmetic of planting could afterwards be applied, rather than a design exercise in which the landscape architect should have a decisive voice from the outset. Now however Telford has, under David Wassell, one of the largest and most exciting landscape sections in the new towns. His total team approaches forty, and as well as landscape architects, assistants and technicians includes a forestry manager, a horticulturist, an ecologist and an administrator; he presents his projects direct to the Chief Officers Board when necessary, and has within those limits total control of his own budget; and it may be significant that, after an initial period working with the Director of Archi-tecture, he sought and got agreement that a more satisfactory and logical place for landscape was under the Director of Planning where he is able to influence decisions at formative state. The land-scape canvas in a new town – and especially Telford – must be painted on a scale bigger than just that of housing layouts.

The landscape team's philosophy of design does however take

profound account of the needs of the new housing neighbourhoods. 'There are two types of landscape,' says Wassell, 'a "settling
in" landscape, which calls for quick results; and a longer-term,
broader landscape structure added to it.' The 'settling in' landscape
is designed to respond to the needs of people moving in to new
houses; to mitigate the inevitable rawness of just completed housing layouts; and to offer a psychological sense of stability and per-
manence to people whose lives are often to some extent in turmoil
because they are uprooting. 'We try to green up the area before
they move in. Some of this settling in landscape is temporary and
therefore expendable,' he says. The aim is to keep it human in scale.
'We use a lot of ornamental trees and shrubs, and daffodils.'

The longer-term, broader landscape is an evolving one, whose
structure takes in the best of the existing features and builds on them
and on such large-scale features of the developing town as the new
road pattern. Land reclamation linked with some open-cast mining
provides opportunities for creative modelling on a large scale. 'We
hope the existing landscape and the new features will lie down
agreeably together. Here at Telford we look on landscape as basic
infrastructure – as basic to the town as main drainage and roads.'

The landscape strategy's overall aim is 'to try to inject nature
into an urban area on a massive scale'. This, the Telford team
believes, has not previously been attempted in this country –
though the aim is shared by Milton Keynes. 'We are creating a
"forest city" or woodland town.' Instead of buildings dominating
the urban scene, it will be trees and nature. 'No-one,' he adds with
candour, 'quite knows if it will work.' But a hopeful sign comes
in the judgement of the Nature Conservancy Council that Telford
now probably contains a markedly richer wildlife than the surrounding agricultural country. As the landscape develops, this
effect should be strengthened. The new town will, paradoxically,
serve as a wildlife reservoir for much of rural Shropshire.

However in many areas poor soil presented almost insurmount-
able problems. In some places zinc levels exceeded threefold those
generally considered tolerable for plant growth; and Wassell and
his team were running out of easily accessible topsoil. On the poor
soil, alders will grow, sometimes pines, but not much else without
excessive effort. In some areas the best hope must be that these
species will in time provide the topsoil for a richer growth.

Part of the Telford strategy aims at providing a countryside experience on the fringes of the designated area, and so muting the

impact of recreational incursions into farming countryside. Facilities for 'passive' recreation including picnic areas form an integral
part of the plan; and in the increasingly popular Ironbridge Gorge,
Telford is trying to blunt the impact of tourist numbers on a basically rather fragile and small-scale landscapes.

The town park, developing to the south of Telford's shopping
centre, is quite another matter. It contains some of the most deliberately exciting effects to be found in a public landscape in Britain
in the postwar years. A trio of what I can only call fibreglass
'temples' in bright primary colours beckon people across a semi-
natural landscape from the town centre; at a confluence of paths,
intersecting circles of trees, intersecting circles of paving, and a
water-garden with a distinctly geometrical formality sit sweetly
into a landscape that is basically English natural-seeming parkland.
The GRP pavilions, justified in utilitarian terms as shelters or perhaps sales kiosks, serve as an eye-catcher and fulcrum between two
vistas. They draw you from the town, and then point you down
the hill to a lake with a concert platform on a floating raft and
a semi-circular arena of seats. The lake, one of an eventual seven,
will have a 60 ft. high fountain; and nearby there are plans for
another eye-catcher, a belltower. The whole thing is a skilful and
imaginative re-writing in twentieth-century materials and styles,
of the classic eighteenth-century landscape where the designer led
the visitor on from one visual surprise or delight to another. In
a situation like Telford's town park, argues Wassell, 'you need to
have a bit of fun. The approach mustn't be too low-key. After all,
what we are trying to do is to extend people's life-styles.'

One device that Telford is using to supply landscape features for
the town park is an annual set-piece garden at the Chelsea Flower
Show. In 1978 it designed and put together a formal, old-fashioned
English rose garden with brick walls and gazebos. As with other
set-pieces at the RHS show, this was dismantled at the end of
the week and has now been re-sited in the town park. Such displays
provide publicity for the new town, foster a sense of pride in its
achievements, and year by year add features of significance, each
with an identity of its own, to the landscape ensemble.

The work of the section does not stop with design. Alongside
design staff works a forestry and landscape maintenance team with
a workforce 150 strong. Wassell's staff are responsible for future
management policies as well as design. 'It is all too easy for landscape designers to turn their backs on what they've produced; then

later have a good moan about how it's being wrecked.' Their guidelines on, for instance, the town park will contain very explicit information not only on how particular sections should be maintained but on what sort of pressures they will stand up to. For instance, the arena area by the lake is maybe designed to stand up to a maximum crowd of 50,000 people; after that the managers should turn people away. 'Success in the design of a public park often creates its own problems such as access, use and safety,' says Wassell, 'and so the situation must be kept constantly under review.'

One of the points he makes most strongly about landscape professionals in relation to the public client concerns the importance of a businesslike approach. The preconceptions of other professionals still tend to label landscape design as an airy-fairy, dilettante operation. 'There's likely to be flippancy towards landscape unless you can talk the language of the financial and administrative people. But, once you get their confidence, it becomes a bandwaggon.' The machinery of decision making is also crucial. As we have seen, at Telford the chief landscape architect has considerable influence, thanks to the corporation's commitment to landscape, the backing of his staff and an early landscape input into decisions.

Milton Keynes, in many ways the most exciting and ambitious of Britain's new towns, has also been planned as a city of trees and woodlands. Its early planning included a large-scale planting programme; its 'string bag' pattern of grid roads bordering neighbourhoods roughly 1 km square leaned heavily on the notion that development could vary enormously in style and even visual quality – given a thick high curtain of trees along the grid road. But some of the original decisions and assumptions of the planners now, from a landscape point of view, appear arbitrary and unjustified. Thus, the strategy for tree planting with contrasting groups of species allocated by zone turned out to have little connection with either the ecology of the region or existing landscape patterns, but it may be argued that it relates strongly to the major development sectors of the city. Similarly, the decision to pile up linear mounds along the grid roads to protect neighbourhoods from noise has now come to seem an arbitrary one, wasteful of land and reducing opportunities for using spoil from roads to create interesting and useful landscape features. What is more, the concept of roadside mounding topped with trees does not altogether work in practice. Sometimes the mounds dry out; the young trees die.

LANDSCAPE BY DESIGN

Another criticism that can be made of parts of Milton Keynes follows from similar causes. In a number of grid squares, what has been built or is building constitutes a highly formalized, geometric layout. The decision to make such neighbourhoods as Fishermead, close to the town centre, firmly urban in character was surely a sound one. Spacious straight residential boulevards have an honourable pedigree, and can be reinterpreted successfully in 1970s styles and materials. But the visitor again has the impression here that the architects and planners took the crucial decisions; that landscape designers did not exercise a strong enough influence on those decisions. The result is that the intermediate scale landscaping at Fishermead often looks like *ex post facto* cosmetic: a tarting-up of spaces left over after architecture. This particularly applies to the internal spaces within the housing blocks. Visually, straight residential boulevards will probably work when the trees are bigger – though the amount and kind of space demanded by the car plainly conflicts with any notion of urban tightness, and the use of space, for instance in the central reservations, appears to have been dictated by parking convenience to the exclusion of visual considerations. But the mechanical application of 'straight line planning' to the interiors of the housing squares produces long empty vistas where tightness and a sense of enclosure are needed; and fosters the impression of space leaking away where it ought to be firmly contained. Nor has some of the landscaping in these spaces helped.

Under the regime of Milton Keynes' imaginative and colourful former chief architect, Derek Walker, the landscape group coined the slogan 'relaxed generosity of scale' which became a guiding principle. Which sounds all very fine and on the face of it helpful to landscapers. The reality is that Fishermead and a number of other developments have proved to be formal architectural compositions so geometrically positioned and widely spaced that it is very hard to tie them in with any meaningful landscape at all. Fishermead, for instance, would have benefited from rather narrower residential boulevards, with strategic setbacks and variations in the front building line but, by contrast, a really firm straight line of trees along the central strip. The central courts, which are really quite big spaces, could have varied in treatment to give identity and could, for instance, have benefited from walled enclosures. Fairly formal walks with pergolas and like features were proposed in some places to break up the spaces and give them much more the feel of town gardens, but have not yet materialized.

If some of the Milton Keynes landscape work, working to decisions of architects and planners with too little eye for the basics of landscape, has produced disappointing results, some evokes admiration. Neath Hill, towards the north of the town, has not only gone for a village feel in the materials, style and grouping of its houses, but fits beautifully into the landscape. Its spaces lend themselves to effective planting; and, though the style of its houses is very different, it is reminiscent in this respect of Runcorn's excellent scheme at The Brow, which spearheaded the battle to reduce the width and impact of housing access roads. 'Relaxed generosity of scale' should not (and need not) mean acres of tarmac with lonely trees and shrubs fitted in apparently as an afterthought.

But to return to the positive features. The concept of a city centre in which boulevards of plane trees overtop virtually all the buildings, and provide a leafy canopy for extensive and convenient ground level parking, will surely in visual terms prove a success, as will the notion of a linear walk alongside the Grand Union Canal, and the use of balancing lakes for visual and recreational purposes. The linear walk will be the more successful because the original idea of a continuous Broad Walk of poplars is now to be modified for both environmental and practical reasons.

One of the difficulties the new landscape unit continually faces is, as already indicated, that landscape considerations did not sufficiently influence some of the early planning decisions; another is that budgets bore little relationship to the ambitious results the landscapers were expected to achieve. 'Budgets are grossly inadequate,' says chief landscape architect Neil Higson, 'and in places landscape work has sunk down to the level of simply designing planting.' This, however, does not apply to bigger public spaces like the town park or Willen Lake on the town centre's eastern side. Here already we see something of the mixture of greensward and formal features which is being achieved at Telford: a promontory, meandering paths leading to an area of fairly geometric planting and hard landscape, rubs shoulders with an ambitious piece of earth mounding intended as an arena round a 'water organ'. An imaginative notion in the best traditions of parks for people; but, alas, the water organ, like the winter gardens Paxton intended for Queen's Park, Glasgow, has been ruled out on grounds of cost – at least for the time being. Instead, rather than leave an unused space, the development corporation has laid a circular tarmac strip for roller skating and skateboarding, which has already proved popular and is helping to bring this part of the park to life. The lake will boast an even taller fountain than Telford's – 70 ft. – and a belvedere formed five years ago from surplus subsoil projects from the high ground close to the town centre to link it visually through the town park to Willen Lake and the north-south linear park.

One of the problems of a new town is to enable people to distinguish between open spaces like the town park which belong to the public, and other open areas – typically land under grazing, crossed by the odd right of way, which the development corporation owns and will eventually claw back for development. Higson believes that the park will need to take on a more distinctively public character quickly to encourage the people of the new town to use it more.

Under Higson (who, though he previously worked as a consultant in Milton Keynes, only became its chief staff landscape architect in September 1977), design policies can be expected to evolve in quite a lively fashion to respond to events. The original choices of planting have seemed to some observers to be rather timid and too chastely orthodox. The new landscape work goes for a richer mixture, avoiding planting schemes which look fine in one season but leave a visual vacuum for the rest of the year. In housing areas, particularly, they favour 'things people can enjoy'. Species include nuts, blackberry and crabapple, for instance. There is strong pressure for richer, more quickly established landscape to boost house sales; and in such rented housing areas as Netherfield and Bean Hill, where many tenants find the built surroundings given them by the architects rather oppressive, good cosmetic landscape work can still help to alleviate this painful sociological condition.

Before working at Milton Keynes, Higson was first at Basildon and then, from 1965 to '73, at Runcorn, where The Brow housing neighbourhood set new standards in landscaping as well as in roads designed to keep motor vehicle speeds down to 20 mph or less. Earth mounding and barrier planting kept incompatible uses separate. 'All happenings in the landscape other than the houses themselves were either soft materials or fluid forms,' recalls Higson. 'Roads and paths flowed over the land in response to its basic form....' Siting of major open space preserved existing landscape features such as a pond and some mature hedges; and the narrow roads were based in character on English country lanes. The Brow still looks good, works well, and is popular.

Private garden in Barnet, 1936 – Robert Matthew, Johnson-Marshall & Partners.

Plate 1

The Water Gardens, Hemel Hempstead, 1957–59, for the New Town Development Corporation – Sir Geoffrey Jellicoe.
Plate 2

Plate 3
University of York from 1966. Robert Matthew, Johnson–Marshall &
Partners/Frank Clark. The Lake.

Plate 4
University of York from 1966. The Planting.

Plate 5
Stirling University, 1965 – Robert Matthew, Johnson-Marshall &
Partners/Ed Hilliard. Campus development in rural setting.

Rheidol Hydro-Electric Scheme, 1957 – Colwyn Ffoulkes. Use of local
materials and sensitive water detail.
Plate 6

Only one of Britain's thirty-odd new towns boasts a seaside location: Irvine, on the Scottish west coast north of Ayr. The inherent advantages and recreational potential of this site were, however, until recently frustrated by a legacy of chronic dereliction. The history of the site is complex, but essentially it was used for the manufacture of acids and explosives and abandoned some time after World War II. Irvine's designation as a new town put more urgency into the wish to reclaim this area, and also provided the administrative machine, in the shape of a new town development corporation, to tackle so daunting a task. In the summer of 1973 the corporation commissioned Brian Clouston & Partners to prepare a foreshore landscape study, and from this came the proposal for Irvine Beach Park.

The 53-hectare site divided quite distinctly into four zones: (1) an area where the sand dunes had been partly removed, leading to the erosion of what remained, and where substantial fly tipping had taken place; (2) an area of old foundations and some chemical waste, low-lying because of extensive sand winning; (3) areas of chemical waste tips; and (4) the site of factory buildings and explosives blast bunkers. The whole, say Cloustons, 'comprised a dreadful eyesore and area of dereliction'.

Phase I, started in May 1975, included basic reclamation works, including the creation of a 4½-hectare lake, which also benefited from a government derelict land grant. Reclamation works comprised three major operations: site clearance, land contouring and drainage; retention and establishment of vegetation; and coastal protection and sand dune re-establishment. The approach was to bury toxic material in deep defiles between existing waste heaps. As not infrequently happens in dealing with chemical dereliction, however, the extent and toxicity of the contaminated waste exceeded estimates. Much of it was highly toxic to vegetation. Working with the contractor and resident engineer, the consultants found to their relief that limey materials which would mask and neutralize these deposits were available on site and, with some adjustment to their plans, could be turned up by the earth-moving machines in sufficient quantities to solve the problem.

As an essential part of their plan, the consultants sought to retain as large an area of existing vegetation as possible. Where this had established itself on sand over chemical heaps, they limited the treatment to filling in deep hollows and to grass cuts and fertilizer applications. They took special pains to select a grass mixture which would stand up to salt winds and poor soil conditions; and provided the development corporation with a maintenance programme using slow-release fertilizers and differing grass cutting regimes in line with the design for different areas of the beach park.

Toxic waste heaps close to the sea also restricted the means to be employed in combating erosion of the sand dunes. One device used was the 'gabion remo mattress' – a mattress-shaped gabion or wire basket. These have successfully withstood the storms of three winters and, being sand-covered, do not attract the attention of vandals during the busy summer months. For reclamation of sand dunes, the consultants tried out a variety of techniques and materials, including a number of different grasses.

Phase II of the Beach Park scheme, which started soon after Phase I, provided car parks, paths, paved areas and picnic facilities; also a considerable amount of tree and shrub planting with protective rabbit-proof fencing. Species planted (all feathered whips or forest transplants) including alder, poplar, sycamore, willow and Corsican pine, with tree planting areas edged with such shrubs as blackthorn, hawthorn, rose, blackberry, willow, tamarisk and elder. Phase III of the scheme, started in February 1978, includes construction of more footpaths, sitting and picnic areas, a dinghy park, and a 'trim track' for jogging and similar activities.

At the time of writing, however, the beach park seemed to have reached a critical stage, resulting from its own growing success. A boat hire operator had been using the lake for one season, and other commercial operators were expressing a wish to establish themselves exactly where they wanted. If all their requests were conceded, the master plan's aim of spreading the activity load over the area would be frustrated. Feeding in the intended commercial element into the park called for a combination of flexibility with sound and consistent overall planning; and the consultants expressed concern that no management team as yet existed properly equipped to carry through this function; nor did very much advice on the park's management 'other than our own, when requested for an input'. The project so far is an undoubted success, both in pure landscape and in recreation terms; but one hopes that Irvine Development Corporation, which ought, if any public body can, to be able to mobilize an effective in-house management team, will not let the park's development drift but put its future management on a firm enough basis to survive eventual transfer of this function to the district council. The beach park received an award in the 1979 *Times*/RICS Conservation Award Scheme.

The problems of handing over to a local authority also worry Redditch Development Corporation's landscape architect, Roy Winter. By the time Redditch was designated in 1964, it was, he says, well established that landscape design should form a major part of the master plan. Michael Brown as consultant provided this sound base and ensured that the new town quickly employed its own landscape team. Winter compares its design philosophy with 'providing a suit of clothes for a purpose, e.g. hard wearing, colourful, stylish and well cut. In other words, part of the living fabric of the town.' He sees one of the prime achievements as 'getting away from the hitherto traditional role of being mere cosmeticians'.

But, he adds, with Redditch new town 'nearing the end of its term, it is with some apprehension that I regard the prospect of landscape assets being handed over to those who will follow on. I do not think our philosophy of "natural" planting design is understood or accepted by our successors in its totality, and I am a little disappointed in the obsession for "neatness" which seems to pervade local authority minds.'

Winter's biggest regret is that in Redditch his team's brief did not include development of open spaces, which remained the responsibility of the local authority. All they could do was to include an open space element in other projects, such as housing. Recently, the job creation programme has, however, given his team the chance to create a small park complete with lakes and play areas. 'We have been able to do this by direct supervision and involvement on the site, much in the manner of the eighteenth-century designers,' he says, adding, 'I would like to think that this method of improving the landscape could be more widely adopted, as it could directly involve the public in creating their own landscape for their own enjoyment.'

Chapter 5

A CLUTCH OF CAMPUSES

New University Landscapes

The great expansion of university education associated with the 1963 Robbins Report undoubtedly produced some of Britain's most interesting and attractive postwar architecture. Whether in social and educational terms campus universities were a success, an unfortunate necessity, or an avoidable mistake, will long be debated. Campuses most of these new universities were, detached and sometimes remote from the towns that lent them their names, and providing, one might have thought, like our new towns, a challenging opportunity for large-scale landscape design. In practice, with a few exceptions, architecture and functional planning have dominated the design of these campuses; landscaping has been a cosmetic – albeit a skilful and very acceptable cosmetic – applied to the spaces left over after building.

To be more accurate, we can distinguish three kinds of campus: those where landscape appears to have been totally an afterthought; those – such as Sussex with its sensitive edge-of-downland setting, Lancaster on its wet and windy ridge, Kent on its heights above the cathedral city of Canterbury, and East Anglia on its sloping greenfield site above the River Yare – where landscape considerations powerfully affected the siting and grouping of buildings, and they and land form interact to great effect; and finally those few where landscape quite as much as buildings is the thing that catches our attention, holds and uplifts us, affects the whole attitude of resident and visitor alike towards the campus. Outstandingly, though for different reasons, York and Stirling belong to this last category.

Stirling is widely, and surely rightly, regarded as the most beautiful of postwar campus universities in Britain – at least from an overall view. The designers (Robert Matthew, Johnson-Marshall) started with a superb site: mature, well-planted parkland laid out in the nineteenth century by the father and son White, from County Durham. White Senior had been a pupil of Capability Brown. The estate belonged to a baronial style pocket castle, Airthrey Castle, built in 1791 to designs by Robert Adam. This stands on a rise to the east of a sizeable artificial, but very natural-seeming loch, which curves round two small hills at its centre. From the loch stretch carefully arranged slopes, running up towards clumps of trees and shelter belts. Away to the south rises the distinctive granite pile of the Wallace Monument, confidently Victorian on its well-wooded hill and serving as an established reference point for visitor and resident alike. A peach of a site! The problem, then, not 'to make something of it', but how not to spoil it: to design a university there that strengthened and preserved the essential quality and character of the place, not dispersed or evaporated it.

This, most visitors admiringly allow, the designers have achieved. Landscape, planning and architecture from the first worked together as one design exercise. Frank Clark, before his death in 1971, had a hand in the early landscape; thereafter the design team led by RMJM's partner John Richards, and including notably landscape architect Ed Hilliard, produced the designs. Richards irreverently but aptly describes the site as 'a saucer with a bump on its base'. This of course gives no hint of the sweetness and maturity of the 'given' landscape. The designers' basic formula is white buildings in a green glen. Residences look out across the loch from a south-facing slope running in a series of inverted U blocks up the lawns towards Hermitage Wood. A service road is hidden behind the bases of the U-plans; though broken with new and existing planting, the landscape here gives the impression of running up from the loch to the very windows of the residences, carrying the greensward in almost Capability fashion into the sunny space within each 'U'. The view of these staggered, carefully stepped white blocks against their green background, with sails of dinghies on the loch in the foreground, is classic and almost magical in its simplicity (see Plate 5).

From near the foot of the residence lawns, a simple concrete bridge strides across the loch to link these living quarters to the university's working and recreational zones. On the 'bump' – a low, flattish hill with water on three sides – shops, theatre (the MacRobert Centre), restaurants, bars and library huddle together in a complex used by the whole university and frequently in part by the general public. Behind the 'pimple' lies the 'ladder' – a line of teaching buildings on a flexible grid round a series of court-yards, in plan like the rungs of a rather wobbly ladder.

Over the centuries most of the original parkland had been given over to agriculture and divided into arable fields. The original woodlands and many trees in the open had, however, been left standing and reached maturity. The Forestry Commission, before the University arrived, carried out work in several areas, thinning and replanting mainly with conifers. Elsewhere on the site beech and sycamore predominated, with large numbers of rhododendron and other typical woodland flowers and shrubs. The island on the loch was and still is a tangled mixture of deciduous and coniferous trees with waterside vegetation where wild fowl and swans nest. Trout abound in the loch; the whole site is rich in wild life.

Three or four scales of landscape make the Stirling site what it is. Its landscape planning has preserved and capitalized on distant views, such as those of the Ochil Hills to the north and east, rising grandly to 1,500 ft. or more; and, in a different way, the royal castle of Stirling on its rock above the town to the south. In the closer landscape, Airthrey Castle and the Wallace Monument provide important visual features. Much nearer is the landscaped terrain provided by the Whites, and especially the mature woodlands to the north of the loch. This the university's designers have reinforced and extended, planting more rhododendrons and azaleas, and trees such as oak, beech and sycamore further from buildings. They have sought to simplify maintenance by using shrubs and ground cover on steep slopes and mowing strips close to buildings.

The designers stress – a point which constantly recurs in these pages – the importance of having an effective and constructive relationship with those who will maintain what they have created. A successful development depends on maintenance of completed areas, setting out and planting of areas nearing completion, and the 'growing on' of plant materials for successive contract stages. They emphasize the importance of their good relations with the University Grounds Department, adding (I quote from the February 1978 issue of *Landscape Design*): 'Close coordination between the landscape designers and those involved in the work has prompted a mutual understanding of the final goals for a planned environment.'

At York, the 'given' landscape formed much less an established asset than at Stirling. Admittedly, just as the architects, Robert Matthew, Johnson-Marshall & Partners, could capitalize on the

substantial but victorianized pile of Heslington Hall, so Frank
Clark, their landscape consultant for the development plan, inherited its small landscaped park with yew topiary, mature lawn
trees and walled gardens. But this feature, like woodlands on the
180-acre campus, had been neglected; and much of the site was
poorly drained. Indeed it is said that when a university was first
proposed for the site, locals shook their heads and prophesied,
'You'll never do it. We've had cows sink up to the knees on that
pasture.'

The answer to coping with such a cow-sinking water table was
a balancing reservoir – and that necessary piece of basic 'infrastructure' the designers made the central and transforming feature of
the campus, accentuating the contrast between the ridge to the
north, on which the library, Alcuin College and the chemistry
block stand, and the flatter area which forms the bulk of the
campus. For speed and availability of materials, York used the
CLASP industrialized system for buildings crucial to the programme. Without the landscape, and especially the lake and its
associated planting, many of those buildings would have appeared
very drab and austere. As it is, the 15-acre lake, with the trees and
plants that border it, pushes its way among and around the buildings, and landscape and buildings have been designed to create one
overall picture. Thus the CLASP panels are a neutral brownish-
pink in colour so that the buildings do not assert themselves but
leave the near greenery and hard landscape features round the lake
to speak for themselves; though at the same time other ingredients
in the built landscape, such as pyramidical roof lights on single-
storey college entrance halls and common rooms do stand out and
thus add a lightness to the scene. Covered ways linking buildings,
which if aligned and designed in a mechanical way, could blow
apart such a visual composition, have been handled skilfully and
imaginatively; and they link with one of the most important elements of all – bridges. In their variety and lightness, the six or seven
bridges over the York lake are a delight (see Plates 3 and 4).

The result, on the main section of the campus about the lake,
is landscape at its best and fullest. The designers, led by RMJM's
landscape architect Maurice Lee, have created an atmosphere that
is relaxed yet immensely civilized; the ripple of water, the lacy
branches of trees, smooth lawns, bridges, stepping stones and terraces, the colours, movement and muted quack of ducks, and a
fountain rising from the centre of the lake against the backcloth

of the central hall's great glass-and-steel A-frame. The scene is one of repose, yet full of incident: at the lower end of the range of scales, bridges, low but eventful roofscapes, and the projecting edges of one or two woodlands; at the upper end, large reference points like the Biology clock tower and an inverted mushroom water-tower, as well as the dark green mass of the denser shelter belts. The campus commands the esteem not only of residents but of a wider public. The walls of the City of York are only a ten minute bus ride away, and on fine summer days families come and picnic by the lake. The university welcomes such visitors, convinced that if you can offer the public an attractive environment, they will seldom abuse it. That act of faith has largely proved justified. A fine manmade landscape commands respect.

We have been looking so far, however, at the main body of the York campus linked together visually by the lake. Much of its sense of repose, as well as the quality of the setting, results from the decision to keep this area vehicle free. The price of that is a large traffic artery, University Road, running across the northern part of the campus. Formerly Heslington Road, it links the little village of Heslington (firmly preserved on the edge of farmland and deliberately not engulfed physically in the university) with the city. The best the designers of the campus could do was to sink this road, so that neither from the lake nor from colleges on the ridge does it obtrude. This part of the campus presented visual problems, not least because the university inherited a large and ugly York Waterworks water-tower on the ridge. The designers did their best to soften and integrate it, but it lacks the sweet, light and delicate touch of the main body of the campus. York, nonetheless, provides an outstanding postwar example of how to re-interpret in mid-twentieth-century landscapist's language the spirit and appeal of the classic eighteenth-century landscaped park. And much of the credit, stress RMJM, must go to a perceptive and sympathetic landscape maintenance department at the university, with whom – here too – they worked closely from the start.

Chapter 6

WHERE ANGELS FEAR TO TREAD

The Landscape Architect in Whitehall

The first landscape architect employed by the government specific-
ally to work on landscape design was former Institute president
Clifford Tandy. Qualifying both as a landscape architect and an
architect shortly after the Second World War, he worked in local
government until invited by Sir Donald Gibson, first civilian director of works at the War Office, to join a team which included
Roger Walters (later GLC chief architect), John Redpath (later of
the Crown Agents) and quantity surveyor James Nisbett. At that
time and for some years afterwards, Tandy recalls, the Civil Service
did not recognize landscape architecture as a professional qualification. Though working a hundred per cent on landscape design,
Tandy got his established Civil Service grade only because he
happened also to be an architect. Before Gibson's day, the Works
Directorate had consisted of army engineers and drawing office
staff, working not in the kind of creative design team he put
together, but to a rigid military hierarchy. The result had been over
the years, in a whole series of military establishments, the complete
antithesis of landscape planning. As the Army wanted extra buildings, orders were given, and the War Office Works Directorate
dumped them down – typically the standard tin-roofed and
wooden-walled hutment – on whatever convenient site happened
to be free.

Gibson's regime changed that. Tandy and his colleagues began
to produce systematic plans for the development not only of buildings but of the spaces about them. At Arborfield, they produced
one of the first development master plans for a garrison, and the
repair and enhancement of landscape as well as the careful siting

of buildings were key features. At Aldershot they brought in Brenda Colvin, who remembers having to battle against the instinct for excessive tidiness – against what was almost a 'short back and sides' approach to landscape maintenance. 'But the military were already changing to our point of view,' she considers. 'And economic arguments clinched it – when we could show them it was cheaper to let things grow.' So the hard rectilinear gridiron of Aldershot has gradually been softened by vegetation. 'Natural regeneration there is very good, if only you can keep soldiers' boots off it.'

Tandy remembers going to a so-called 'planning meeting' in a garrison town, which shall be nameless. He quickly discovered that this particular garrison commander's notion of planning consisted of placing on a table in the centre of the room a model of the camp, providing loose blocks of wood to represent buildings, and then encouraging more than thirty senior army officers to push these wood blocks about with their swizzle-sticks as if they were planning a battle. Tandy 'refused to play', which the army took very badly. An official complaint about his conduct landed on Sir Donald Gibson's desk. 'He just laughed,' recalls Tandy. Another fruitful outcome of the early days of the Gibson team came in the 1960s when James Nisbett, the quantity surveyor in the team, devised the first system of elemental bills of quantities for landscape work on which the professions's current procedures rest.

Eventually, because RAF and Navy Works Directorates refused to combine under Gibson, the government lost patience and merged all three into the Ministry of Works, where Tandy became landscape architect serving all government departments. Much of the work went to outside consultants, and several leading practices owe their early success – even sometimes survival – to the enlightened patronage guided by Tandy's recommendation. Another important step forward during that time was the writing of landscape cost limits into budgetary procedures for building projects. For whereas architects frequently chafe against cost limits as constraints on good and creative design, for landscape architects they constituted much needed defence against the attitude that, as soon as economies were called for, landscape – as a 'frill' – could be axed with impunity.

The contrast between 1959, when Tandy found himself pioneering landscape architecture in the Civil Service, and today, is remarkable. Then he was the one and only landscape architect in government service, and there only as a result of a piece of administrative sleight of hand. Now Michael Ellison, as the Property Service Agency's Chief Landscape Architect, has a professional team of twenty-nine; Michael Porter at the Department of Transport, sixteen; and there are probably half a dozen more Civil Servant members of the Institute lurking in sundry other government departments. But, believes Tandy (now consultant to the Forestry Commission and principal with Max Nicholson and John Herbert in the multidisciplinary practice, Land Use Consultants), their status and numbers are 'still nothing compared with what they ought to be'.

Michael Ellison joined PSA from the GLC in inauspicious circumstances: the establishment he had been led to expect fell victim to a moratorium on all recruitment. He filled in the time until the ban was lifted by devising ways of releasing the potential for use of landscape design skills in PSA, getting to know and develop a fruitful relationship with administrative civil servants, and mastering the implications for landscape architects of PSA cost control disciplines. One of the keys to development of the profession, he believes, is having the right mix of jobs for in-house landscape designers, so that they not only develop experience and versatility but end up firmly 'in the black' by the standards the Civil Service uses to test cost effectiveness.

The Property Services Agency – with new construction worth more than £400m on its books ranging from embassies abroad to army married quarters, government office blocks and post offices, and an annual maintenance bill of over £300m – can claim to be the largest building and property organization in Britain. There are those who argue that creative design can scarcely flourish in such a set-up. For instance, in his presidential address to the Landscape Institute in July 1978, Professor Arnold Weddle said, 'I confess to some doubts that any large, central organization, especially Civil Service, can consistently produce high quality designs of any kind.' We need to weigh this instinctive, and often well-founded scepticism about large public organizations against the efforts of Dan Lacey, the PSA's Director of General Design Services, and his Director of Architectural Services Geoffrey Woodward, to keep things fluid and creative – notably through the Design Office, based on the model of an interdisciplinary professional partnership, which Woodward originally headed. Ellison is one of the 'partners' in this set-up, and has landscape architects working as equal members of the design team on two of the Office's biggest projects: the Liverpool Exchange station site which is being redeveloped at a cost of some £25m to accommodate Civil Service departments dispersed from London; and a design project of comparable size at Middlesbrough. 'My own view,' says Ellison, 'is that the landscape architect needs to be inside. Landscape design can't be understood from a distance. You lose the magic of the architect, landscape architect, QS, civil engineer and administrator all sitting down and discovering how much they can achieve together.'

Ellison now has three main roles at the PSA. He is 'line manager' to nineteen landscape architects, including the small studio cheek-by-jowl with his own office at Lunar House, Croydon, which serves as a 'test laboratory' for clients' needs and strives to look after research and development. He is responsible for the results and design quality of these nineteen. His second role is to advise on the use of consultants. Some of them, he says, are excellent, but others have not in practice produced results that their reputations promised. His third role, as head of profession, has two particularly significant facets. He controls recruitment, sifting all applications for landscape jobs in the PSA, and has deliberately been 'very, very fussy' in order to keep the profession's reputation within the department high. His files in July 1977 contained sixty application forms for PSA landscape jobs; only four of them had been successful. The other facet of his 'head of profession' role involves advising the directorates who are his clients whether they have the kind of potential workload to justify starting their own landscape sections. Here lies the potential for growth of the profession within the agency; but Ellison sees this as no empire building exercise. Again the mix of work must be right, both as between types and sizes of design job and between work that is 'productive' by Civil Service accounting standards and the 'non-productive' advisory and monitoring side. Growth of this kind brings a double benefit. Carefully chosen landscape architects are on hand to advise client directorates at an early stage as to the landscape potential of a project, and are better able than architects, engineers or administrators to monitor the performance of consultants and judge whether their designs or performance come up to scratch; and, Ellison believes, the unlocking of potential for landscape work in PSA projects, achieved by a strong in-house team, will produce so much extra work that consultants too will stand to gain more and bigger commissions. At present, the division of work between inside and outside designers normally runs about fifty–fifty.

One promising new client from outside the circle of PSA directorates is the Post Office, for whom Ellison's team are carrying out a range of work, including two large and particularly significant jobs. At the Post Office's huge Radio-Telecommunications Centre at Martlesham Heath in Suffolk they are producing an overall 'steering plan' for landscaping a collection of quite sizeable Spaces Left Over After Planning. And at Newbold Revel near Rugby they are making an overall landscape plan into which will be fitted new buildings round an existing mansion. This commission also includes a management plan for the long-term after care of the estate.

Asked for good examples of design for the public client in his field, Ellison suggested two schemes carried out under his predecessor, architect/planner/landscape architect John Higgins: work for the Army at Larkhill in Wiltshire and Maidstone's Invicta Barracks; and two by consultants: Brian Clouston & Partners' work at Catterick Camp; and William Gillespie & Partners' scheme for the then Post Office Savings Bank at Cow Glen near Glasgow. At Cow Glen Gillespies have produced a setting round buildings full of skilful changes of level and shrewd planting, and marked by the retention of existing trees among roads paths and parking spaces. At Catterick, Cloustons have developed and exploited the experience of earlier consultants that landscape can be the key element of any overall development plan for a garrison or camp. The Army's land holding at Catterick covers some 1,000 hectares, and the Landscape Master Plan commissioned by the old Ministry of Public Works in 1970 concentrates on the actual 770 hectares of the Garrison itself. The consultants, working with the PSA's Garrison Town Planning Unit, drew up a programme of landscape development and improvement which extended over the ten years to 1980 and costing £700,000 at 1971 prices. Catterick won Cloustons and the Army one of the Civic Trust's 1978 awards, and it seems that the Army at Catterick now understands and respects landscape design and landscape planning in a way that most clients still do not; so that the CO, points out Michael Ellison, takes VIPs not to see his new hospital but on a tour of the camp's new landscape.

No attempt, however partial, to survey the role of central government as the client of the landscape architect can fail to mention the Scottish Development Agency. Speaking to the Landscape

Institute early in 1978, its chairman Sir William Gray remarked that while everyone knew about the SDA's role in financing industry, most people were much less aware that it had also been charged with 'reversing the trends of dereliction in cities, towns and villages throughout Scotland'. Indeed in the two years up to February 1978 when he was speaking, the agency had committed some £36m to reclamation of abandoned coal, shale and slate workings and a wide variety of derelict and degraded land in both town and countryside. The SDA's usual approach is to grant-aid reclamation or improvement schemes put forward by local authorities, using either their own landscape architects or consultants; and there is little doubt that the agency has pushed and cajoled many of the new Scottish local authorities into employing landscape architects where their predecessors would not have done so.

The SDA employs three landscape architects, who act in some schemes as designers, in others for the client in briefing consultants. The agency even offers, in selected projects, a three-year after-care service; but requires undertakings from local authorities that they will then take over the schemes and maintain them to specified standards. It has also found, encouragingly, that communities respond to an upgraded environment. For instance, tenants in Govan, by tradition one of Glasgow's toughest areas, have actively safeguarded their new River Clyde Walkway; and at Dykehead Cross near Motherwell reclamation of derelict land has stimulated interest from private housebuilders. The agency sees repair of landscape as complementary to its task of industrial development because, to quote its chairman again, environmental improvement is 'a most effective double-edged weapon in removing the worst of the industrial past for the good of the industrial future of Scotland.'

On the face of it, central government in Wales is less appreciative of the skills and potential contribution of landscape architects than in Scotland. The Welsh Office has attached to its planning staff a landscape adviser, Charles Smart, who has to try to spread his time and energies over a whole range of topics, from overall landscape planning for the whole Principality, down to influencing particular planning decisions or the siting and designs of specific government buildings. The Welsh Office clearly should have more than one landscape architect; and yet Smart's appointment in 1973 was a welcome step in the right direction.

So, are landscape architects now welcomed and appreciated in all departments of central government? Ray Miller, landscape architect with Surrey County Council, has his doubts. He cites a Civil Service Commission leaflet inviting applications for posts in the Planning Inspectorate. These are the men and women who hear planning inquiries and either write the report on which the Minister generally bases his decision or – in an increasing number of cases – give a binding decision themselves. Apart from such eminently desirable qualities as good presence, sound judgement and the ability to think clearly, this document, issued as recently as August 1978, requires candidates to be 'member of the Royal Town Planning Institute, the Royal Institute of British Architects, the Institute of Civil Engineers, the Institution of Municipal Engineers or the Royal Institution of Chartered Surveyors (any branch)' or be barristers or solicitors. The implication is clear. The Civil Service Commission considers, that in deciding planning and environmental issues, engineers, lawyers and perhaps even surveyors running an estate agency business are suitable as inspectors but landscape architects are not. Miller also analysed all appeal decisions relating to the Waverly district of southwest Surrey, which contains much green belt land and land in Areas of Outstanding Natural Beauty. Of the inspectors who heard the appeals, 11% were surveyors, 17% engineers, 22% town planners, 6% each lawyers and architects, 5% architect-planners, and 33% other, mainly with no professional qualification. None of the inspectors had a landscape qualification. Does the Civil Service Commission, then, still regard landscape architecture as for some purposes 'not quite a profession'?

Chapter 7
IN CAHOOTS WITH THE HIGHWAYMAN

Landscape and Roads

Few areas of government activity illustrate the transformation which has occurred in attitudes to landscape design better than road building. Concern about the impact of new roads on landscape began to find strong expression already in the 1920s, and the first positive response from government came with the passing of the 1925 Roads Improvement Act which gave power to sow grass verges and to plant trees and shrubs alongside roads. In 1928 an enlightened Minister of Transport, Colonel Wilfred Ashby, persuaded various bodies then campaigning to improve the appearance of highways to amalgamate into the Roads Beautifying Association; and in the following year a former curator of the Royal Botanic Gardens, Kew, Mr. W. G. Bean, was appointed on a retainer to advise the Minister on roadside planting schemes put forward by local authorities. It should be noted that he was an acknowledged authority on trees and shrubs, rather than landscape; and indeed until the 1960s the approach remained that of applying cosmetic improvement after the event to the artefact created by the road engineer – as indeed the name Road Beautifying Association implies. Mr. Bean's role was by no means lavishly funded. His visits to roads under construction depended on the courtesy of the chief engineer in sending his own car; and the basis of planting was often (as departmental correspondence reveals) that the foreman on this or that length of road was 'doing a very thorough job of double-digging', or that a local nursery had some suitable trees and would be sending a batch along.

One aim of the campaigners seems to have been to secure a woodland margin which would prevent or at least disguise the ribbon growth of bungalows along new highways. Economic depression slowed new road building during the 1930s, but 1935 saw a significant step forward when the Restriction of Ribbon Development Act gave power to plant on land acquired *outside* the limits of the road. In 1938 the Minister secured the advisory services of the Roads Beautifying Association by paying them an annual grant of £200. The RBA continued this role until 1947.

The advice the Association gave did not, however, commend itself to everyone. It remained horticultural in its bias, and it often favoured exotic species inappropriate to rural landscapes; its treatment was 'gardenesque'! Avenues of flowering cherries really had little to do with the landscape of the North Downs, pointed out the critics. After the Second World War the Ministry, in anticipation of a greatly expanded road building programme, appointed its first full-time horticultural adviser, Mr. W. Sheet His appointment met with a barrage of criticism. 'Is it not a monstrous thing,' asked Mr. Patrick Thorneycroft in the House of Commons in 1951, 'that poor people should have to pay purchase tax in order to pay the salaries of gentlemen who then go out and plant highways?' A great many people still regarded roadside planting as a lot of pretty-pretty nonsense or, at best, a desirable but luxury extra.

In 1956, the postwar road building programme did at last get into top gear, with the building of Britain's first stretch of motorway, the Preston bypass and the start of the M1. And at this point came the Ministry's most important step forward to date – the appointment of an Advisory Committee on the Landscape Treatment of Trunk Roads. Its chairman, the Hon. David Bowes Lyon, set it firmly in the right direction by expressing, at the Committee's inaugural meeting, a firm preference for indigenous trees. Foreign species, however attractive and adaptable, should be discouraged because they were uncharacteristic of the region through which a road passed. He urged the Committee to take a long view for posterity's sake, and suggested that fast highways demanded a fresh approach to landscape so that it was geared to what a driver in a fast vehicle saw, not designed for a static viewpoint.

So incongruous exotics were out; scale and spacing of planting were to match the speed of modern roads and vehicles – but, it may be noted, all Mr. Bowes Lyons' emphasis was on the view *from* the road. The importance of the view *of* the road from the surrounding countryside only fully occurred to the Committee later.

LANDSCAPE BY DESIGN

It did not take them very long to discover that comment on cut-and-dried schemes would not suffice: the Committee needed to involve itself actively in all stages of the engineering design process, from choice of route onwards. They clearly needed a skilled professional to act for them – a landscape architect. This did not, however, happen for another five years: in 1961 the Ministry of Transport appointed Michael Porter its first Landscape Adviser. Then he was a one-man band, rushing from engineer to engineer and scheme to scheme, trying to achieve an improvement here and prevent a disaster there. Now he has a team of sixteen, including six horticulturalists and nine other landscape architects, seven of them regionally based.

To most motorists, landscaping – in so far as they think about it – probably means trees and shrubs. The change in official thinking over the past three decades or so stands out well from statistics on this. In 1946 when the Ministry contemplated 3,000 miles of new road over the next ten years, they estimated (basing their calculations on the three miles of prewar Southend arterial road, which had 60 trees) that about 60,000 trees would be needed for the ten-year programme. Contrast that with the actual use of trees and shrubs in the 1960s and '70s. For instance, in the 1963–64 planting season, trunk road schemes used some 402,000 trees and shrubs; in 1977–78, the figure was more than 2 million just for that year.

But Porter's first few years at the Ministry were also a battle to get in earlier and earlier on the design process. In the urgency of getting roads built, the Ministry were generally not too impressed by environmental arguments; what did gradually win them over was results. Thus one of the first things the newly appointed adviser did was to look at the crucial stretch of M6 route through Cumbria, then on the drawing board. The first stretches of M1 had disturbed many observers by their visual crudity, and brought protests such as an article by Sylvia Crowe in *The Architects Journal* of 10 September, 1959, where she wrote:

It is obvious that the present line [of the M1] is the logical result of applying the simplest, speediest and most economical engineering technique to the problem, regardless of other factors. The need for adjustment to meet the landscape occurs only on limited stretches, and even then involves only a comparatively narrow area on each side of the curtilage line ... Some ill effects can never be changed. The severance of complete landscape compositions by the great barrier of the road embankments is one of the most damaging....

These embankments, especially those carrying slip roads, formed 'major and often clumsy shapes in the view', she considered. An ILA deputation led by Richard Sudell (president 1955–57) had earlier been to see the Minister; and all these pressures strengthened the hand both of the advisory committee and of the adviser. Porter was able to argue that the Cumbrian stretch of the M6 called for exceptionally sensitive treatment; and a gratifying accolade came when the engineers were about to open the road, having adopted most of his and the Committee's landscape recommendations. They asked him to look them over once more to make sure that the landscape advice had been correctly incorporated. They were clearly rather pleased with the result (and did not want to spoil the ship for an accidental ha'porth of environmental tar). In the event, the road – with its spectacular Shap summit, its vertically separated carriageways, and its graceful sweep into the Lune Gorge – won a Civic Trust Award. Porter pays special tribute to the consulting engineers for the scheme, Scott Wilson Kirkpatrick & Partners, who right from the start appreciated the landscape challenge of the M6 and began to talk the same language – a skill, it may be added, that some road engineers even today have not managed to achieve.

The time scale in the landscape of roads is as little understood by the general public as in other areas of landscape design. Thus Michael Porter says frankly that, though it must obviously be designed to have a visual impact on the day the road opens, planting will not be at its best for fifty or sixty years. Here the Ministry of Transport team have one great advantage denied most other designers. Land acquired for the road and its landscape remains the Department's in perpetuity, and the Department of Transport's landscape team continues to exercise control. They can not only advise a regime of maintenance, but have *locus standi* to see that it is carried out; they can also review planting to see whether it still fits what is often a changing landscape around it. Their contractors for most purposes are the Forestry Commission, which by its nature and size is well equipped to do this job. At the other end of the time scale, the passing motorist scarcely appreciates that landscape design of the road he is using may have begun ten years before the road opened. Influence by the advisory committee and the landscape team is now considerable. No longer do they have to struggle to argue a more acceptable route against objections of extra cost; they have their say from the moment routes first begin to be considered. They also influence the choice of alignment, both horizontal and vertical, the shaping of earthworks, earth moulding and the alignment of fences; besides designing planting on and off site and indicating what additional land needs buying to produce an acceptable planting scheme. Good landscaping has become part of the highway engineer's credo.

As to results, we need only contrast the early M1 sections – long, boring straights connecting radii; structurally economical but ugly bridges; vertical alignments designed chiefly to match the cubic quantities of cut and fill – with the sinuous, graceful and often dramatic qualities of the M4 or M6 to realize how far road land-scape has advanced. The item that remains least satisfactory is motorway service areas. The early M1 service areas were incredibly crude and rushed in design. Original plans show that, for instance, at Watford Gap someone simply stuck a compass point on the mid-way point of the road and drew a circle. The arcs on either side of the motorway became the boundaries of the two sites. Porter's team does its best, within the limitations of a tendering system where developers can rarely be persuaded to take landscape advice for their initial submissions; and some of the best results – for in-stance at Leigh Delamere and at Aust on the M4 – stem from the Ministry landscape men drawing up the zone plan within which buildings, car parks and service roads must be fitted.

Once on the road the picture, as we have seen, is happier. The designers have mastered the art of manipulating the distant view, rather than features in the foreground which, for a motorist passing at speed, are frustrating, shortlived and sometimes even dangerous. At a distance there can be drama without distraction. Thus at Bre-don on the M5 tree planting is deliberately used to postpone a dramatic view of the church steeple: its impact is the greater for coming at the end of a long, tree-screened curve. A basic technique is, in Porter's words, 'to take what you find and emphasize it. Otherwise at 70 miles per hour, it all comes to seem much of a muchness.'

The depth of the landscape belt which can be related to the road has also increased out of all recognition. In the 1930s, the 'beauti-fiers' were fighting for a narrow strip of land for planting, and to deter or screen ribbon development. Even before the 1973 Land Compensation Act, Porter and his team were sometimes able to obtain parcels of land adjacent to the actual road line by letting district valuers know what they would like. Ministry road engineers

have thus moved in less than two decades from regarding landscape
as a dubious cosmetic ('A good, honest piece of civil engineering
has no need of "tarting up",' was a not untypical attitude in the
early sixties) to an axiomatic assumption that it is an integral part
of road design. We can detect two main reasons for this. First, the
thoroughgoing professionalism of Porter and his team has won
them over. They accept expert landscape advice almost in the same
way that they accept expert advice or expert judgements on
geology or structural calculations. Secondly, the ever-increasing
difficulty of getting road schemes through public inquiries against
more and more resourceful and well organized environmental
objectors makes it essential for them to take the best landscape
advice and implement it unstintingly. Porter says he has never been
kept short of money for landscaping; on the other hand, he has
clearly always been understaffed for the amount of work his team
is expected to do. His original estimate at the time of his
appointment was that he needed twenty professional staff to do
the job thoroughly. The present team of sixteen has to cope with
a much bigger workload which, as we shall shortly see, the slowing
down of the roads programme has not at all lightened.

One of the big challenges in designing road landscape schemes
today stems from recognition that the country on either side of
the road may be in transition – notably from modern agricultural
methods and the transformation of field patterns it brings. A road
landscape scheme which relates to an eighteenth-century enclosure
pattern of hedgerows and hedgerow trees can come to look distinctly out of place if neighbouring farmers root up those hedgerows and fill in ditches to create a 1,000-acre field for ease of
mechanized harvesting. Equally, if all the elms are dying, the landscape architect for the road needs to know what plans, if any, landowners or local authorities have for replanting.

But it is not only in unspoiled country that road landscape
schemes are important. A stretch of motorway running through
a depressed or derelict industrial area may demand every bit as careful treatment. A poor or unsuitable scheme may retard, impede or
even scupper plans to rehabilitate and upgrade the adjacent environment; a skilfully designed scheme can assist and stimulate them.

The Leitch Report of early 1978, with its emphasis on non-quan-
tifiable environmental and other factors and a fairer deal for objectors, has generally been welcomed by landscape architects as by
other environmentalists. It will, however, mean a much heavier

workload for the Department of Transport's landscape team. They are now, for instance, having to produce photo-montages not only of the 'preferred route' put forward by their own department but of alternative routes urged by objectors. Already by June 1978, six months after Leitch, Porter had come to the conclusion that this would triple his team's workload. Some people would say it also put the Ministry landscape architect in an invidious position. It is one thing to argue with your engineers on the right and necessary treatment of a road from the landscape point of view; quite another to satisfy a group of often suspicious objectors that you, the salaried servant of the promoting department, have conscientiously and honestly done the best you could in working up their rival alignment. The profession's job thus appears akin to that of the politician: the art of optimizing the inevitable.

Chapter 8

POWER, STEEL, RAIL, CANALS AND AIRPORTS

The State Corporations as Clients

After roadbuilding, perhaps electricity generation and transmission has had a bigger impact on Britain's landscape than any other activity. Pre-1939, power stations were local and relatively small scale. Then, as with most of the postwar power stations built in the forties and fifties both by the old undertakings and the newly nationalized electricity supply industry, landscaping meant to all intents and purposes gardening. Flower beds appeared in front of power station administration blocks; the Roads Beautifying Association sometimes planted some trees. Only in a few sensitive spots, such as the hydro stations at Ffestiniog and Rheidol, or where the impact of a very large station on its surroundings seemed to call for special attention, was anything more attempted (see Plate 6).

The creation by statute of a new structure for the electricity industry changed this picture. People saw that the scale of power stations and transmission lines was, as it were, making a megajump. The Central Electricity Generating Board which superseded the Central Electricity Authority in 1958 had two significant statutory duties: (1) to develop and maintain an efficient, coordinated and economical system of electricity supply; and (2) to take into account any effect which their proposals would have on the natural beauty of the countryside and on flora and fauna. This second duty – what today might be summed up as a duty 'to show concern for the environment' – was in its time unique as a statutory goal. Here was a major state industry, set up by Parliament to construct what was virtually a new national electric power system, working under statutory guidelines which required it *not* simply to produce electricity as cheaply as possible, with a little cosmetic landscaping tacked on as a gesture; but consciously to balance in each project the twin objectives of cheap electricity efficiently produced and respect for the environment.

The first sign of how seriously this new duty was to be regarded came with the appointment of Lord (then Sir William) Holford as member of the CEGB with special responsibility for architecture and amenity. Holford, it will be remembered, had played a crucial role in getting landscape design built into the planning of the post-war new towns. In Sir Christopher (later Lord) Hinton he had a chairman keenly aware of the impact of the CEGB's development programme on the environment; and in two papers presented at the Royal Society of Arts in November, 1959 – *Power Production and Transmission in the Countryside: Preserving Amenities* – they spelled out the problems and laid down principles and guidelines for meeting them. From that time on, the early appointment of landscape architects for power stations projects became the rule; on occasion the Board appointed its landscape consultants before its civil engineering consultants, so as to benefit from their advice even at site selection stage.

At first public opinion was sceptical of the CEGB's new enlightened attitude to landscape, but Michael Shepheard, the CEGB's first architect, believes the dynamism of Hinton and Holford, beginning with their RSA papers and thereafter going on to demonstrate environmental concern in actual projects, soon 'began to turn opinion round'. Shepheard, CEGB Architect from 1959 to 1970, saw his office grow from a three-man band to a team of eighteen architects and two landscape architects at head office, as well as a team of twelve (mostly landscape designers) working on transmission lines, switching stations and the like. Shepheard, who had got to know Sylvia Crowe while working on housing at Basildon New Town, now met her again in the very different context of Trawsfynydd and Wylfa power stations. Other landscape consultants for CEGB schemes during his time there included Brenda Colvin, Kenneth and Patricia Booth, Frederick Gibberd, Derek Lovejoy, Peter Shepheard, Peter Youngman, Colwyn Ffoulkes, Gordon Patterson, Arnold Weddle, Sheila Haywood and Milner White.

The procedure for power station design is now well established. Every 'Section 2 consent' contains conditions which make a landscape scheme an integral part of the proposals and require the agreement of the local planning authority. Schemes must frequently run the gauntlet of public inquiries, with landscape architects called to give evidence as expert witnesses.

At an early stage in a power station project, the design team, which includes architects and landscape architects as well as engineers, obtains and analyses a comprehensive range of data about the site: its geology, topsoil, existing vegetation, drainage patterns, land use and visual and ecological characteristics included. They then make an analysis of the environmental impact of the proposed new structures on the ecology and appearance of the site, using computers and photogrammetry to analyse zones of visual influence. Architects and landscape architects as members of the project team advise on site layout, orientation and shapes of buildings, and the choice of texture and colour in the station's main visual components. The landscape architect's proposals comprise detailed design and maintenance proposals, including conservation of existing trees and shrubs, ground contouring and tree planting, both on site and, wherever agreement can be obtained, in strategic positions off site. In the Trent Valley, for instance, the CEGB commissioned Derek Lovejoy to prepare what amounted to a regional landscape plan, and contributed to the cost of extensive off site planting. The County Council carried out the work and remained responsible for maintenance. The care taken in siting and design of the board's huge 2,000 megawatt stations is well demonstrated by one of the Trent Valley stations, West Burton. Its designers used a device called a heliodon to view the station's main components in model form so as to assess various groupings from different viewpoints and under a wide range of light conditions. They paid particular attention to the grouping of cooling towers, and it was at West Burton that the CEGB experimented (not in this author's view by any means unsuccessfully) with colour mixed into the concrete used for the towers. These eight huge structures they eventually arranged in two dissimilar groups, one of which rises out of a large pond. This, combined with ground modelling, creates a dramatic approach to the station. West Burton eventually won the CEGB a Civic Trust Award as 'an immense engineering work of great style which, far from detracting from the visual scene, acts as a magnet to the eye from many parts of the Trent Valley ...'. That success, believes the Board's present Architect, Howard Mason, was in no small measure due to Derek Lovejoy's imaginative landscape design as well as consultant architects Gelsthorpe & Savidge's design of the actual buildings.

Other landscape honours followed West Burton: Didcot (Frederick Gibberd), Wylfa (Sylvia Crowe), Cottam (Kenneth Booth) and Trawsfynydd (also Crowe). Originally three project groups handled power station design and construction contracts, with architects at CEGB headquarters coordinating architectural and landscape aspects. Shepheard's first landscape assistant, John Herbert (now a principal in Land Use Consultants and landscape professor at Nottingham University) possessed both landscape and town planning qualifications and handled preparatory work and research outside the scope of consultant landscape architects' commissions. In 1970 project groups and HQ Generation Design Department merged into a single Generation Development and Construction Division, now based at Barnwood near Gloucester. Its architects section includes landscape staff under divisional landscape architect Ronald Hebblethwaite, who carry out some 'executive commissions', previously the preserve of consultants. Hebblethwaite's team has also undertaken research on techniques for establishing trees in pulverized fuel ash (a byproduct of coal-burning power stations), cracking the hardened layers with small gelignite charges and adding various organic ameliorants to the ash in the tree pits. Other research it has carried out includes work on establishing trees in the specially difficult conditions of draw-down areas at hydro-electric stations; and on the computer/photogrammetry techniques of visual impact analysis already mentioned.

Electricity transmission poses in some ways greater amenity problems than generation. Overhead power lines are, with very few exceptions, linear intrusions into the landscape. Society has required large new power stations (particularly nuclear ones) to be away from centres of population, and their operation requires large sources of cooling water; therefore the grid linking them to big towns and cities often inevitably crosses attractive or vulnerable stretches of countryside. With the bigger scale of generation, transmission also needed to increase in scale, first from 132 KV to 275 KV, then from 275 KV to 400 KV. Higher voltages increased the size of pylons and thus the potential impact on the countryside. So, conscious of this, the Generating Board set up in 1961 a separate Transmission Project Group (now part of the Transmission Development and Construction Division) which included right from the outset 'in-house' landscape architects and architects working as members of project teams. The ideal solution for power lines would, from a landscape point of view, be to bury them. But undergrounding costs upwards of sixteen times as much as overhead transmission, largely because cooling them underground is an expensive business. The Generating Board, inspectors at public inquiries, and ministers in making the final decisions, have all concluded that in most circumstances such a disproportionate spending would tip the balance too far away from efficiency and cheapness. Even so, out of 12,100 km of high voltage power line in England and Wales, the CEGB has put 1,100 km underground – one kilometre in every eleven; and Britain's total of underground high voltage cable exceeds the equivalent total for the whole of the United States.

Where power lines do go above ground, the choice of route largely depends in the first instance on the judgement of CEGB wayleave officers – men and women chosen partly because they have an 'eye for country' – and Lord Holford said publicly on at least one occasion that he considered in most cases their route could not be bettered. On rare occasions, for particularly sensitive stretches, where the CEGB wants to investigate alternative routings, it may commission consultant landscape architects to give advice. In choosing routes it carries out extensive consultations, with landowners, local planning authorities, and on occasion the Countryside Commission and other public and private bodies concerned with amenity. The CEGB's landscape designers on the transmission side, however, spend much more of their time on designs for major substations and switching stations, where power lines converge or the voltage is reduced for distribution into networks of the area electricity boards. These artefacts, bigger in area and larger in scale than the actual generating stations of earlier decades, can have a profound impact on their surroundings – which skilful design can do wonders in softening. For instance, the switching station at Wymondley in Hertfordshire (which won a commendation in the 1973 RICS/*The Times* Conservation Awards) uses large-scale ground modelling and extensive tree planting to render its array of large-scale busbars and switchgear all but invisible from most points of the compass.

Power stations you cannot generally hide. Their chimneys, their generator halls and, in the case of thermal stations, their cooling towers – all are nowadays of a scale to defy any screening or tucking away. But designers can do three helpful things at least: architects can make the buildings themselves exciting, inspiring and in harmony with their surroundings rather than drab, ugly and at odds;

they and landscape architects can work together to fit the buildings into the landscape to best effect, in terms, for instance, of colour, position and profile; and skilful landscape design can hide some features of the station and enhance others, as did Sylvia Crowe at Trawsfynydd, the 580-MW nuclear power station completed in 1964 in the midst of the Snowdonia national park at a cost of £69m. The lake from which the station draws its cooling water appears at first sight from its southern end to be a natural stretch of water. It is in fact a dammed valley created in the 1920s for the purposes of an early, small hydro-electric power station. The nuclear power station's buildings, designed by Sir Basil Spence and clad in concrete panels made on site with a coating of grit from local stone, stand behind the lake embankment in a deliberately compact grouping. Dame Sylvia's landscape design aimed at achieving a direct union between the main buildings and the wild Welsh mountain landscape about them. She shunned any formal frame of lawns or flower beds; and the sitting out garden she has provided for staff nestles in the shelter of the embankment between it and the reactor and turbine buildings. The approach road to the station follows the contour; and is free of kerbs and lamp standards; car parking is partly masked by a gatehouse block; and the unsightly tangle of switchgear that forms the substation stands on low ground, partly hidden by an existing spinney, partly by extensive ground moulding and new planting.

Security fences had long been a problem in landscaping power stations – especially nuclear stations. For the first time at Trawsfynydd the board agreed to accept a much tighter perimeter, with a new and less obtrusive design of fence carried relatively close to the buildings, and often hidden amidst tree planting or by the fold of the ground. Other landscape recommendations resulted in the pumphouse going underground; the pylons and girders of the substation switchgear being painted grey, and much of the ground between them sown with dwarf clover; and the skilful fitting in of the transmission lines which carry power from the station to the grid using the least obtrusive route and a short underground stretch of line close to the station. Tree planting, carried out by the Forestry Commission, continues up the hill behind the reactor buildings, absorbing some of the buildings' bulk into a bowl of forest; the low siting of the main buildings means that the clutter of engineers' impedimenta which seems to be inseparable from any industrial complex remains out of sight until you are actually standing under the buildings' walls; and in reinstating ground disturbed by construction work, Dame Sylvia specified use of gorse, rowan, birch and heather. With local vegetation steadily recolonizing slopes left bare by the building process, it has become virtually impossible – fourteen or sixteen years later – to tell where the disturbance occurred. The central artefact constituted by the reactor and transformer buildings, too big to hide, nonetheless sits naturally in a landscape that gives the illusion of never having changed.

Modern power stations, we have seen, are generally too big to be hidden. There are exceptions. The greater part of the new £200m Dinorwic pumped storage power station scheme in Snowdonia is underground, in huge manmade caverns beneath the mountain. Dinorwic which takes its name from slate quarries close to Llanberis, a village in the very shadow of Snowdon, shows how sensitive landscape issues now are, how seriously the Board and the local planning authorities treat them, but how, at the end of the day, the sensible solution is often a compromise that satisfies neither the test of maximum efficiency in electricity generation nor all the demands of the conservationist lobby. Indeed, Dinorwic, as a pumped storage scheme, represents a conflict between two different kinds of conservation: energy conservation, which it serves handsomely; and landscape conservation, where despite all the efforts of the Board and its consultants, a price remains to be paid.

Some rural conservationists argue that the Dinorwic scheme, even in its present form, is a disaster and should not have been allowed to go ahead. Against this we must consider the remarkable changes for the better which the efforts of local planners, conservation groups, the public inquiry process and, not least, the CEGB's consultants and its own design staff, have achieved since the original proposals were put forward. The most crucial of these concerns Llyn Peris, the lower reservoir for the scheme, which with a second lake, Llyn Padarn, forms a key element in the beautiful valley running down from the Pass of Llanberis to Llanberis village. Llyn Peris has over the years grown smaller in size as waste material from nearby slate quarries pushed forward its eastern banks. The original CEGB proposal would have used that diminished area of water, and would have necessitated a 9-metre high dam or embankment across the valley. Cherished and time-honoured views down the Pass of Llanberis would have been wrecked, argued objectors. Caernarfon County Council put forward proposals for a lower dam and for removing some of the slate deposits so as to increase once more the surface of the lake. Sir Frederick Gibberd's initial reaction was to point out that the county schemes damaged the landscape seriously in other ways; but eventually he was able to produce an amended scheme using a 3.5-metre embankment and eliminating some of the uglier civil engineering features required by the county scheme.

The most remarkable feature of Dinorwic remains, of course, how much is not seen. A power station with a capacity of the order of Didcot's, or about treble Trawsfynydd's, has been almost completely tucked away inside a Welsh mountain. Its turbine hall alone (measuring 179 × 23.5 m and 51 m high) could accommodate the nave of Westminster Abbey and leave room to spare. Think of the impact such a power station would have on virtually any landscape, let alone Snowdonia's.

The investment programme of the British Steel Corporation is comparable to that of the CEGB, but its effects on the landscape are very different. Michael Shepheard, who left the CEGB in 1970 to join the British Steel Corporation as Manager of Land Development and Architecture under Lord Melchett's chairmanship, makes the point that, unlike CEGB, British Steel is for the most part developing on sites where steel works already exist – no national parks or areas of outstanding natural beauty, but rather established industrial areas. For this reason, amenity is only occasionally a critical issue.

Shepheard (now BSC chief architect) recalls that Melchett was, in implementing his 1970 'Plan for Steel', keen to emulate the CEGB's concern for good design and sensitive approach to the environment. He consulted the presidents of the RIBA, Town Planning Institute and Institute of Landscape Architects about the best way of preserving amenity and of employing land use techniques to avoid the kinds of dereliction that heavy industry had in the past all too often created. From these consultations grew the idea of establishing an architectural and landscaping 'presence' at BSC's head office.

Hunterston on the Clyde (where the landscape scheme, now completed, had a budget of over a million pounds) is one of the rare cases where a large new steel works was proposed for a green field site; and the consultant architects appointed for this job, Sir Frank Mears & Partners, include a partner who is a qualified landscape architect. BSC's largest investment in landscape work, however, is going into rehabilitation schemes, such as those at Irlam,

Shotton, Skinningrove and Ebbw Vale. Apart from its two 'macro-landscape' schemes, at Hunterston and Redcar (discussed below), the corporation has also commissioned, or plans, landscape studies at Llanwern, Port Talbot, Scunthorpe (the Anchor scheme) and elsewhere. Landscape architects currently commissioned by BSC include Peter Youngman at Anchor; David Thirkettle at Port Talbot; Sir Frederick Gibberd at Frodingham (Scunthorpe); Ralph Colwyn Ffoulkes for the industrial trading estate at Shotwick; Wyn Thomas Associates for the Ebbw Vale works; and Brian Clouston & Partners for Redcar, for the research laboratories at Grangetown and Ladgate Lane, Teesside, for the rehabilitation of Skinningrove works, Cleveland, following the end of iron-making there, and more recently for a new industrial estate in Hartlepool.

Redcar, indeed, provides a striking example of the scale of BSC development and the way in which the corporation treats landscape as a key factor from the outset. The development, on a 46-hectare site on the southern side of the Tees estuary will eventually be one of the largest steel making complexes in Europe. The first part of the landscape commission consisted of a comprehensive study of the impact of the development and proposed an environmental buffer zone between the works and residential areas. This would accommodate screen mounding, wildlife areas, a golf course and Redcar beach.

The first phase of landscape development is adjacent to the Trunk Road, on land which was a mixture of old slag banks, a disused refuse tip, marshland and a small-holding. It was extremely exposed with virtually no trees or shrubs, and suffered from salt spray, industrial air pollution and bad ground conditions.

Extensive large-scale mounding has been formed using about a million tons of slag arising from British Steel Corporation's Teesside operations. This provides an effective screen to the new works as well as improving the micro-climate. A large lake has been excavated and the soil used for covering the slag, and the site has been grassed and prepared for tree planting. Special studies are being undertaken in order to develop suitable techniques for establishing vegetation in such a difficult environment.

The area is of considerable wildlife interest, and the new site is to be run by the Corporation as a nature reserve. The value of the landscaping contract is £200,000.

The National Coal Board is another nationalized industry which has contributed to the growth of the landscape profession. Lord Robens, NCB Chairman from 1961 to 1971 and Frank Baker and Don Davison, successive Managing Directors of the Opencast Executive, have also been among the profession's patrons. The decision by the Board to use a multi-disciplinary firm of landscape planners had only just been taken when the disaster at Aberfan occurred. Tragic though this event was, it sparked off the demand for reclaiming derelict pit-heaps – firstly for safety reasons, then for amenity purposes. The firm of Land Use Consultants, who had already begun planning for the restoration of opencast coal sites, were appointed to deal with the reclamation of Aberfan and subsequently worked on numerous schemes of derelict land reclamation as well as the restoration of opencast sites to various use, including recreation instead of the routine 'return to agriculture'. Other landscape firms were engaged on similar work in the Northeast and in Wales.

At first the 'deep mines' regions of the NCB did not show the same interest as the Opencast Executive – probably because they were not in as healthy a financial position and were preoccupied with pit closures. Nevertheless they commissioned studies for several collieries, and consultants visited nearly a hundred of them with a view to creating new industrial 'parks' on the sites of closed mines.

Public inquiries generated a heavy workload; they took place whenever the NCB proposed coal working on a new site. Landscape consultants took part in most of these, acting either for the developers or for objectors. In preparing reports for the NCB on proposed new workings, consultants (mostly LUC) produced a form of analysis and assessment of environmental factors very similar to present *environmental impact statements*, and these gained considerable respect from planning authorities and even from objectors.

In recent years the Opencast Executive has employed more firms, but the amount of work given out has been much reduced, because the Executive now has its own staff and has adopted the skills learned from landscape consultants. The NCB's deep mines management, however, have been handing out more commissions. They have engaged Shepherd Fidler & Associates for the environmental aspects of the new Selby coal mine; Owen Luder's landscape team on the Vale of Belvoir project; and Land Use Consultants to prepare an environmental assessment on a 25 sq. mile search area for a new colliery in Staffordshire. Cliff Tandy of LUC comments: 'The encouragement given to the profession by all departments of the National Coal Board is much appreciated.'

The use of landscape architects by the gas industry is a recent development brought about by the need to exploit offshore natural gas discoveries and by increasingly acute public concern on environmental issues. Throughout the past decade, say British Gas, it has been their policy to use the expertise of landscape architects to produce a large number of landscape schemes, each designed to suit a particular gas installation and its location. The British Gas Corporation's Assistant Chief Environmental Planning Officer, Charles Hibberd, stresses that the corporation attaches the utmost importance to the initial search for a site. This, he says, allows them to make the best of the 'very difficult compromise between technical, economic and environmental considerations'. One purpose of this search is to find a site whose land and tree topography will help as much as possible to harmonize the proposed structures with their surroundings.

'Once the site has been chosen,' continues Hibberd, 'the role of the landscape architect is not necessarily to further screen the installation (which is near impossible anyway) but to utilise his or her expertise in assisting with the visual composition of the new artefact in its landscape setting. Landscape schemes involving tree and shrub planting plus earth mounding have formed an essential part of all British Gas projects, and since 1969 up to 500,000 trees have been planted and at least another 50,000 are planned.'

British Rail, not having constructed any major new railway lines for a century or more, has not until lately seen the need to make much use of landscape architects. The abortive proposal for a Channel Tunnel, with its huge terminal area at Cheriton near Dover and new high speed rail line from there to London, changed that situation radically. The proposals provoked widespread concern as to environmental impact, and prompted all manner of questions which, with the best will in the world, plain straightforward railway engineers found they could not answer convincingly. So in the summer of 1974 British Railways Board commissioned Derek Lovejoy & Partners to prepare an environmental assessment of all the route options proposed – one of the first major environmental impact analyses to be carried out in the United Kingdom.

'Many fundamental short- and long-term proposals were recommended to ameliorate visual and audible intrusion,' recalls

Lovejoy, 'for example the consultants were able to suggest that the only effective method of reducing visual–audio intrusion in the centre of Tonbridge was to deck over $\frac{1}{4}$-mile of the railway and use the deck as part of the expansion of the existing congested town centre.'

At about the same time, British Rail engaged Building Design Partnership to design the terminal, at which up to 2,000 cars and lorries per hour would arrive from an extended M20 motorway for marshalling on to trains. BDP in turn commissioned Brian Clouston & Partners as landscape consultants. The design team early seized on the fact that the terminal's landscaping and general design would have an important psychological effect in 'winding down' drivers and passengers after their 70 mph journey; but from a broader environmental point of view the terminal's impact on the pastoral Kentish landscape was clearly going to be immense.

In 1976 economic and other considerations led the government to abandon the 'Chunnel'; but recently there have been increasingly strong suggestions that the European Economic Community might provide money to revive the project in modified form. Such a scheme might or might not include a high speed rail link. If it does, the lesson will have been learned that railway lines (which give little scope for sharp changes in gradient) are much more difficult to integrate successfully into the landscape than are motorways.

All in all, British Rail have in the past few years shown markedly more environmental awareness – in no small measure thanks to their chairman Sir Peter Parker, who quickly appointed the Board's former Chief Architect Bernard Kaukas to the new post of Director of Environment, with a roving brief to discover and sort out environmental problems and failures, and to show rail engineers and managers how to do the right thing environmentally and reconcile it with sound operating practice and economics. Some British Rail regions and divisions have lately begun using landscape architects or assistants on a small scale, for instance to redesign forecourts to enhance some of their better station buildings; and there is increasing awareness in BR of the value of railway verges, especially cuttings and embankments, as reservoirs and corridors for wildlife.

The British Waterways Board has also, in a steady, quiet way, been improving the appearance of its own canalside land, and in cooperation with local authorities and adjacent landowners. Its problems are, of course, very different from those of the railways. For the most part the canal and inland waterways system antedated the railways; and its linear, manmade landscape has a visual graciousness, harmony, maturity and sense of repose which, to leisure users, is a great part of its attraction. But for many years, the Board's engineers, working on a shoestring to preserve the system from decay, resorted to 'patch repair' solutions of a visually disruptive kind.

In 1970, however, the Board for the first time appointed an architect, Peter White, with a keen instinct: for and understanding of the character and materials both of canalside buildings and of the whole canal landscape. Two-hundred-year-old canals, he stresses, had their buildings, towpaths, walls, locks and other artefacts built in local materials, so that each of these waterways has a distinct personality of its own. White has been able to guide his engineer colleagues into looking always at the environmental effect of functional changes and repairs. Much of this guidance comes in an admirable loose-leaf *Waterways Environmental Handbook* in which White's own pen-and-ink drawings spell out the seemly and the clumsy ways of doing things. He now has a qualified landscape architect working under him. The watchword in landscape design at BWB, he says, is: 'Foster the indigenous qualities of the canalside scene.' The Board undertakes an annual environmental programme, including several minor and two 'major' (but still modestly budgeted) improvement schemes – improvements always eschewing the mere cosmetic and providing for functional needs as well as enhanced appearance (see Plates 7 and 8).

By contrast airports – perhaps even more than railways – are difficult places to bring any visual consistency to. The busiest airports like Heathrow and Gatwick have been in a state of continuous redevelopment virtually since they first opened. They are also often huge: Heathrow, for example, has a 15-mile perimeter. They also pose technical problems like 'bird strike' which may further inhibit a landscape architect's freedom of manoeuvre.

Professor Peter Youngman is the main landscape consultant to the British Airports Authority. He first became involved in work on airports as consultant to planners engaged on the location studies for a third London Airport, and later served on a five-man advisory committee (planner, ecologist, sociologist, noise expert, and landscape architect) which examined very thoroughly the implications of building at Maplin. Thereafter BAA asked him to advise on developments at Gatwick, including the new road approach, entrance and exit buildings, and car parks east of the railway; and he has since increasingly been involved in longer-term plans for expansion at Heathrow, Gatwick, and Aberdeen.

At Heathrow the BAA has begun gradual improvement of perimeter areas, and is carrying out a scheme, designed by Darbourne & Darke, for the improvement of the airport's central area. At Edinburgh the Authority is screen planting round much of the airport boundary, and carrying out a large scheme prepared by Robert Matthew, Johnson-Marshall (landscape architect Ed Hilliard) for the recently completed new terminal area. Airports, says Youngman, so easily can – and often do – look like battlefields. There is always construction work going on; and lessees of individual sites, such as airlines and cargo handling firms, may or may not employ landscape architects when they put up buildings. Even where they do, their designs need coordinating. On the other hand, well-designed and consistent landscape can immensely improve the overall look and atmosphere of an airport.

Chapter 9
WOODS AND WATER

The Forestry Commission and Water Authorities as Clients

Another area of state activity where the whole approach and attitude of a public client has lately been transformed concerns forestry. In 1919 when Parliament set up the Forestry Commission, the prime aim – in the aftermath of the First World War – was clearly a much expanded production of home-grown timber. This remains a prime aim, and more than $3\frac{1}{2}\%$ of the surface area of England, Scotland, and Wales is today covered by the Commission's plantations. For the first four decades of its existence the Commission and its foresters pursued policies largely dominated by commercial considerations: choice of species, pattern of planting, and the shapes of plantations – all aimed at enhancing productivity and profitability. In the last twenty years or so, two things have changed. The Commission now has a statutory duty to concern itself with rural amenity and with recreation. The state foresters have been learning that functional efficiency and a high standard of workmanship are not enough. An increasingly critical public demands that afforestation should take pains to attune itself with its surroundings, harmonize with and if possible enhance the existing scene.

The Commission's foresters have on the whole learned these lessons more readily and less superficially than other 'developers'. The main credit for that must go to a landscape architect, Dame Sylvia Crowe, who held the post of consultant to the Commission from 1963 until 1976. The Commission appointed her in response to a mounting tide of criticism of the pernicious effects which 'functional' geometric planting of conifers was having on cherished and beautiful landscapes. Even in the interwar years, resentment and concern at the 'march of the conifers' had been growing. The

Second World War understandably muted such criticism: the nation's survival depended in some measure on timber production unfettered by environmental scruples. But in the 1950s, with afforestation taking place on an altogether larger scale, the alarm bells began to ring again. Organizations like the CPRE and the Ramblers Association protested ever more vigorously; but so too did influential individuals with an eye to the landscape.

It is not clear to this author, nor indeed to Dame Sylvia herself, who it was that finally influenced the Forestry Commission to appoint a landscape consultant. 'I've met at least ten men who all said it was they who told the Forestry Commission to seek my advice,' Dame Sylvia remarks. Her appointment seems to have been the culmination of widespread and energetic lobbying by a number of people who cared and could bring pressure to bear. The Commission itself was by no means deaf to criticism nor blind to the impact of its work. 'When I first went there, there were some members of the Commission who had a great feeling for landscape; and indeed some of the older forests were beautifully done, especially in Wales.' Concern, and the wish to do better, certainly already existed. But foresters, rather like road engineers in the same period, had become prisoners of their own professional discipline. Dame Sylvia remembers that, 'while many foresters had an appreciation of the landscape, there was a widespread idea that what really mattered was production of a big and profitable bulk of timber. That was efficiency; and one shouldn't be diverted by any other consideration. Foresters were trained in this way.'

How was one woman, wearing the misunderstood and then little regarded label 'landscape architect', to alter generations of traditional forestry practice – even if she were so relatively well known as Miss Crowe? For she did. 'My chief work,' she says, 'was getting there and talking over the technical problems with the foresters. There had to be give and take. Their job is to produce timber, and they have got to do it in an economic way.' But unlike the more extreme preservationists, the Commission's new landscape consultant was not telling them that they shouldn't be planting conifers in this or that beautiful stretch of mid-Wales or northern Scotland. She was saying: It will look better and not cost much more or unduly prejudice your efficiency, if you follow the contour, loosen the edges of your plantations, and plant a rowan, birch and other native or broadleaved species to give variety, colour and a link with the traditional landscape. The gospel she preached, from detailed

knowledge, experience and example, was (to use her own words):
'You can have good landscape and conservation with no extra cost
or loss of efficiency, or with a slight loss of efficiency which is really
only marginal.'

The word conservation is crucial. Though foresters look to a
longer time scale than most people in an urban, instant-results
society, their traditional training in some respects failed to teach
them to look far enough. Dame Sylvia showed them that their
practice of clearing extraneous saplings to secure a 'tidy' effect in
their plantations was ecologically unsound; and that the supposed
economic penalty of planting broadleaved trees among their cash-
crop conifers could actually help to enrich the poor soil of a planta-
tion. But from a landscape point of view, her achievement can be
summed up in the words 'making the connection'. Foresters often
perceived and understood the landscapes on which they had to
work; but they also knew their commercial and professional duty
to produce timber efficiently. They could not generally connect
the two. Dame Sylvia, in thirteen years as the Commission's consultant, showed them how to make that connection. She taught
them a new language, which may be best understood by quoting
briefly and at random from the booklet *Forestry in the Landscape*
which she wrote for the Commission in 1966. Thus in discussing
tree species, she said:

The value of broadleaves in a forest is both biological and visual...

Biologically their contribution to soil fertility and to a wide range of wild
life is recognised. Visually their value lies in their form, their colour and the
beauty and interest of their seasonal change.

The softer, rounded form is in sympathy with the gentle topography of much
of Britain, particularly on the skylines of low hills, and where the forest merges
into open ground.

The colours of broadleaved trees fall within the range of the browns and yel-
low-greens of grasslands, heaths and moors. Their seasonal change is particularly
important in Britain where the changing colours of spring and autumn extend
over half the year.

The colour value (though not the shape) is shared by larches, which can be
used to break the heavy blue-green of other conifers.

And she then goes on to demonstrate, in detail and with diagrams
and photographs, specific situations of ground form and forest
where larches can emphasize attractive features, soften the impact
of the main commercial forest, and add variety and colour to the
overall scene.

In 1976 Dame Sylvia, by then in her 70s, retired as the Commission's consultant, and was followed in that post by Clifford Tandy of Land Use Consultants. 'I came in knowing very well what Sylvia Crowe's work had been and with every intention of carrying it on with the least possible disruption,' he says. 'She had a remarkable personal influence on our foresters, and the effect of her tenure made itself felt right from the top down to working foresters on the ground.' The amended brief to which they were now working also transformed the prospects for forest landscapes. 'Once relieved of the burden of producing trees only for timber, they were very ready to do other work in the best interests of good landscape and good countryside,' explains Tandy. 'After all, foresters are on the whole countrymen and not businessmen selling cubic feet of timber.'

He points with satisfaction to the fact that the Commission now picks likely candidates from among its district officers, and sends these trained foresters to take a degree course in landscape architecture at a university. The first of these, Duncan Campbell, has already been in post for about two years at the time of writing and a second newly graduated forester/landscape architect is just about to join him. The Commission has moved from being a body which regarded landscape design as a desirable but impossibly expensive luxury to accepting it as a necessary and integral part of its work.

Dame Sylvia's was, necessarily and rightly, a 'one person, individual, man-to-man approach'. The nature of the workload in what was essentially a personal consultancy made that inevitable. 'Sylvia was obliged to go round and throw off sparks from the top of her head, which was the right and only way.' Now the client, with its own design section, has changed; the workload has increased; and the new consultant comes with the benefit of backup from a large, multi-disciplinary practice. He is able and determined to base his solutions on very thoroughly researched analyses of local conditions: visual factors, geology, soil conditions, climate, exposure and characteristics of species. Dame Sylvia, Tandy says, gave an ecological basis to forest design and for the first time integrated designs – the forests integrated into the wider landscape and ecological and visual factors brought together in that process. But whereas she, lacking the resources to carry out complete analysis at every site, had to 'use instant judgement, quick assessments', Tandy, with the Commission's own landscape staff, proposes to do it all more systematically. 'Our solutions will be "derived" rather than spontaneous, in a way that the Commission's district officers can follow and apply for themselves.'

Tandy also points to one far-reaching change in the nature of his public client. The Forestry Commission, bidden by government to take greater account of the nation's recreational needs, now gives these almost equal weight in some areas with timber growing. Some stretches of forest will always be reserved for straight commercial timber growing; others are being designed to provide a variety of attractive forest walks of varying length and difficulty, as well as such features as scenic drives. In these new forests, no longer will the rambler feel hemmed in by impenetrable walls of conifer, forced to follow excessively long straight 'rides', and with his occasional glimpse beyond that of ugly, square plantations spoiling distant hillsides. His paths will be pleasantly eventful, his viewpoints frequent and affording vistas of a landscape where the art and science of the landscape profession have produced a landscape more attractively natural than nature herself could provide. It will not, of course, satisfy those who detest all conifers and oppose all change. Most people will enjoy it, and not even realize that it is 'landscape by design'. Unfortunately, trees being what they are, it will not happen overnight.

The water industry, like electricity generation, is one in which attitudes to the environmental and visual aspects of civil engineering have changed beyond recognition in the past thirty to forty years. The present author, before straying permanently into the paths of journalism, worked briefly for the Bristol Water Company as an administrative trainee. They used to quote the tale in those days of the old lady living in Clifton who protested to her good old-fashioned, blue serge-suited and peak capped waterman about an increase in the rate. 'I don't see why we should have to pay all this money,' she said, 'after all, the Good Lord sends down the rain from heaven.' 'Ah, but 'e don't pump it up from Cheddar, do 'e ma'am?' replied that sterling representative of the men who did. Cheddar, built in 1934, was the old type of supply reservoir: earth banks thrown up in a huge, roughly circular shape from the flat of the plain, puddle clay applied inside as a seal, and the outside grassed over. Even after half a century or so, it remained plainly an artefact, unsympathetic to the nearby Mendip landscape; its recreational use limited to very popular coarse fishing from the bank. In the right situation, of course, the water engineers of forty, and indeed eighty years ago, did very much better. Flooded valleys dammed, for economy's as well as amenity's sake at a narrow point, are often as attractive a feature in the landscape as what preceded them – many would say more attractive. Lake Vyrnwy in Wales is a superbly mature example; Blagdon Lake in the Mendips (completed 1904) was the example I got to know when in Bristol. After the Second World War, while the consumption of water and therefore the need for new and larger sources of supply, grew rapidly, so did public opposition to reservoirs, the loss of agricultural land they involved and their impact on landscape, the patterns of movement of local communities and disruption to wildlife. So Bristol's next big supply reservoir, Chew Valley Lake (opened 1956) demanded and got more skilful handling – albeit still from engineers without any professional landscape advice.

The nature of the changes which even a skilfully landscaped and integrated reservoir makes to the natural scene were well analysed by Sir Frederick Gibberd in an address to the Institution of Water Engineers in London on 2 December, 1960. They are: (1) The change from land to water, which for most people only really becomes a cause for objection if it is badly designed. (2) 'That it obliterates a stretch of countryside that has generally taken centuries to develop' including loss of such intimate details as 'a tiny waterfall cascading between rocks and stones worn to the most beautiful colours and shades'. (3) Change in the marginal areas or fringes of the lake ('There will be a sudden and sharp change of character between the edge of the water and the land. Land form and plant material which has become balanced over the years will be abruptly and illogically terminated'). (4) The character of the dam itself ('Not the largest element, but is large and is an intrusion into the scene'). (5) The objection that 'the reservoir demands all kinds of structures that are foreign to a rural environment, such as the draw-off tower or control house'. Sir Frederick, however, dismisses this last change as less significant 'because, with sensitive design, they need appear no more foreign to the landscape than, say, a group of farm buildings'.

The questions that must be asked, he concludes, are: Does the landscape suffer through construction of a reservoir on this site? And if it does, are there other interests that outweigh that loss of amenity?

At his 1960s Llyn Celyn reservoir in Wales, Gibberd was not able to influence siting, though he has on other occasions been asked to advise on the environmental pros and cons of alternative locations being considered by the engineers. Nor was he able to influence the water level, which can be crucial to the ultimate effect. But by this time such arguments as those of Sylvia Crowe against straight, concrete embankments and in favour of contoured and planted dams, were beginning to convince the engineers. With Gibberd's Derwent Reservoir on the Durham/Northumberland border, they had been persuaded to smooth the grassed slope of the dam out into the uneven shoulders on either side of the valley; and in his IWE paper Gibberd felt able to stick his neck out before the assembled engineers and say marginal additional cost involved 'is not an extra over contract; it is the minimum standard at which design starts'. At Llyn Celyn landscape went one stage further: the engineers curved the dam itself. The Llyn Celyn curvature, Gibberd pointed out in his IWE paper, 'was regarded by the consultants as an essential part of the appearance of the dam, and no cost comparison has been made with a straight bank'.

Other points in the paper which show the way landscaping of reservoirs has been developing concern 'draw-off', and the principles of planting around the banks. Draw-off – the 'tide-mark' between high and lower water levels – is, as we have seen in looking at the Dinorwic hydro-electric scheme, on the face of it an intractable problem; but landscapers have found some ways of mitigating the worst and most obtrusive effects. Thus at Dinorwic the consultants are seeking to use the same covering material at each point in the tide-mark as predominates in the landscape above and behind it. Another device is to foreshorten it by reducing it not vertically (which is impossible) but horizontally. Where existing contours would produce a shallow, gently shelving margin, a little excavation and the consolidating of earth into spurs or promontories can mean both a more interesting shoreline and a much steeper bank. This reduces the tide-mark effect. Another approach, mentioned by Gibberd and increasingly used by him and other consultants, uses water-loving trees and plants which both look right in or near water and can be expected to survive when the water reaches its top level.

As to planting generally, Gibberd felt it necessary in his IWE paper to explain: 'Trees, shrubs and carpeting materials like grass or gorse are the materials of the landscape architect. After any land shaping that may be necessary or desirable, it is with them that he forms his compositions – *forms compositions, not decorates*', he stressed.

LANDSCAPE BY DESIGN

A much more recently completed reservoir, Brenig, lies some 10–15 miles north-west, and illustrates another significant change in the character of reservoirs. Brenig (landscaping by Colvin & Moggridge) was first conceived seventy years ago as a straight-forward supply reservoir to feed water to Birkenhead; but it was eventually built, in the mid-1970s, as a river regulation reservoir, used to keep the level of the Dee always high enough for towns like Birkenhead and Liverpool to take water supplies from it. This has two sets of 'amenity' advantages: it sets recreation free from the constraints imposed on reservoirs that feed drinking water direct into trunk mains. Since this water goes into the Dee in any case, there is little point in being over-fussy about minor pollution at the reservoir. And from a visual and ecological point of view, Colvin & Moggridge's 1971 outline report on the Brenig site may be quoted:

The attraction of Welsh rivers derives from their romantic lack of constraint. From a landscape point of view, we consider that regulating rivers is much superior to taking water direct from storage reservoirs, as the health of the rivers tends to be enhanced. The river does not lose water and is saved from droughts.

They support regulation of the Dee, but add the rider that some Welsh rivers should be left in a natural, unregulated state, and suggest scheduling some for 'preservation from all interference'.

The Brenig scheme was unusual in that it envisaged a two-stage reservoir and dam – the initial stage being required to meet short-term needs for abstraction from the Dee; the second stage, involving a much higher and longer dam, to meet longer term needs by raising the water level and flooding a larger area of ground. Construction, concluded the consultants, would create a new landscape 'and, possibly, if the two phases are implemented, two new landscapes'. Their aim was 'to ensure, by careful forethought and design, that the landscape ... of a lovely area of Wales ... shall not be degraded but rather enhanced'. They took it as axiomatic that conservation of wildlife and ecological balance as well as conservation of landscape should be inherent in this as in all present-day development; and their brief extended to the siting and landscaping of pumping stations, some quite remote from the reservoir, as well as the landscaping of the reservoir itself. The sense of positive change, of enhancement, comes over strongly when they say:

74

In our opinion existing views, pleasant but without any great distinction, can be enhanced and improved by the proposed new water surface. *Reflections in still water, or the movement of waves and ripples when the wind rises,* would introduce a dramatic character to the scene, and the rim defining contours would, with suitable care, give added character to the land forms.

The 1971 report is also of interest as making explicit features that the visitor to Brenig today may well miss or take for granted. For instance, it urges the salvaging and reuse of stone from farmsteads demolished in the flooded area; proposes that realigned roads should have rough edges and no kerbs; and recommends that foot-path diversions should 'be laid out in detail by walking the route and pegging it, so that irregularities dictated by features on the ground are incorporated into the tracks. Thus the paths will be real footpaths like those existing, and not survey lines which would look incongruous.'

Paradoxically, Brenig's most remarkable new landscape feature – a large hill part way along the dam, covered in grass, planted on the top and on the downward side with young trees, and known to water authority employees as 'Mount Moggridge' – came about at the suggestion of the engineers. The consultants' 1971 report recommended a rocky treatment for the high east end of the dam with a steep front face; but suggested that the long west end should be softly moulded with its base curved into the land. It added: 'We should like to see a block of trees on the face of the dam above Bryn-hir dividing these two parts.' The aim was to break up visu-ally the long line of the dam rim. The clients accepted this recom-mendation, but then realized the implication of losing the trees at Stage 2, just as they were becoming mature. They therefore sug-gested constructing the centre of the dam to its bigger, Stage 2 dimensions from the outset, so that the maturing wood could be conserved when the water authority needed to enlarge the dam.

The origin of the 'Mount' also says something about the charac-ter of this particular public client, the Welsh National Water De-velopment Authority. Its chief executive, Dr. H. H. Crann, who as chief officer of the former Dee & Clwyn River Authority was the key man in commissioning and setting the brief for the land-scape consultants, cared deeply about the impact of the reservoir on both landscape and communities. As a result, Colvin & Mog-gridge not only found themselves engaged early in the day and working with design engineers whose environmental awareness Dr. Crann encouraged and supported; but found themselves also expected to act as intermediaries between the client and affected parties not just on landscape matters, but on the impact of the scheme on farming, communications, wildlife, recreation and a whole range of other matters. The client chose consultants whose skill and judgement he respected, gave them a remarkably free hand, and took their advice when they gave it.

Two other large-scale reservoir schemes may be mentioned, not so much for their detailed design as to demonstrate how the scope and influence of landscapists have increased in recent years: the Northumbrian Water Authority's Kielder scheme (landscape consultants again Frederick Gibberd & Partners); and the Anglian Water Authority's Rutland Water. Both are river regulation schemes; both conceived on a scale with few precedents in Europe. Kielder is in fact more than a reservoir; it is the biggest river regulation scheme so far undertaken in Britain. The reservoir itself creates a lake six miles long buried in the largest manmade forest in Europe, and with a storage capacity of forty-one thousand million gallons. But a very large proportion of its £115m cost goes not for the lake or its dam, but on a system of tunnels and pipelines to take water from the Tyne, thirty-six miles downstream from Kielder, across country to feed the rivers Wear and Tees and the populations and industries of Wearside and Teesside. The scheme caused much controversy; objectors urged other sites, using several lakes instead of one. Sir Frederick, having personally looked at the options, advised the water authority firmly in favour of Kielder. In his inquiry evidence he said:

I cannot understand anyone advocating that four distinct landscape valleys, each with its own character, should be fundamentally altered instead of one. Water has to be provided for the North East. Kielder can provide it for the foreseeable future. Were it constructed, there need be no fear of the familiar situation in which the construction of a reservoir is followed almost immediately by the stress and conflict of the proposals for another one. The combination of one of the most beautiful lakes in the country with an immense forest could make Kielder a major recreation centre in the North East. None of the alternatives compare with it. I can understand that a scheme of such magnitude as Kielder should come under attack but here is a case for 'thinking big' if ever there was one. Not only could the reservoir itself form, with the forest, one of the finest landscapes in the country but that landscape could be a source of enjoyment to thousands.

Regional Water Authorities now take very seriously their duties, spelt out by the 1973 Water Act, to provide both for wildlife conservation and for recreation. Even though commercial prudence sometimes seems to make them excessively cautious in the latter area, as compared say with some water undertakings in Germany, they certainly research both very thoroughly, and this must tend to extend the role of landscape consultants. The North Western Regional Water Authority for example, in investigating four possible strategies for expanding its resources to cope with demand to the year 2000, commissioned Land Use Consultants to make a parallel study of what may loosely be called 'the amenity factors'.

Rutland Water, with a surface area rather larger than Kielder's (but a smaller volume), is another large river regulation reservoir, completed several years earlier than Kielder. The words 'river regulation' may conjure mental pictures of wears, sluices, embankments and other devices of the drainage engineer. In fact, Rutland Water (landscape consultant Sylvia Crowe) is perhaps the most natural-seeming flooded valley-reservoir in Britain. Here the consultant's job included setting out zones for such potentially competing uses as boating, fishing, picnicking and wildlife conservation; and, in consultation with the Nature Conservancy Council and local naturalists trust, Dame Sylvia reserved one end of one of the lake's two long 'legs' of water as a 350-acre nature reserve, creating a system of bunds and lagoons carefully designed to provide hospitable habitats for a wide range of species. Creeks, marshes, mud-flats, reeds, osiers, pasture, undergrowth and woodland – they are all represented.

In visual terms, Dame Sylvia took very great pains to make the new lake sit well in the existing green and gently rolling farming landscape. The site selected left a three-mile long peninsula stretching eastwards from the western shore two-thirds the length of the lake: a low, well-farmed and tree-grown ridge, sufficiently broad to support continued farming of the high-grade agricultural land and to provide a generous and natural landscape feature.

Sylvia Crowe's plans were directed to a number of quite specific aims. 'The conception,' she has written, 'is that the reservoir, with all its works and its recreational facilities, must form a unified landscape whose components come together into an overall composition with the surrounding countryside, without visible boundaries or jarring notes.' Essential to this end was close working between her and engineers and architects from the very inception of the scheme. This, she says, enabled landscape considerations to be incorporated into the engineering works – for example, surplus soil has been used to form a low hill near the pump-house, reducing its apparent size and tying it into the scale of its surroundings; a canalized stream has been designed on easy curves instead of a straight line; the working road over the dam looks to the eye like a grass track, though under the grass are mono slabs; and the grass slope of the earth-fill dam appears to sweep right up to the wave wall.

At Rutland, Dame Sylvia was very lucky in the Water Authority's choice of architects for features like the intake works, pumping stations and 'amenity buildings'. Pick, Everard, Keay & Gimson of Leicester have adopted two styles; for larger buildings away from the lake, they have produced a series of simple pitched-roof buildings that look very much like the best of modern farm buildings in the area; for buildings closer to the lake, including 'amenity' buildings, they have gone for octagonal structures in local stone with pitched roofs rising to a cone, sometimes above a band of louvred, clerestory glazing. Fitting in with low stone walls, these buildings are an adornment to and a natural part of the lake landscape. Two factors, of course, make them a success visually: their intrinsic architectural quality, and skilful placing in the landscape, which in the case of the intake and pumping station buildings much reduces their apparent bulk.

Dame Sylvia's attitude to recreational use is that it should be catered for positively and this provision integrated in the landscape design; but that there is a limit to what it can absorb. Thus of Rutland Water she warned even before the reservoir was finished:

If the quality of the site and its neighbourhood is to be maintained, constant vigilance will be needed to ensure that the value of this outstanding resource is not destroyed by overuse or unsuitable development. The demand will, I believe, be insatiable, and the determining factor should be the site's capability of absorption without losing its character as a magnificent sheet of water in a landscape neither wild nor grand, but representing the best of rural England.

Shortly after the reservoir's completion, someone working in Sylvia Crowe's office met a man who had spent a week fishing there. 'Lovely spot, Rutland Water,' he said. 'Oh, you've been there, have you?' said the woman from Dame Sylvia's. 'I know the person who designed that.' 'Designed? What do you mean, designed? It's a natural lake, Rutland Water!' Dame Sylvia regards that as the greatest compliment possible on her work there.

But Rutland and Kielder are high spots. Frank Shaw, a leading Landscape Institute member and regional architect to the Severn-Trent Water Authority, points out that the overall picture in the water industry is patchy. Quoting Sir Colin Buchanan's descrip-

Plate 7

British Waterways Board. Hard Landscape details – British Waterways Board.

Plate 8

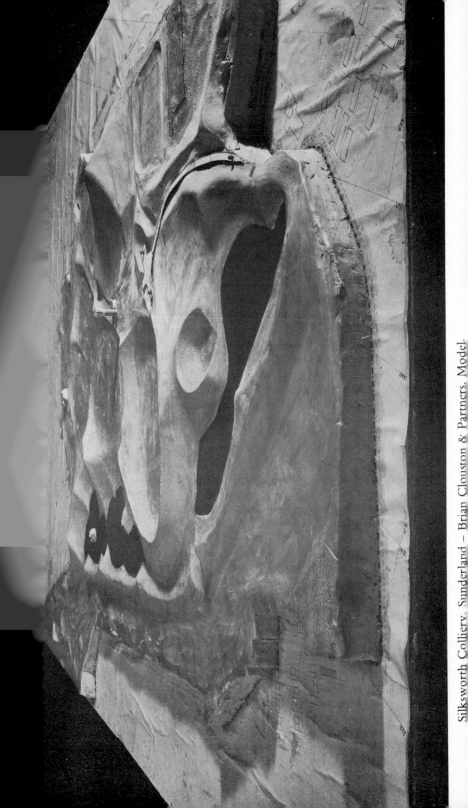

Silksworth Colliery, Sunderland – Brian Clouston & Partners. Model.

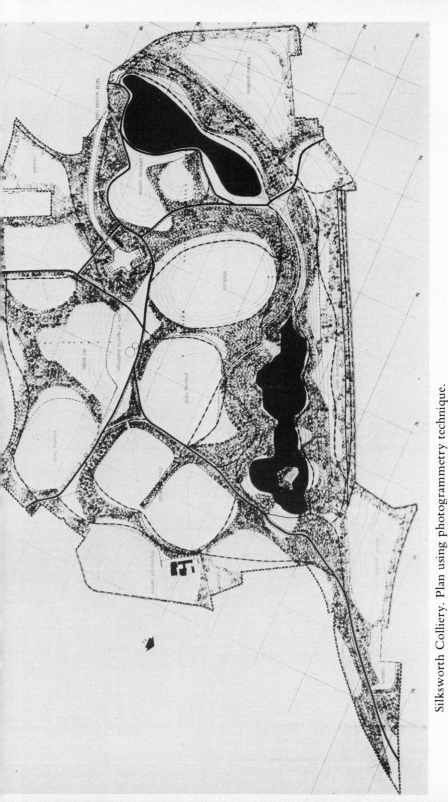

Silksworth Colliery. Plan using photogrammetry technique.
Plate 9b

tion of reservoirs in the hills as 'surely the softest form of all intrusions into the landscape', he makes the point that the 'clean
water' (that is, water supply) side of the industry had a reasonable
record before the 1974 reorganization, but that the 'dirty water'
side had a less happy one, with treatment works that often looked
as bad as they smelled. The former River Boards and River Authorities generally had a narrow view of their job – flood prevention
and land drainage – and were not much aware of either landscape
design or nature conservation.

Under the 1973 Water Act which created them, however, the
ten Regional Water Authorities of England and Wales have an
explicit duty to promote 'amenity'; and, as we have seen, their attitude towards water-based recreation has been transformed. Shaw
pinpoints a crucial change in organization – from one-purpose units
towards multi-functional divisions handling all aspects of the water
cycle for a given geographical area; but he adds that multidisciplinary working of engineers and others such as landscape architects
and architects 'has little penetrated the water industry yet'.
Although, for instance Thames Water Authority inherited architects from the old Metropolitan Water Board, and the North West
Water Authority employs two landscape architects primarily on
the recreation side, Shaw believes his own water authority is
farthest advanced. It has a headquarters group of architects and
landscape architects who oversee the engineering work carried out
by divisional staff and also carry out projects of their own. 'By this
combination of advising and demonstrating, we have had some
success in raising standards of architectural and landscape design,'
he says.

In his personal view, problems remain in two areas. First, the
vast bulk of the work is done by engineers whose training and in-
stincts lead them to seek functional solutions without adverting sufficiently to the visual implications and possibilities. 'It is difficult,'
says Shaw, 'to improve the vital small details of design such as fencing and architectural "trim".' Land drainage he sees as the second
problem area, partly because RWA land drainage committees are
still anomalously separate and semi-autonomous. Even here, he
adds, awareness of natural and landscape values has improved – a
tendency that will be reinforced by the ministerial decision not to
allow comprehensive drainage of the Amberley Wild Brooks area
in Sussex. Shaw sees this side of Water Authorities' landscape work
as generally not a matter of stopping land drainage schemes (they

LANDSCAPE BY DESIGN

are valuable for food production and not intrinsically unacceptable environmentally) but of getting in early enough and strongly enough to ensure that 'the positive opportunities inherent in change are taken'.

Chapter 10
TOWN HALL, COUNTY HALL

Local Authorities as Clients

Local authorities, in so far as they use landscape architects, use them in two ways. A council may be the client in the accepted sense for a scheme which is either primarily a landscape project or is an architectural or engineering scheme with landscape as a more or less important ingredient. The role of client holds good whether the landscape designer is an employee or an outside consultant. The second way in which local authorities may use the skills of a landscape architect is in formulating policies and advising it on planning and other decisions which have a landscape aspect. These two obviously overlap; but whereas landscape *design* is clearly a growth industry, with for instance an important role in the revitalization of inner urban areas, landscape *planning* too often, like the unsung rustic genius in Gray's *Elegy in a Country Churchyard*, 'is born to blush unseen' in some corner of a town or county hall 'and waste its sweetness on the desert air'.

That is not to say that landscape considerations go unconsidered in specific town planning decisions. Planning inspectors do now quite often have an eye for landscape and are occasionally landscape architects. Let me cite a case that occurred near my own home. It concerned proposed development in the grounds of Vanbrugh Castle, a house in castellated Gothic style built by the Restoration architect-painter-dramatist Sir John Vanbrugh for his own use in 1719 and overlooking the east side of Greenwich Park. The inspector's report, cited in the Minister's decision letter, based rejection of the scheme on the certainty that it would be 'destructive of the romantic silhouette of the castle in relationship to the nearby trees'. Not too elegantly expressed, perhaps, but testimony to the fact that development control now weighs landscape considerations quite heavily in the balance. The inspector, Miss Jessica Albery, is both an architect and a landscape architect.

But though landscape finds a place in structure plans, generally in the form of statements of broad policy, a gap all too often exists between this and the occasional defensive stand in planning committee or at a public inquiry. What is usually missing is a strategy and mechanism for implementing those policies: for stopping or diverting development proposals which would damage good landscape or result in poor landscape – stopping them consistently and not just in random or socially controversial cases; and for repairing and developing existing landscapes in a purposeful way.

Take for instance the experience of Ray Miller, landscape architect for Surrey County Council. The position he holds was created in 1969 because of growing concern about the effects of highway improvement schemes and other developments on that county's well-treed landscape. The county council saw the need to employ a professional who could make an appraisal of the landscape impact of schemes; and also make professional advice available to district councils lacking this expertise. Miller works primarily for the Planning Department, but also advises the county engineer on new roads, and to some extent all other county council departments except architects, who have their own landscape section. Miller has another landscape architect working with him, a Newcastle postgraduate diploma holder (who, though he does not qualify for Associate status of the Institute under ILA criteria, ironically has the background necessary to qualify him as a Science Member under the rules of the expanded Institute).

Miller thinks the best achievements of his section so far have been the complete revision of the county's landscape conditions for planning control, and implementation of its planting schemes in the countryside. His biggest disappointments have been the fragmentation of responsibilities for the landscape, with design resting largely within the architects and planning departments, and management (which in itself entails considerable landscape change) resting within a number of service departments. No fewer than five departments, operating independently of each other, carry out tree, shrub and hedge planting, and care for mature treescapes. 'This has meant,' he says, 'that there is no integration of policy or purpose, and considerable variation in maintenance standards.' As to land-

scape advice to district councils, most of the Surrey districts instinctively shy away from involving county personnel in their activities – and, since reorganization, development control *is* mostly
a district function. In the result, observes Miller, 'Most development is permitted with insufficient landscape appraisal.'

Ken Fines, Brighton's Borough Planning Officer, has been in
town and country planning for thirty years and a qualified landscape architect for twenty-five of those thirty. From 1950 to 1969
he worked in East Sussex county planning department, for much
of that time as assistant county planning officer in charge of the
development plan division, but also with a responsibility for landscape matters. That brief included landscape; conservation and
recreation policies; tree preservation; overhead electricity lines;
radio masts; mineral workings; and the landscape aspects of major
planning applications.

One big problem he and his chief, the then county planning
officer Leslie Jay, had to cope with was pressure for development.
The metropolitan green belt protected large swaths of Surrey and
Kent from development, which therefore tended to jump over into
the areas beyond. Throughout much of the fifties and sixties,
pressure for residential and recreational development was intense;
and the power and telecommunications industries also threatened
the Sussex landscapes of weald and downland in a more pervasive
way. Much of Fines's work at East Sussex concerned the making
and implementing of policies aimed at curbing 'adventitious' development and ensuring that such development as the local communities needed would be integrated into the landscape.

The success of such policies, he realized, would be greatly strengthened if he could devise a method of evaluating landscape qualities. He therefore carried out private research and came up with
a method of evaluation which he has used extensively in his work,
not only in preparing development plans but also in finding routes
for electricity lines and roads and to identify landscape conservation
areas – such as the High Weald AONB. He described these evaluation methods in a paper published in 1968 which won the county
council a Countryside 1970 award; and used it again when in 1969
he was appointed director of the Greater Brighton Structure Plan.

Among his successes Fines would include the routing of a 400KV
power line from Dungeness nuclear power station across the
county from east to west. 'The route originally proposed by the
CEGB would have been very intrusive,' he considers. The county

council, however, engaged Sylvia Crowe as consultant, and together she and Fines worked out a new route which was finally accepted after public inquiry.

Another plus was at Brightling, an attractive and sparsely populated parish astride the Southern Forest Ridge of the High Weald. An existing gypsum mining company proposed in 1959 to open new workings, transporting the ore three miles by road to the old works. A succession of heavy lorries along the narrow country lanes would have severely damaged the character of Brightling, says Fines. He put forward the notion of an aerial ropeway, and worked out a route through dense woodland, passing via screened tunnels under the lanes which follow the ridges. The ropeway, now operating, is scarcely noticeable to casual visitors.

Perhaps the worst minus in his score-sheet concerned the ancient pollarded beeches of Balcombe – great gnarled specimens of tremendous girth, reputed to be over four hundred years old, and a legendary and well-loved feature of the Wealden scene. When landowners threatened to fell them because of the cost of maintenance, the county council surveyed the trees and proposed a tree preservation order, payment of compensation and a programme of tree surgery. But after a public inquiry the Minister refused to confirm the TPO, and most of the beeches were felled.

Ken Fines recalls the difficulty experienced by landscape architects in getting recognition from the public patron in the early years. He himself qualified as a landscape architect in 1953, four years after qualifying as a planner. 'I was then employed at £500 a year as a planning assistant, and was informed that henceforth in addition to my normal duties I would be the council's (one and only) landscape architect – with no increase in salary!' These days county councils generally employ landscape teams of several professionals to deal just with what was for him an unpaid extra.

He also has memories of using helicopters to carry out a one-day survey of car-borne recreation and its impact on the landscape ('Leslie Jay never did things by halves!'). Fines was in charge of operations, the base was a field at police headquarters at Lewes, surrounded by trees. But because of hot weather, landing in this enclosed space became hazardous. With one helicopter due back from a sortie, he had to find another site – and quickly. 'My only choice at hand was a children's playground, which I quickly cleared of children, much to their annoyance.' (Not exactly the use of statutory planning powers). 'Unfortunately,' he adds, 'the playground adjoined both a rubbish tip and a council estate. The effect of the one on the other, under the influence of the rotors, was quite spectacular.'

John Lodge, County Planning Officer of Northumberland, is also an Associate of the Institute, and sees landscape as a key ingredient of planning, ranging from preparation of broad county policies down to design advice to developers and the public.

Capability Brown was born and practised in Northumberland. His influence on landscape thinking is still reflected in the attitude of local people, who are very responsive to environmental issues. The county council has recognised the need for landscape design at both policy and implementation levels and has employed landscape architects for many years.

Lodge's patch – 2,000 square miles of it – has great diversity of landscape, from the Cheviot Hills in the north, upland moors and forests in the south and west, to the mixed farming country of the lowlands, attractive north-east coastline and the urban south-east corner, ravaged over a long period by mining and industry. All call for policies of either landscape conservation or rehabilitation.

Northumberland evidently cares about trees, for it almost alone among local authorities has – with Countryside Commission help – been meeting the entire cost of removing diseased elms, including carrying out of replacement plantings agreed with landowners. This determined campaign to restrict the spread of the disease has really got a grip on the public, who – often through parish councils and other local organizations – report trees that look diseased and enable the county to take prompt action. Lodge also reports that his county has developed a good working relationship with the Forestry Commission, with an agreed consultation procedure keeping it *au fait* with felling licence application in private woodlands, dedication schemes and new planting, so that it can make preservation orders where this is needed to safeguard trees or woodlands significant from an amenity point of view or to encourage their sensible management. Northumberland has also tackled the problem of derelict land with some vigour. The county can now boast more than 710 hectares (1,750 acres) of 'Dead' land restored, of which 280 hectares (690 acres) is newly created amenity woodland with a prodigious 2.5 million new trees.

Throughout north-east England land reclamation has been one of the major tasks presented by the local authority client to landscape architects. Sunderland Borough Council's Silksworth Colliery scheme (landscape consultants Brian Clouston & Partners) must be regarded as one of the most impressive and genuinely creative of these. The 64-hectare (160-acre) site lies south-west of Sunderland town centre and consisted of a disused colliery, derelict pit-head buildings, a huge shale heap set against the valley side and dominating the scene, and some adjacent low quality farmland. The client's brief called for reclamation for future industrial use and public open space (see Plates 9a and 9b).

Silksworth illustrates vividly the problems that the landscape architect working in this field faces, and the environmental and technical expertise he must deploy in addition to a grasp of the aesthetics of landscape. The shale heap was burning, with very high temperatures internally; its surface was saline to a level toxic to plants, and also unstable; and acid drained from it. The valley bottom below suffered frequent flooding. The consultants demonstrated with their preliminary study that, nonetheless, the site had great recreation potential; and the client accepted this in preference to the original industry-plus-parkland idea. They proposed a layout which basically divides the site in two. On the flatter areas to the east will be a stadium and sports pitches as well as an equestrian centre and funpark. On the longer western side earthmoving on a very large scale has created a very natural-seeming linear landscape, with sinuous lakes curving through what, during the construction stages at least, could have been taken for a pass in the saddle of some remote mountain range – though with a ski slope just round the corner! Yet that landscape had not only to look good; it had to overcome the pollution problems just cited; it had to provide for effective land drainage; and, in order to keep costs to a reasonable level, it had to maintain a balance between cut and fill over a complex site, and with the volume of material to be moved exceeding one million cubic metres. It is sometimes rather assumed that today's landscape architect is either an artist in the classic style, composing poetic arrangements of plants and simple manmade components, or a technician – frighteningly competent on a technical level, but with no poetry or hint of the artist's eye about him. Silksworth, among other schemes, triumphantly disproves this, and has received a *Times*/RICS Conservation Award.

Durham county's systematic appraisal and planning for its landscape during the late fifties and early sixties, leading to policies which concentrated reclamation where it would have most effect, notably on the main motorway approaches, shows how powerful a weapon well-deployed landscape work can be in transforming the image and reputation of a region. The decision makers, it was reasoned, would often approach the north-east by motorway; their attitudes towards locating employment there would depend in some measure on how it struck them as a place for themselves and their families to live in; and a harmonious, generous landscape on the approaches – with wooded hills rather than black pit-heaps on its horizon, for instance – could well be a decisive factor.

Less successful has been the attempt, begun in 1964, to carry out coordinated landscape improvements on the banks of the River Tyne within the Tyneside conurbation. The attempt started bravely, with a River Tyne Banks Improvement Committee representing riparian local authorities, appointing a leading consultant, Ian Laurie, to make a comprehensive study and recommend improvements to the landscape on either side of the tidal river from its mouth at North and South Shields some twenty miles upstream to Wylam. Laurie's report, which the committee and its constituent authorities in principle accepted, gave a great fillip to landscape work in the area. Gateshead County Borough, for example, has transformed such former riverside eyesores as the seventy-nine acres of former chemical waste, coal shale, abandoned shipyard and eroding river embankments which have now become Gateshead Riverside Park. This scheme (again designed by Cloustons) demonstrated the difference between straight land reclamation as often carried out by engineers and creative land reclamation deploying the skills and experience of the landscape architect. Major earthmoving transformed the chemical and coal waste tips into a rolling parkland landscape. A ski slope rises gently on the horizon overlooking the surrounding playing fields and giving splendid views over Tyneside. Adjacent to the Gateshead Stadium, the site has become a popular training and meeting place for national and international sports events throughout the calendar. Further facilities allowed for in the scheme include a maritime museum, motor-boat club, public house and improved stadium accommodation.

Gateshead also took on in 1969 their own staff landscape architect, and after the 1974 local government reorganization, the new Gateshead metropolitan district covered a much bigger area than the old county borough, containing more countryside but also more derelict land. It therefore began to build up a specialist team, working under an assistant director of planning who is also a landscape architect. At present the team, led by Robert Brandt, is only four strong. Apart from Brandt, the only other professional is a qualified forester. At the same time, Gateshead parks department, which carries out most non-reclamation schemes on a direct works basis, has lately recruited two graduate landscape assistants; so the professional landscape presence in this local authority is clearly growing.

On the other hand, many people in Tyneside – not least the landscape profession – feel disappointment and frustration that Laurie's overall plan has not been more quickly or completely implemented. It contained, for instance, fairly specific recommendations for a derelict area on the Newcastle bank of the Tyne slightly downstream from Gateshead's Riverside Park – but at the time of writing, nine years later, very little seemed to have happened.

In Scotland also the notion of transforming the 'image' of a region by landscape surgery along its main approach roads has been eloquently demonstrated. Strathclyde Park, which stands astride the new M74 motorway as it passes between the towns of Hamilton and Motherwell, comprises an area of some 1,600 acres along the Clyde Valley upstream of Glasgow – an area full of history, but on which nineteenth- and twentieth-century coal mining made the biggest impact. By the time the last pit closed in 1958, the landscape was a mess – spoil heaps and collapsing galleries, sometimes with subsidence as deep as five metres – enough to swallow an ordinary two-storey house. On the other hand, flash ponds caused by subsidence gradually attracted a wide variety of wildlife, and local angling clubs stocked them with fish. By 1973 this 140-hectare reserve contained seventy-seven different species of birds, sheltering a heronry of regional significance, and serving as an important staging post for flocks of migrant waders.

The origin of the regional park can be traced to Abercrombie's Clyde Valley regional plan of 1946, in which he proposed a public open space in the area known as Hamilton Low Parks. In the early 1960s, plans for the M74 once more focused attention on the area, and the Scottish Development Department then revived proposals for the area's recreational development. A large part of the area had become liable to flooding, but at the same time contained extensive domestic rubbish tips, which were thus contributing to river pollution. The SDD suggested creating a loch in this low-lying area and raising the rest above flood level. Rehabilitation of this despoiled landscape would thus serve two ends: it would provide a pleasanter approach for motorway travellers heading for the Glasgow conurbation; and provide recreational facilities for more than two million people within a 20-mile radius.

In 1965, prompted by the SDD and with the promise of government cash backing, a joint committee of three local authorities, Lanarkshire County, and Hamilton and Motherwell Burghs, commissioned first a feasibility study for the loch from consulting engineers, then a general planning study. In 1970 the main contract started and only then, six months later, William Gillespie & Partners were appointed landscape consultants. By this time many of the basic elements of the plan had already gone beyond the possibility of unscrambling. Not only the loch was an already fixed element in the scheme, but also the parcelling out of sporting provision into three separate complexes, each needing separate access roads, car parks and other supporting facilities. The park's internal road system, designed by engineers, is on a scale that neither fits park landscape nor is in any way justified by traffic. All it achieves is to make enforcement of speed limits needlessly difficult. One section of road, constructed at considerable expense, now leads nowhere and is blocked off. That said, Gillespie's landscape master plan, produced in May 1974, did represent a clawing back of some funds for this purpose. Original budgets, in contrast to the £500,000 spent on that misguided park road, allowed only some £50,000 for planting. Gillespies managed to get this increased to £250,000 over four years. The aim of the master plan was to fit a wide range of active and passive recreation into the available land, not merely the water-based recreation centring round the 1,000-metre rowing course of the new loch. Planting aims to strengthen existing woodlands and provide a strong visual framework, as well as shelter and enclosure for visitors. Because a high proportion of the park's visitors arrive on foot, the consultants gave great attention to the design of footpaths. They range from relatively wide, asphalt-surfaced paths in intensively used areas down to narrow gravel paths among woodlands; and wherever possible are kept apart from the park road system. Designs for park 'furniture' aim at simplicity, robustness and resistance to vandals, with stained timber as the dominant material. The plan required that such manufactured items as lighting columns, balustrading and signs be placed as specified by the landscape architect to ensure visual consistency. Car parking uses terracing to avoid expensive excavation, but with earth mounding and planting of trees and shrubs to break up wide stretches of asphalt and screen the lines of cars.

As to the loch itself, the consultants have sought to vary the edge treatment with two objects in view: counteracting the dullness that could have come with such a huge stretch of water, and encouraging people to enjoy it in an informal way. On the advice of the Nature Conservancy Council, the designers created shallows, both for visual and nature conservation reasons. The client was persuaded to expand the woodland management plan called for in the original brief to cover management of new as well as existing woodland, and also of shrubberies, grassland, footpath maintenance, the loch shore, and park furniture and signs. The consultants also proposed a system of zones, in some of which nature conservation has priority, while others are primarily for recreation and amenity (see Plate 10).

Strathclyde Park offers two lessons. First, landscape expertise allied to recreational planning can transform the lives and opportunities of thousands of people as well as transforming their landscapes. Second, the client should call in his landscape consultant much earlier than was done at Strathclyde Park. He stands not only to secure a better result, but to avoid unnecessary expense.

One of the most impressive exercises in upgrading urban landscape must be that at Stoke-on-Trent. Arnold Bennett in *Anna of the Five Towns* described the townships (there were in fact six of them) that federated to become the City of Stoke-on-Trent as:

mean and forbidding of aspect – sombre, hard-featured, uncouth; and the vaporous poison of their ovens and chimneys has soiled and shrivelled the surrounding country till there is no village lane within a league but what offers a gaunt and ludicrous travesty of rural charms.

Bennett wrote that in 1902. By 1966 the position was in some respects worse. While the ovens were alight and the coal mines working, people could see some justification or consolation for the grievous wounds they inflicted on the landscape. But by the midsixties many of the mines had been closed as uneconomic, leaving their black and angular spoil heaps as ugly legacies of the singleminded entrepreneurs to whom land meant much but landscape nothing. Pottery marl-holes, abandoned once clay extraction became uneconomic, left grim chasms in the shadows of the very tips. The complex pattern of branch railways which had linked potteries to collieries and other industries became redundant and fell victim to the Beeching Axe. Of the city's 22,927 acres, a daunting 1,746 officially ranked as 'derelict'.

The burden of clearing this fell mostly on the city council, whose efforts redoubled when the government started giving grants for derelict land reclamation. The 75% grants which applied from 1970 allowed the city council to tackle the problem with imagination and resource. In quantitative terms, the achievement since 1966 has been impressive. Stoke has spent £4.5m of its own and the government's money and has reclaimed 1,700 acres of the 2,700 at one time or another officially declared derelict. Of this reclaimed land, about 200 acres accommodates new or relocated industry; the remainder forms part of the city's new and more generous open space provision. This has raised the ratio of public open space in Stoke from 2.1 acres per 1,000 people in 1968 to 7 acres per 1,000 in 1978. So far, the council's contractors have shifted an estimated eight million cubic metres of spoil, earth and other materials.

But quantity is not all. The most impressive aspects of the Stoke achievement are the quality and the comprehensively planned nature of the reclamation programme. For councillors and officials had the wit to realize that bulldozing away the muck was not enough. They looked around for design and recreational consultants, and picked Land Use Consultants, then landscape consultants to the National Coal Board, whose services the NCB had made available to the city for a small, 2-acre site at Dividy Road in the south-east of the city. With the Coal Board playing fairy godmother, Cliff Tandy, the LUC principal in charge of the job (and more recently ILA president) was able to 'sell' Stoke's land reclamation committee the idea of a comprehensive design strategy – a strategy for which, over more than a decade, he has been responsible. But neither he nor the Institute have yet succeeded in persuading the Department of the Environment to allow fees for such overall design work to rank for grants just as individual projects do.

The Six Towns form a loosely strung out collection of settlements, the spaces in between largely occupied by coal mining, the pottery industry, and railways and canals. Stoke's consultants hung their strategy on two main elements: a 'greenway' system of pedestrian footpaths tying the six towns together along the routes of the old railways; and Central Forest Park, an 87-acre open space created of colliery pit-heaps, whose inspirations are perhaps Hampstead Heath crossed with Amsterdam's Bospark. The consultants' approach from the first was, as is generally now accepted, to mould rather than flatten the pit-heaps which had so overshadowed the edges of Hanley, sowing them with grass and planting forest-type trees, mostly as whips. The stolid people of Stoke do not habitually display emotion over such matters as landscape; but as oppressive black mountains were transformed into seductive green, tree-planted hills, they became noticeably more enthusiastic about the whole programme. Land reclamation gained political muscle in the city – the more so when it became apparent that houses round the fringe of the new park were selling at a marked premium.

The public of the Potteries did not, however, always quite understand what LUC were at. In the first growing season of any stage of the project, a scatter of little trees, generally only a foot high, lost itself in a sea of unmown grass. 'Why the long grass if it's meant to be a park?' people asked. 'Where are all the trees if it's meant to be a forest?' These two remarks reveal both the town-man's clichéd concept of 'park', and his failure to understand nature's time scale and ecological chain. That grass was sown on to a thin topsoil over raw colliery shale. Gradually, season by season, plants have established themselves and created a thicker top-soil. With each season came more food for birds and insects, especially butterflies; and in turn these helped to fertilize plant growth. Forest Park was not the kind of municipal park, with flowering cherries and herbaceous borders, that Potteries folk at first expected. It was a stretch of landscaped countryside, with the sights and smells and sounds and life cycles of the countryside – yet close to the centre of a linear conurbation of a quarter of a million people.

Central Forest Park is only the largest of more than thirty reclamation sites in Stoke. Westport Lake, which won a Civic Trust Award in 1972, has been equally successful but in a very different way. Before reclamation it was a huge water-filled hole, disfigured by industrial tipping and fed by a badly polluted stream. Reclamation cleared up the mess, rerouted the stream, and reshaped the banks to provide an attractive 25-acre lake with quay for boating and a sandy cove for children to play at the water's edge. There as elsewhere in Stoke one appreciates the unifying effect of a consistent design policy. Items like bollards, seats and litter bins have a family likeness throughout the chain of parks and greenways: simple, robust, using materials like old railway sleepers, they leave the walker in no doubt that here is the footpath he wants to follow. Within that pattern, the uses and characters of the sites vary greatly: here a playing field, there a sports stadium, over there a 'kick-about' for kids from a neighbourhood previously short of play space and, for that reason among others, long plagued by vandalism.

In addition to greenways, LUC's strategy also ties in the Potteries canal system with three small rivers to form a complementary 'blue ways' network of towing paths and footpaths. The canals, it should be added, demand a rather different landscape treatment, having a strong and on the whole urban character of their own.

Comparable in its scope to Stoke's land reclamation programme, though of more recent date, is Greater Manchester Council's for the Mersey and other river valleys which reach into the heart of the conurbation. In the past, such river valleys as the Mersey and the Tame provided the focus for industrial development; then as they declined they were used as dumps for industrial and domestic refuse, became derelict and neglected, and their waters were polluted. More recently, public and official opinion recognized their potential for recreation and the need to upgrade their landscape. The pre-1974 fragmentation of local authorities in what is now the GMC area made this difficult; but one should pay tribute to the ginger-group activities of a number of bodies, notably the Civic Trust for the North-West, which pioneered a strategy of landscape 'repair' and development for the Tame Valley.

Reorganization here, though a mixed blessing in many ways, has certainly provided in the GMC an authority with the resources and remit to look systematically at the whole problem of the river valleys and the recreational needs of the 2.7 million people within its five hundred square miles. Greater Manchester has within those boundaries 8,500 acres of derelict land of which it considers about 8,000 worth reclaiming. On reorganization, the new GMC tried to hold on to the old Lancashire County reclamation team, which had worked to a considerable extent within what is now Greater Manchester County. The present team serves both counties and consists of some 35–40 people, including engineers, surveyors, an ecologist and supporting technicians, with additional inputs from planners and landscape designers; and landscape and reclamation work comes very much within the County Planning Department's overall strategy for environmental upgrading in the conurbation. Even when one takes account of inflation, its spending in recent years on the river valley schemes and country parks remains impressive: £295,000 in 1974–75, £263,000 in 1975–76, £939,000 in 1976–77 and £1.4m in 1977–78.

Let us look in rather more detail at one GMC scheme: Daisy

Nook country park, south of Oldham, in the Medlock Valley, the first stage of which was opened in 1977. Local people frequently recalled, 'It was nice at Daisy Nook when I was young'. What had happened? No single big environmental disaster, but the Ashton Canal disused and derelict; the landscape gradually slipping from the agreeable and seemly to a state of neglect; and all the time recreational pressures from horse-riders, walkers, kids seeking adventure and freedom from supervision. The country park scheme, like other GMC projects of this kind, operated as a joint county/district project, with GMC team doing most of the design work, the district councils involved taking over maintenance, and much of the money coming from derelict land grants (now at 100% of approved costs) or from Countryside Commission grants. The designers have here kept the line and feel even of the stretches of canal that have been filled in, using fairly straight, formal arrangements of post-and-rail fencing to separate footpaths from bridle paths; have left a flight of locks as much as possible undisturbed as a 'water feature'; but otherwise have largely contented themselves with restoring and reinforcing with suitable planting what remained basically a pleasant rural landscape. The much needed car park, with its information centre and lavatories, fits in quietly at one end of the site. Tangible upgrading of the first section of Daisy Nook brought out higher public expectations. It also brought political commitment. Stage 1 as executed by the GMC team convinced the two district councils concerned that they should give much higher priority to Stage 2.

Two other river valley/country park schemes may be briefly mentioned to give some impression of the range of problems and opportunities presented. First, the Lower Croal Valley. This is a 450-acre site which would seem to have run almost the complete gamut of dereliction: domestic refuse tipping, mine shafts, chrome waste, old bleach works lagoons, derelict works buildings, quarries and old brickworks. The reclamation scheme and subsequent development carried out over the last five years at a cost of approximately £250,000, provides boating and fishing lakes, a nature area, picnic spots and footpath systems. Chorlton Water Park, a scheme of comparable scale, aims at upgrading typical down-at-heel river valley land alongside the new M63 motorway in the Mersey Valley. The construction of the motorway offered opportunities for using spoil for land-moulding and noise-screening; while on the north side of the river the team has already created a pleasant lake and country park alongside an existing golf course. Success in this kind of scheme depends as much on drawing together under-used or derelict parcels of land and negotiating with public authorities and others for better access, as on actual landscape design.

Some landscape design now goes into the development of most local authority schemes – though whether it goes in early enough or whether the designs are done by qualified landscape architects is another matter. One big step forward in recent years has been the realization that landscape design has a part to play in inner city revitalization. Thus Glasgow City Council brought in Brian Clouston & Partners to play a key role in the upgrading of areas of depressed and substandard housing in the Greater Possil area of the city. Over the years many of Glasgow's housing areas have suffered from lack of maintenance and outdated facilities. A special grant was awarded to rehabilitate areas which, though in poor condition, had a useful potential life. One of these areas, Possil Park, contained some 3,000 1930s dwellings arranged in around thirty-five 'back courts' whose degraded state contributed to dragging down the whole neighbourhood. Preparatory work included the holding of sixteen public meetings to encourage tenants to discuss the proposals at different stages and to form associations to represent their interests. The consultants regarded this as crucial, and rightly so. For while landscape works can transform housing environments more quickly and cheaply than almost any other means, they are in some respects especially vulnerable to disenchantment expressing itself through vandalism and lack of respect.

The eventual design centred on the provision of new facilities for each group of six flats (known in Scottish housing terminology as a 'close') – a drying area and dustbin enclosure – together with children's play and sitting areas. Footpaths, play areas and grass mounding run the full length of each oblong court, but with screen planting of trees and shrubs breaking up any excessively linear effect. The scheme has provided new fences and gates on the previously very run-down street frontages, with turf laid in place of derelict and overrun gardens and occasional shrub beds and tree planting used to break up the drab vistas of these long straight streets. The scheme also develops local open spaces positively for children's play. This £4.2m scheme formed the wider part of Greater Possil's environmental improvement exercise including rather similar tenement courts at neaby Keppoch and Cowlairs (see Plate 11).

No survey of what local authorities are doing in the landscape field, however partial, can omit to consider pedestrianization and paved zones. But here the heart sinks. British towns and cities have made huge strides in the last decade in creating paved zones and footstreets in shopping and historic areas; and the relief that it brings to shoppers and other pedestrians is substantial and undoubted. But as for landscape quality, the results are mostly disappointing. The procedures used to bring about exclusion of vehicles, with their emphasis on reversible experiment, may be partly to blame, and also the practical demands of fire brigades and refuse departments for unobstructed access lanes. But few schemes have bettered the pioneer, Norwich's London Street, which former city planner Alfred Wood hoped would be an example which others would improve on. Some schemes show a nice eye for the detail of hard landscape – for instance, in the Leeds paved zone, bands of brick paving relate to the vertical divisions in the townscape; and where the buildings of the central arcade area use terracotta, an orange brick displaces blue engineering brick. But mostly the impression given by Britain's paved zones and footstreets is of *ad hoc*-ery and always of excessively tight budgets. Nowhere do we come near to the quality and consistency of overall design in hard landscape shown in Munich's superlative and popular *Fussgängerzone*. Even where, as in London's Leicester Square, money in reasonable quantities was evidently available, the *ad hoc*-ery persisted. We have bits and pieces of paved space tacked on round the still railed-off original square. The result is an improvement; but by contrast with what could and should have been achieved, a dismal disappointment.

Among the biggest and most impressive of local authority landscape projects must be counted Nottinghamshire County Council's National Waters Sports Centre at Holme Pierrepont near Nottingham. This was very much the product of a county planning department whose chief officer, Jack Lowe, was both planner and landscape architect; the man who designed and coordinated the project, Charles Smart, is now, as we have seen, landscape architect at the Welsh Office. The Holme Pierrepont scheme started with 101 hectares of land left derelict, chiefly by gravel working, alongside the serpentine line of the Trent, and ended up by supplying, to a very tight deadline, a rowing course to Olympic standards but at only a fifth the cost of the Munich Olympics course – which it technically surpasses. The 2,000-metre rowing course grandly dominates the scene, but around it the landscape architects created a country park which, by changes of level, use of retained tree clumps and new planting, and the creation of smaller pools and lakes, avoids being dominated by the great broad canal. The designers had to cope not only with conflicting technical requirements from various user organizations – their specifications were actually changing as the designers worked – but with such problems as finding a bank profile which minimized wave bounce, and minimizing the differential effect of wind on lanes occupied by competing boats. Fortunately the designers and their clients, the county council and the Sports Council, felt able to take a fairly robust view of the possibility that a particularly fine block of mature trees might bend the air currents unfairly against some competitors and not others. The effect was shown to be slight and uncertain; the trees remain, a very necessary natural antidote to the straightness of the rowing course. Apart from the course, Holme Pierrepont includes walks, trails, fishing areas, picnic spots, and facilities for other water sports such as sailing, water-skiing, power-boating and sub-aqua training. Sports Council and derelict land grants ensured that the county council paid only a relatively small proportion of the total cost. The landscape architect now responsible for Holme Pierrepont, Clive Gordon, works under the reorganized local government structure not for the Planning but the Recreation Department of the county, which he regards as a sensible and satisfactory arrangement.

One of the pioneers among local authorities in the use of landscape architects was the London County Council and its successor the GLC. Before 1965 nearly all the council's landscape department was the responsibility of its parks department; but in the late 1950s the LCC, then planning its own new town at Hook in Hampshire, engaged Peter Youngman as consultant and also employed Michael Ellison as landscape architect to the new town planning team. When the LCC was thwarted at Hook, it turned with all the greater energy to 'town development' – the expansion under the Town Development Acts of smallish country towns mostly ringing London in partnership with the local authorities. It re-engaged Ellison to head a landscape group and, influenced by the Hook experience, the members of the group worked from the first as a matter of policy as members of an integrated design team for each expanding town. John Medhurst, Ellison's successor, comments: 'This principle of landscape architects working at the elbow of their design profession colleagues has been one of the major reasons for the success of the profession in this division and for the high standard of work they produced.' The expanding town of Andover in Hampshire represents some of the best results of a team which, at its peak, built up to a strength of more than twenty landscape architects and three landscape clerks of works. The group also acted as a training ground and sponsored many students; and through it passed many members of the profession who now hold top landscape posts in local authorities, new towns and higher education.

When, however, the GLC – frightened by increasing symptoms of inner city decay – precipitately reversed its overspill policies, it unhappily did not sufficiently grasp the full potential role of its landscape team in inner city renewal. Medhurst's landscape group has therefore declined in numbers; and only belatedly have policy-makers perceived that the landscape techniques and approaches developed for town expansion can be very fruitfully applied to inner area housing and environmental improvement.

Though it is not strictly within this chapter's ambit, we must not leave London without mentioning the Lee Valley Regional Park, a major exercise in landscape repair and recreational provision along a river valley that traditionally served as the 'dustbin' of east and north-east London. Landscape skills constitute an important part of the regional park authority's design approach; and while some of the ugly visual features that edge this linear park are difficult to remedy, it is important that the authority's designated area has been based on terrain and not the vagaries of local government boundaries. Much of the credit for the creation of the Lee Valley park belongs to a voluntary body, the Civic Trust, which first demonstrated the needs and possibilities and brought together the local authorities concerned. Voluntary ginger groups can sometimes make the running in such cases. The Scottish Civic Trust are currently working as consultants to the Scottish Development Agency at Lesmahagow in Lanarkshire, using a Project Officer to promote environmental improvement with the local community's cooperation and involvement.

Few consultants have made more of an impact on the profession's and its clients' thinking in a particular area of landscape design than Mary Mitchell in the field of children's playgrounds. In 1957 she became the first landscape architect to be employed by the City of Birmingham Architects Department, directly responsible to the Chief Architect, then A. G. Sheppard Fidler. The city's policy, agreed between the designers and their client the Housing Department, was to provide a toddlers' playground with every new block of flats of four storeys or more; playgrounds for older children according to the size of an estate and proximity of other parks and open spaces; and playgrounds in older housing areas, in existing parks, and using derelict sites.

Miss Mitchell's own design philosophy, developed over her period with the city from 1957 to 1963 and since then as a consultant, is nothing if not 'user oriented'! Playgrounds, she writes, should be simple, natural outdoor living spaces where children may play near their homes with seats for their mothers. They should be designed to provide spontaneous, natural play so that the children can develop their own imagination, expression, individuality, communication and a feeling of achievement. They should provide a challenge with a slight element of danger as a counter-attraction to deadly games on roads and railways.

Simplicity gives more scope for the child to use its own initiative: 'The elaborate fussy and grossly expensive layout and equipment may be fun for the designer on the drawing board,' she says, 'but it can be deadly dull for the child on the ground.' She points to the analogy of an old saucepan giving a child hours of creative play, while an expensive, elaborate toy is often soon discarded.

She stresses the all-too-familiar point that the landscape architect should be brought in early at the initial design stage of a project as a member of the team of architects, planners and engineers to advise them on the siting of play areas in relation to buildings, paths and roads. This can ensure that they allocate suitable sites, and not just unwanted scraps of ground that no-one else can make use of; and ensure too that playgrounds are designed into the landscape and form part of the overall layout. They should be sited close to their users' homes so that small children do not have to cross even estate roads; and their design should shelter them from winds, noise, dust and traffic fumes, and be in sunny positions. She stresses the importance of adequate financial provision, with play facilities treated as just as much essential components of a development as drains.

On the programming of playground construction, Miss Mitchell makes the important point that, whereas play facilities ready when children move into their new homes help them to settle into their new environment, a child who has grown up among the bricks and rubble of uncompleted construction work is much less likely to show respect for its surroundings. In terms of maintenance costs alone, timely provision pays off. Economies can also spring from the landscape designer being brought in early, since he or she can remodel the site using surplus excavated soil from roads and the foundations of blocks of flats and schools – materials which would otherwise need carrying away at considerable expense. Such remodelling also gives the designer a chance to make play spaces interesting and attractive. For instance, in the Birley Street playground she designed for the Borough of Blackburn, a mound paved in local stone setts and supporting a slide contains all the rubbish from the site and, with the sinking of the playground, helps to shelter the play area from wind tunnelling effects round adjacent tall blocks of flats.

The scope for well-designed play facilities is, says Miss Mitchell, enormous. Just three of her schemes may be cited as showing the variety of schemes possible: Markfield playground in Tottenham, created for the London Borough of Haringey out of a derelict sewage works and using some of the concrete tanks to create intimate and attractive 'outdoor rooms' for small children and their mothers; Booth village green in Cumbria, created and financed by the village and with much of the work done by residents; and Robin Bank at Darwen, where the Borough of Blackburn remodelled a whole hillside to include such features as sitting areas alongside the river for old people and a 116-foot long zigzag children's slide following the line of the bank.

How can the potential for well-designed play space be realized? Planners could well insist on adequate provision in housing schemes submitted for planning approval, she suggests. All too often submissions show playgrounds as flat macadam surface and arbitrarily chosen items of play equipment sited with no relation to their surroundings. She adds: 'Play facilities should be thought of on a very much broader scale today, and not simply as isolated pockets here and there. Each town or city should have a master plan for this purpose.' At Blackburn, in association with the Director of Environmental Services, she drew up the initial sketch master plan – the ideas of which were later incorporated into the official town plan.

Apart from making the play environment more interesting, mounds and earth-moulding provide shelter and a sense of enclosure without being overlooked. The surrounding banks form the boundaries and are (I quote Mary Mitchell) 'fun for rolling down'. Little mounds and other more subtle shaping within the play space, with areas around trees, form pockets round which toddlers can tricycle, run and play with each other. The design should also provide sand pits large enough to have a good depth of sand with adequate drainage, where air and rain can percolate to prevent stagnation; spaces for 'games of fantasy' or playing with their own toys, and quiet corners with benches where children can draw and make things. (see Plate 13).

Chapter 11

SEEKING AND WINNING

The Corporate Client in the Extractive Industries

The large corporate client for landscape design is almost wholly a product of the period since 1945. It results from the same pressures of planning law and public and official concern for the environment that produced the big public client. And, as with big state organizations, it is the increasing scale of the corporate clients' operations or development that has widened and deepened public concern about their impact on the environment. A quarry 100 yards across with an entrance just big enough to admit the occasional 10-ton lorry, collecting gravel for local use, is one thing. A quarry, like Batts Coombe above Cheddar, which makes a 500-yard gash in the side of the Mendips and unleashes a constant stream of heavy lorries through country lanes and village streets – that is quite another matter. Figures produced by Dr. William Stanton of Bristol University indicate the change of scale. In 1947 the total limestone quarried in Somerset was 1.2 million tons; by 1972 it was 12 million tons. In 1947 all the centuries of small quarrying that had taken place in those Somerset uplands amounted to no more than 50 million tons; twenty-five years later the cumulative total had doubled. Society demands sand and aggregates, cement and limestone, coal and oil to maintain it in the style to which it has become accustomed: to build its roads, schools, hospitals and houses; to power its industry and carry its goods and people about. But society also – or a significant and articulate section of it – objects to the impact that this large-scale extraction and exploitation makes – and makes, unfortunately, on what are generally our more attractive rural landscapes. It cannot forbid such activity, for it needs its products; but it calls in planners and, more positively, landscapists to regulate, repair and redeem.

Already in 1947 this process began to be formally embodied in statute. The 1947 Town and Country Planning Act, cornerstone of comprehensive land-use planning, made planning permission necessary for all new mineral extraction. Planning authorities had in mind two main aims: minimizing the impact of extraction while it continued, both on people's lives and on the landscape; and ensuring so far as possible the reinstatement or conversion of the site after extraction to something both beneficial in use and acceptable as landscape. So already by the 1950s a number of commercial undertakings engaged in mineral extraction deemed it prudent to seek advice from the landscape profession.

One example is the firm of Hall & Company, now part of Ready-mix Concrete Ltd. It had an extensive sand and gravel business in south-east England, and in the mid-1950s went to a leading landscape architect, Leslie Milner White. Over more than a decade he, the firm's general manager, Gerald S. Smart, and company executives developed new techniques for planning, operating, and restoring gravel, and later also chalk, workings. In the past, piecemeal mineral extraction had caused serious visual and noise intrusion, and in many cases quarrying companies made no real provision for reinstatement or after-use. Hall & Co. on Milner White's advice planned extraction as an orderly progressive process which Frank Marshall, now principal of Milner White & Partners, likens to 'domestic double digging of a vegetable garden, though on a much larger scale'. The area to be worked was divided into sections, the first positioned close to the site's access point. Here you normally established processing plant for washing and screening the extracted mineral. You stripped topsoil and overburden from the first section, often using it as banks and mounds to screen the plant or sensitive sections of future workings. In removing sand and gravel from this first section, the company could often form a pond into which it could pump silt from the processing plant.

As extraction proceeded, so topsoil, overburden or subsoil were carefully removed. They could be used in two main ways. If the site lay in a river valley and other land with a high water table, you could use them, suitably graded and contoured, as banks to edge the lagoon that would be formed when mineral extraction ended. If the working was dry, you followed one of two courses: either to lay these materials in suitable thickness on the bed of the quarry immediately behind the latest workings, or – if it was available – bring in other filling material to raise the floor of the quarry nearly to the level of the surrounding terrain, then finishing off with the salvaged topsoil.

Hall & Co. and other companies were thus as never before finding themselves expected to plan ahead not just in a functional way but 'thinking environmentally'. You could rarely, says Marshall, commit yourself precisely in the initial planning application to a particular after-use. The whole process might take ten years or more and involve some unknowns. But you could generally indicate the 'after-use potential' of a working – perhaps sailing, water-skiing or fishing for a 'wet' site; for a 'dry' site working, agriculture, housing or playing fields. As restoration proceeded then Milner White would specify the planting of indigenous trees and shrubs to suit this probable after-use.

The Milner White practice provides a striking demonstration of the changing nature of landscape design over the past century or so. Edward Milner, engineer, was partner to Joseph Paxton in a garden design business, and eventually took over the practice as Paxton became more immersed in politics and business interests. For three generations, this family practice lived almost exclusively on a diet of garden and park design, but in the fourth generation, Leslie Milner White (an ILA founder) expanded its scope to include the landscaping of the surrounding of factories, offices and power stations – as well, of course, as gravel extraction.

From pioneering new techniques for aggregates, the practice went on to develop and modify them for use in chalk quarries such as those of Rugby Portland Cement at Kensworth near Dunstable, Pring Quarry near Rochester and Barrington near Cambridge.

Kensworth Quarry, near Dunstable in Bedfordshire, provides a good example of mineral extractors, consultants and planning officers working together to achieve solutions giving some satisfaction to all involved: the industry, the local community and conservationists. The client, Rugby Portland Cement, wanted to extend the quarry in order to continue to use it to supply their main cement works at Rugby and Southam. This would mean either working much deeper in their existing 60-acre quarry, or seeking a new planning consent to extend the quarry's area over 230 acres and work it for a longer period. On the face of it, this second option, preferable to the company, might seem less acceptable to planners and conservationists. But here again, an agreed plan providing for progressive extraction and reinstatement section by section met most of the objections; and RPC got their planning permission without the need for a public inquiry, even though the extended quarry amounted to a departure from the county development plan. Key features of the proposals included: (1) careful pre-planning so as to cause the minimum disturbance to the landscape; (2) extraction of the chalk by a machine called a face shovel, in benches or terraces, moving first in a northerly direction, then eastwards, then southwards, so as to screen the working face as far as possible at all times from outside view; (3) restoration of land to agriculture as soon as possible after the chalk is extracted, on a seven-acre annual cycle of overburden stripping, chalk extraction and restoration (this means that no more than 21 acres are out of agricultural use at any one time – less than 10% of the total quarry area); (4) using overburden to make a contoured bank screening any view into the quarry from houses in the southern part of the town of Dunstable; and finally (5) a tree-planting scheme, on a forestry basis, designed for two purposes: (*a*) to screen certain parts of the quarry reserved for later working, by which time the trees will have grown sufficiently to be effective; and (*b*) to enrich the landscape which eventually emerges when the quarry has been fully worked out and its reinstatement completed. The first trees planted, in the areas north and east of the quarry, were mostly beech, ash and sycamore, with some Corsican, lodgepole and Scots pines, larch and sycamore as pioneer species. Readers will notice that tightening planning control over mineral extraction has changed the client's attitude. Instead of regarding landscaping as an 'extra', he now sees it as a necessary ingredient of the whole extraction process. It is not an 'on cost' to be added to the price of the contract, but a cost as basic as plant or land acquisition, without which extraction cannot begin. The staged section by section clearance-extraction-reinstatement seems, wherever it is practicable, both a better guarantee of a satisfactory result and a means to minimizing visual impact at any given time.

The extent to which various sections of the extraction industry have built the new approaches into their *modi operandi* is well demonstrated by the action of the British Quarrying and Slag Federation – the trade association representing companies quarrying and processing granite, limestone, and slags used in steel making and blast furnaces. The BQSF commissioned Sheila Haywood, a Fellow of the Institute and consultant to Blue Circle Industries Ltd., to write a guide to landscaping for the industry. In this book, *Quarries and the Landscape*, published in 1974, she both sets out

clearly the scope and benefits of comprehensive landscape planning
for the industry and goes ino such details as the importance of keeping good topsoil separate and not mixing it with intractable subsoils
and debris, or the need to bear in mind the rabbits' menace to
vegetation, particularly on chalk. She demonstrates some common and less common after-uses of old quarries and quarry land
– for example, Chelmscombe, a former limestone quarry near
Cheddar, provided an ideal site for the Central Electricity Generating Board to tuck away a tower testing station largely out of sight
below the Mendip skyline. Other after-uses Mrs. Haywood
suggests include agriculture, forestry, woodlands as landscape
features, water storage and recreation, picnic sites, nature reserves,
factory farming, industrial and storage uses, car and caravan parks,
sites for holiday chalets, and houses and depots for forestry workers.
The value of any book like Mrs. Haywood's must be that it opens
up the horizons of what is possible to the client in a clear and comprehensive way, so that he can brief his consultant and make his
key decisions in a positive and unblinkered way.

She cites picnic parks as one potential after-use. It is easy to be
a little superior about such places, on the assumption that the landscape architect designs them for other people and other people's
children, then goes off and enjoys the real countryside. Let anyone
who shares that view divert – just to take one example – from the
A21 Sevenoaks Bypass to Dry Hill Picnic Park near Chipstead.
Aggregate for the bypass came from Dry Hill Quarry; Kent
County Council, whose 922,000 acres are on the whole curiously
short of public open spaces, turned that extended quarry into an
attractively informal place for motorists wanting to get off the dual
carriageway and taste a little of the sights, smells and sounds of
the Garden of England. The landscaped remains of the quarry
(designed by the county council's Estates Landscape Branch) provide boulders and cliffs which children (and some adults) seem to
love scrambling on; cars are kept firmly but quietly in one corner;
the path that leads gently upwards away from them opens up a
sequence of spaces rich in wild flowers, grasses and other flora and
fauna; and the whole place is mercifully free of any of those straight
edges or artificial materials which can so easily fracture the illusion
of countryside.

Conservationists have often had cause to lament that the best deposits of certain sought after minerals all too often coincide with
Britain's finest stretches of wild, unspoiled countryside. That con-

flict, and the strong feelings it arouses, were the occasion of a pioneering landscape plan for an industrial complex: Geoffrey Jellicoe's scheme for the Hope Cement Works, in the Peak District. The original client, G. & T. Earle of Hull, had built its cement works before the Second World War on its site in the Hope Valley, one of the most attractive of the Derbyshire Dales because it had limestone, it had clay, and it was well sited geographically for them to transport their cement to the several conurbations and large towns that ring the Peak District. When however the works opened, the company began cutting away at the limestone hillside, digging their clay pits, and spreading their tips, sidings and clogging film of white dust over the landscape: public opinion began to kick. The CPRE in particular lobbied the Minister of Works and Planning, who seems to have been able – in that wartime situation – to persuade the company to appoint a landscape consultant. He invited Geoffrey Jellicoe, then almost single-handedly representing the Institute in an extended wartime term as president, to undertake the commission. Jellicoe went to Hope in 1943, and found that: (1) the buildings were at odds with the landscape, and proliferation of buildings about the site promised to aggravate this. He recommended that all additional buildings be grouped within the existing complex; (2) clay excavations had created a derelict area on the floor of this fertile valley; he proposed recreational lakes and playing fields as a means of using these excavations and bringing them into harmony with the wider landscape; and (3) the limestone quarry as then being worked disrupted the contours and destroyed the sense of loneliness. He proposed that future excavations should fan out behind the valley entrance, leaving the entrance as narrow as possible and keeping the summit of the quarry below the skyline. The company had an industrial development plan, and Jellicoe worked out with them a landscape plan to cover a span of fifty (or possibly even a hundred) years to complement that, and looking forward to the after-use of a site which by then would once more have a mature landscape. Not only were Earles sympathetic, but, as Jellicoe pointed out at the time, the detailed proposals of his plan in most cases came in suggestions from company staff. The design comprised several layers or bands of landscape: near the buildings it is, by today's fashions, curiously formal, with straight parallel lines of pleached limes lining the approach roads and the private railway line that serves the works; furthest from the buildings the scale is larger and the style more natural, blending in with the hillsides to the west and south. But one change that has made all the difference to the scene Jellicoe could scarcely have foreseen: a drastic increase in the size of the works and its production, involving in place of the original two 150-foot high chimneys, one 400-foot chimney which now dominates the valley.

Revisiting Hope with twenty-five years of the fifty-year landscape programme gone, to reassess the scheme for the then *ILA Quarterly*, G. Oldham and R. Walker pronounced the 'fan-shape' excavation urged by Jellicoe a qualified success. It had prevented the worst visual damage to the front of the hillside; but, they warned 'the quarry continues to eat into the back of the moor ... and is encroaching dangerously near to the crown of the hill'. They were worried about the effect of ancillary buildings and waste, and observed, 'It appears that there is no policy of large-scale landscape maintenance to combat this.' The original features best maintained, they noticed, were the relatively small-scale sports fields, tennis courts, lawns and planted areas close to the main group of buildings. Of the series of lakes formed out of old clay pits, they remarked that a judicious combination of new planting and natural regeneration had succeeded in making these bodies of water look part of the valley landscape (see Plate 14).

Some more years have passed since then, and solutions to some of the criticisms are beginning to emerge. Woodland is by now well established on the worked out shale quarries, while a golf course provides a more natural transition between the formal playing-fields and the new, wider, landscape of woods and water. Contoured banks enclose car and lorry parks, the substation, and much of the movement inseparable from a working quarry. The works waste area, of necessity an eyesore from the debris of building maintenance, has been transferred as backfill to a section of the shale quarry, while its former site is being planted up. Most important, a landscape manager has been appointed by the parent company with overall responsibility for landscape maintenance.

Events at Hope nonetheless point to one of the hazards of long-term landscape planning, especially for a site in commercial ownership. The client is the company, but he speaks through individual managers, who may retire, move, or be superseded or (as in the case of Hope) the corporate client itself may change as a result of merger or takeover.

At about the time Oldham and Walker were commenting on the implementation of Jellicoe's plan for Hope, in the late 1960s, planning authorities had to decide on proposals for a different kind of mineral extraction in or on the edge of another national park: potash mining in North Yorkshire. Here in a sense the basic question was the same as at Hope: is the need to mine potash from British sources so compelling as to rebut the presumption in favour of conserving landscape so special that we have attached the label 'national park' to it? Or, seen the other way: is the moorland landscape on the fringe of a national park so important that we must veto home production of potash and import it, at great cost to the national economy and balance of payments, from abroad?

The answer given those twenty-five-odd years later remained basically the same: you can extract your mineral, but you must do it with as little disturbance to the landscape as possible. What had changed was, first, the effectiveness and stringency of the planning apparatus; second, the techniques and resources available to landscape designers; and third, the complexity of the environmental factors. Three firms sought, and got, planning permission to mine potash on the North Yorks. Moors: Shell, RTZ and Cleveland Potash, a joint venture of ICI and Charter Consolidated. All three employed landscape consultants – in the first two cases, Derek Lovejoy & Partners, in the last Frederick Gibberd and Partners – not only to represent them at the inquiry, showing how the mines could be fitted on to chosen sites with least visual damage; but also, much earlier in the day, to advise them on choice of sites. As a paper on the Boulby mine by Sir Frederick, his partner J. W. Grimes, and two former executives of the client company put it in 1974, 'Consultant architects were engaged at a very early stage to advise on all visual aspects of the project, consistent with basic technical requirements.' The weight given to landscape advice, and, perhaps more important, the scope given them and wide terms of their brief, seems to show that – in highly sensitive areas such as national parks – the corporate client *is* prepared to listen as seriously to his landscape consultant as to his accountant. The accountant will be telling him which courses of action will or will not be profitable; his landscape consultant will be telling him which are likely to get planning permission and which are non-starters.

The Boulby case illustrates well the diversity of environmental factors of which an industrial developer now has to take account. At least five different types of objection could be raised against Cleveland Potash's plans: visual disturbance of views from a national park; possible air pollution; possible pollution of sea and beaches by effluent from the potash treatment plant; disturbance caused by transporting out of the finished product; and noise from the mine. The last concerned Gibberds primarily as designers of buildings; the other four all had direct implications for them as landscape consultants. Measures against air pollution involved two 220-foot chimneys. The company decided to ship out its products not by lorry but by a reopened and extended railhead, whose sidings therefore needed screening; and effluent (the subject of a delayed, very stringent and limited-period detailed planning permission from the Secretary of State) goes out to sea through a mile-long pipeline which requires installations in conspicuous positions on the cliff top.

As to siting of the main installations, the consultants found themselves assessing the relative merits of three positions, two of them on the seaward side of the main A174 Redcar–Whitby road, and one further back towards the edge of the moors and below Boulby Hill, which carries the road down towards the sea. Of the two seaward sites, they concluded that one encroached too near to the picturesque fishing village of Staithes; the other would seriously interrupt the view of the coast from the moors. The more inland third site promised to be much less conspicuous – or, as Brenda Colvin put it in the *Architectural Review* of August, 1974, while any incursion into a national park was to be deplored, 'the precise siting by Sir Frederick from three possible positions, on landscape considerations ... is by far the best of the three'.

Once the site was chosen, arrangement and design of its new ingredients followed. Site layout was a matter of 'close collaboration between management, technical staff, architects and landscape architects. An exchange of ideas must take place during the whole process of the design so that the best possible compromise between technology and art can be reached.' Also, one might add, between art and economics. But essentially the designers, whether engineers, architects or landscapists, *worked together*.

One striking result of this collaborative approach, and of the increasing influence and standing of landscape designers, is to be found in the placing of the Boulby installations. Traditionally, engineers had always taken the mine shaft or shafts as the centre of their surface works, and arranged the buildings they needed around them. 'The visual effect of this, 'remarked Sir Frederick, 'tended to be chaotic, particularly when seen from a distance.' Handling of the potash between the main shaft and treatment and

Possil, Glasgow, 1976 – Brian Clouston & Partners.
Landscape rehabilitation; interwar housing.
Plate 11

West Hill Park, Highgate, 1976 – Derek Lovejoy & Partners.
Plate 12

Children's playground, Blackburn, 1970 – Mary Mitchell.

Plate 13

The Grave at Walmer, in which the Body lies. Much of soil . . . . to a . . . . Sir Geoffrey Jellicoe

storage buildings is by conveyor which, in order to feed in at the right level, rises to a height of around one hundred feet. The consultants' final preference was for a layout, unorthodox but acceptable to the engineers, which placed shafts at the edge of the complex and ran the conveyors on a straight grid alignment across the site, at the same pitch as the roofs of the largest buildings. Like the choice of a stone grey colour for the cladding of the main buildings, this arrangement has at least as much to do with the art of landscape composition as with architecture.

Its aim was, in Gibberd's own words, to 'integrate the large plant complex into the landscape'. We should be clear what this does and does not mean. It does *not* mean hide it. That, for a complex which includes 200-foot chimneys and 100-foot mine shafts, was clearly impossible. What it does mean is playing visual 'tricks' to reduce its visual impact. From certain viewpoints, mounding and tree-planting can either partly or wholly hide the plan, and this will increase as some of the tree screens to the seaward, which have been slow to 'take', begin to prosper and mature. More basically, however, the shape arrangement and colours of these buildings achieve a rare combination of intangibles: their shapes are dramatic in a way that reminds us that industry need not be (and has not always been), ugly and squalid; and yet (at least in profile) they attain quality of repose which derives from sympathy of colour with landscape colour, and roof and conveyor pitch with natural gradients. In profile – but not from up on Boulby Hill. From that almost bird's-eye viewpoint, the plant looks huge and very much an intrusion; and it is a view that every motorist heading south along that road is likely to see. But, as the Cleasby/Gibberd/Grimes Cuthbert paper puts it, from Boulby Hill 'there are views down on the mine and, at the same time, panoramic views of the coast. It is not possible to provide any planting screen to the mine without obscuring the view of the coast.'

Over the last ten years fundamental changes have taken place, both in extractive industry and in its related planning policies. The overall trend has been towards concentration into much fewer and larger enterprises, with huge resources of technology. With this goes the closure of small works and quarries. Major expansion on existing sites is thus more likely than the opening of new quarries in undisturbed locations.

The landscape problems will be of ever-increasing scale, and of longer duration, and must be met with boldness and determination on the one hand, and scrupulous attention to detail on the other. But it is illusory to suggest that such landscapes can remain unchanged. They should instead develop as something fine in their own right, unashamed of their industrial connection. The other side of the coin will be that other parts of the country will have a far better chance of remaining undisturbed, while the older, smaller, sites, no longer needed, can be more rapidly returned to other uses.

Chapter 12
SPEC AND BESPOKE

Other Corporate Clients

During the nineteenth century, industry's attitude to landscape was
to do one of two things: ignore it, or dominate it. Lister's great
mill on the heights above Bradford illustrates the second approach;
the first was much more common. Measures by industrialists to
improve or adorn the landscape were rare, and generally took the
form of parks for their people along with the model villages of
philanthropic employers such as Titus Salt at Saltaire (Roberts
Park, whose tranquillity is now threatened by the Aire Valley bypass), the Levers at Port Sunlight, or the Cadburys at Bourneville.
The twenties and thirties brought a rather different approach, Great
West Roadery, the essence of which was that you put a smart or
impressive façade on the front of your works, to hide away the
practical mess behind. This smart-façade-to-the-world approach
sometimes included lawns and rosebeds, but seldom involved professional designers.

Postwar, the industrial client slowly started to change – first in
his attitude towards architecture, which the more enlightened
companies began to see as good both for their 'image' and as an
aid to recruitment; more slowly in his attitude to landscape architecture. The Guinness brewery at Park Royal provides a pioneering example. Not only did the corporate client here take the step
of employing a landscape architect to handle the surroundings of
an industrial building, but responded to his unorthodox suggestions. The consultant, Geoffrey Jellicoe, was briefed to do designs
for an awkward parcel of land left over by construction of the new
A40. It would, he perceived, mean traffic noise and visual disturbance; but it would also mean a large volume of excavated soil. This
the contractors would normally have to pay to dump away from
the site. Jellicoe hit upon the idea of taking the soil on to the brew-

ery's land and mounding it to form both a barrier to the road and an interesting visual feature. 'At that time such an idea was all very experimental,' he recalls. 'I asked the clients, and they said "Go ahead and do it." ' The contractor proved only too delighted to get rid of the excavated material, and the result – a (for that time) large-scale exercise in earth-mounding and sculpturing – was a resounding success. Known as the Guinness Hills, they are now taken for granted as part of the local landscape.

The greatest successes of landscape designers on behalf of industrial clients have generally been for the company developing its own 'campus' complex of manufacturing, research and/or headquarters buildings. This situation lends itself to the employment of a landscape architect. The company is starting afresh on a – generally spacious – site which it controls; going for prestige architecture; anxious, in recent years at least, to win over the planning authority and conservationists; and working with a budget which can probably absorb without really showing it the relatively small percentage that even a generous landscaping scheme requires.

One relatively early example, dating from the mid-1960s, was the Hayes Park research and administration centre for H. J. Heinz Co. Ltd. (Skidmore Owings & Merrill/Matthews Ryan & Simpson). Two low, large white buildings of classical simplicity sit in the existing parkland of a demolished Victorian house. 'Superb,' said the Civic Trust assessor after visiting the site in 1967. 'The atmosphere achieved by the new buildings and landscaping are in the best traditions of English country house design.' The executives I spoke to at Heinz were in no doubt that in their case the individual client, Mr. H. J. Heinz himself, both chose the designers and greatly influenced the design.

The Parke Davis pharmaceuticals group's manufacturing and research complex near Pontypool (architects, Percy Thomas Partnership) provides a good example of a campus development in open countryside, with the buildings arranged in the landscape and their materials chosen in such a way as to enhance the overall picture rather than damage it or introduce any jarring element. A factory with a floor space of 400,000 square feet and employing 1,300 people set down among the gentle Welsh lowlands could easily have been a visual disaster. The siting of the buildings retained many existing trees, some of which are used in the foreground where the designers have created several small lakes which serve both as

a water supply in case of fire and part of the site's surface water
drainage, as well as enhancing views from administration and staff
restaurant buildings over what would otherwise be rather uneventful
ful farmland (see Plate 15).

Finally, for a third example of the campus approach to industrial
development, we must turn again to Skidmore Owings & Merrill,
this time with Yorke Rosenberg Mardall as executive architects in
Britain, and this time in a suburban situation. W. D. & H. O.
Wills, a major and semi-autonomous unit of Imperial Tobacco,
wished to move out of their crowded and out-of-date factory and
office premises at Bedminster, close to the centre of Bristol, to a
campus site at Hartcliffe, closer to the southern edge of the city.
Among the factors that gained planning consent for this at first
controversial scheme was the imaginative and in some ways lavish
quality of the landscape.

As you approach Wills Hartcliffe from the centre of Bristol,
your first impression is, on the hill ahead of you, a huge, dramatic
but unashamedly industrial skyline: a vast shed and a row of chimneys.
neys. But you do not at that stage realize quite how big it is, because
the parkland campus swallows it, shrinks it in size.

Across the campus from the factory, a seven-storey headquarters
office block spans a valley with a stream; and here the designers
have really played tricks with the landscape. From the factory or
the bus/car park between them, the office block looks only five
storeys high. The other two are in a wider podium bridging a lake
formed by the damming of the stream. Here restaurants, staff
lounges and some offices look out on the tree-fringed stretch of
water where wildlife thrives. This side of the campus is more parklike, and the office block less overwhelming than the factory and
adjacent power-house – a fact which helps to integrate it into the
edges of the adjacent residential areas.

Even in the hearts of cities, landscaping in at least two senses can
enhance commercial office building. A notable and pioneering
example in Britain – though no more than following a lead set
in New York and other American cities – is to be found where
land is dearest, in the very Square Mile of the City of London.
Two large commercial companies commissioned the same architects, Gollins Melvin Ward & Partners, to design them prestige
headquarters offices on adjacent sites. GMW persuaded their
clients, Commercial Union Assurance and P & O, the shipping line,
to let them treat the combined site as one. This made for a very

much more effective use of the site visually – better 'townscape', if the expression can be legitimately applied to arrangements of tower blocks; and allowed them to provide what is by City of London standards really a rather spacious piazza with lime trees. On warm summer days it makes a welcome and well-used sitting space for city workers.

Roof gardens seem to have been coming back into fashion again recently with commercial clients. One of the postwar pioneers of this genre was Harvey's department store in Guildford, whose roof water garden by Sir Geoffrey Jellicoe in the 1950s gained a lot of attention in the press. It was almost as if he had re-invented roof gardens; and indeed the realization of what could be done on a suitably constructed roof came as a surprise not only to the lay public but to members of the various professions.

One of the purest pieces of roof garden design to have been carried out in recent years, delightful in its simplicity, covers not an office block, but the car park of an office block. The Scottish Widows Insurance Society's new headquarters on Edinburgh's South Side by Sir Basil Spence, Glover & Ferguson, is a series of interlocking hexagons of various heights. The company wanted car parking for 250 of the 1,200 people working in the building, and only a small proportion of this could be placed under the building. The site is, however, overlooked from Arthur's Seat as well as Salisbury Crags – two important and popular viewpoints – and the city's planning committee was most concerned at the impact that a couple of hundred parked cars might have on those views. The client engaged Dame Sylvia Crowe as landscape consultant for the development, and she, her assistant Sally Race and the architects worked closely together from early on in the project. The crucial decision was to sink the two storey car park and cover it with a roof garden. Visually this gave a double benefit: the massed parked cars would not be visible from the Crags, and nor would they stand in the foreground of the view from the offices of that magnificent landscape feature. The consultants had two aims: '(1) to merge the composition of the [office] building and the landscape together, so as to do justice to the very important site, both at close quarters and from ... the Crags and Arthur's Seat; and (2) to provide pleasant places for the staff to sit and stroll in their lunch hour'. The means chosen was to design the roof as 'a somewhat stylized heather moor', with groups of rowan, birch and sycamore. An informal path of grey chippings, their edges broken with drifts of thyme and sedum, wanders up over the car park roof and then down again by flights of light, open wooden steps.

Finally it would be a grave lacuna not to mention a very different kind of commercial client – the speculative housing developer. The demands of planning authorities, notably Essex County Council in their Design Guide for Residential Areas, have done much over the years to nudge and shove the ordinary housebuilder towards an appreciation that siting and grouping of dwellings is more than just a functional jigsaw; and that a little cash spent on planting and, better, on professional landscape advice can pay off handsomely in enhancing the product for sale.

But probably the greatest influence in a cumulative way here over the years has been the example set by Span Developments, their architects Eric Lyons & Partners, and in particular Lyons himself and his partner Ivor Cunningham, who is both an architect and qualified ILA member. It was a source of wonder to the house-building and architectural world when Span was building its first estates at Ham Common and Blackheath, first that here was a developer prepared to build terrace houses for sale to young professionals; and second that they were willing to spend the then incredible sum of £100 per house on communal landscaping! The two, of course, connect. Lyons's tight grouping of houses into short terraces, as well as being economical, left real spaces for estate landscape and features like play areas (an amenity which owner-occupiers' children had hitherto curiously been assumed not to need). The cachet and reputation Span rapidly developed, and the way in which they were (with greater or lesser success and understanding) imitated, drove home one lesson. Householders, whether tenants or owner-occupiers, are profoundly concerned about and affected by the quality of 'the estate outside the dwelling'; and owner-occupiers, having some freedom of choice, are prepared to pay somewhat over the odds for an attractive setting. Span's success in the fifties and sixties owed as much to skilful, generous landscaping and the creation of overall ambience, as to the design of the houses themselves (see Plate 18).

Finally we cannot leave this consideration of the commercial and industrial client without looking at one of the newest developments which makes perhaps a bigger impact on fine, unspoiled landscape than any other – oil. Right from the start, exploitation of oil reserves under the North and Irish seas was seen by environmentalists as double-edged: it might provide Britain's economic salvation, but because of the location of oil fields, the limited number of deep water sites for terminals, and the sheer size of the installations required, it threatened severe visual damage to some of Scotland's finest stretches of unspoiled coastline.

Whether government and society have struck the right balance between economic benefit and environmental considerations will long be debated. Two results of the Scottish oil boom are clear: landscape architects have gained a great deal of work out of the government's concern to minimize the damage and the oil companies' concern to demonstrate that they are doing their best by the environment; and without the work of the landscape profession, both in influencing choice of sites and in integrating the installations into their surroundings, the results could have been quite disastrous. What also becomes more apparent as we consider their work is that the oil boom has significantly enhanced the art and science of landscape – as consideration of a particular commission, W. J. Cairns & Partners' work on the Flotta marine oil terminal in Orkney, demonstrates. The developer, Occidental, had selected the island of Flotta not because it was their best site in capital cost terms, but because the two other short-listed sites had met more strenuous opposition. Facing a highly complex and entirely unfamiliar planning situation, the company decided that environmental impact assessment provided the most convenient and effective method of evolving the best design for the terminal. The Cairns practice, which significantly now styles itself 'environmental consultants – planners, architects, landscape architects', was able to devise assessment procedures which both allowed the design to incorporate environmental criteria at an early stage, and enabled the consultants to investigate the issues jointly with the planning authority and other consent or licensing agencies. The study comprised four areas for examination: engineering needs and limitations; a general 'environmental' assessment including climate, drainage, soils, solid and 'drift' geology, vegetation, wildlife, marine ecology, as well as landscape character and the nature and needs of the local population; a more detailed study of the effects of any release of oil into the sea from the terminal; and a visual impact assessment.

A key question with visual impact was whether the development should be 'featured' or 'hidden'. The consultants tested various layouts in relation to eight criteria: profile, bulk, sharpness of edges, overlap, 'depth in relation to foreground and background, colour (including the hue, colour intensity and lightness or darkness of the changing natural scene), texture and shadow;' and they evolved a technique which put much of this information on one drawing – a great help in decision making.

Orkney's landscape, observes Cairns, is outstandingly beautiful, but this results not from a vividly contrasting and diverse topography and ground cover, but from

complex permutations of simple forms. The treeless islands have simple elevational profiles and there is variety in their size and shape. With the seas, channels and inlets which separate the islands and reflect the changing pattern of light, the landscape is one lacking in visual containment: it is expansive and open.

Lack of trees deprived the consultants of one of the landscape architect's most useful tools. The solution adopted used ground modelling, following natural contours, to break up the horizontal lines of the bunds surrounding the oil tanks and to hide lower elements in the associated plant. As to the tanks themselves, cost ruled out sinking or burying them; instead the consultants employed two main techniques to reduce their impact. They sited these vertical features so that as far as possible they would line up with existing features of the landscape and not be silhouetted against open sky; and they chose a colour which would merge the installations into the landscape as much as possible. For this they used a simulation technique, employing high quality colour photos of the landscape in many different lights and seasons, mounting the outlines of tanks on them in eleven British Standard colours, and getting independent assessments from two groups of trained observers. The resulting choice – walnut brown – has been used for all structures apart from one relatively small unit, the operations buildings and permanent residential quarters. This was painted white, a contrasting colour indigenous in the landscape, on the simple but sound principle that, if you cannot entirely hide large artefacts, you can at least divert the eye towards something smaller and less visually disruptive. Cairns concludes:

The design of the Flotta terminal and its successful integration into a small and primarily agrarian community has been largely due to the effective synthesis of engineering and environmental skills right from the inception of the project.

Chapter 13
FIFTY YEARS A-GROWING

Development of the Institute and Professional Education

The first thing to be said about the Institute of Landscape Architects is that it nearly wasn't. As an organized professional body, the Institute had its origin in a meeting of some thirty or forty people interested in landscape design at the Chelsea Flower Show on 23 May, 1929. Brenda Colvin recalls her assistant Kate Hawkins drawing her attention to

... a notice in the *Gardeners Chronicle*, that a meeting was to be held in the Design Tent at the Chelsea Show, to consider the formation of an institute. By that time, there were a number of other small practices, so we met – standing in the centre of the design tent – and had an informal talk which led to the launching of the project with R. Sudell as president.

That meeting, however, had it in mind to call the new body the 'British Association of Garden Architects' – or was it perhaps 'of Landscape Gardeners'? Miss Colvin, admitting frankly that her memory is unreliable on events now so distant, writes: 'I feel sure that at the earliest stage of the discussion the term Landscape Gardeners was the title considered, in continuation of the Capability Brown and Repton tradition.' In the event, however, Thomas Adams persuaded the founding members to follow the American lead and opt for 'Landscape Architects' – a decision more far-reaching than even Adams and those with knowledge of the more developed profession in the United States can possibly have dreamt.

'Most of the people who started the institute were only doing private gardens, you must remember,' recalls Miss Colvin. 'If we had called it Landscape Gardeners, it would have taken us much longer to arrive at the full scope the profession has today – if we had arrived at it at all.'

What led to that momentous meeting at the Chelsea Flower Show? One of the ILA's founders, Stanley V. Hart, had been much disturbed by a lack of unity in the British section of the 1928 International Exhibition of Garden Design, and came to the conclusion that they needed a professional organization. A similar idea had occurred to students at a course in garden design which Miss Colvin attended at Swanley Horticultural College. Madeline Agar, a contemporary of Gertrude Jekyll, ran this course, and having trained with engineers in the United States was 'much more professional than Jekyll – she did working drawings for construction and taught her students to do the same'. In the early years of the twentieth century, the practice of landscape design in the States had moved far ahead of that in Britain, and involved work done here by engineers.

Brenda Colvin recalls that she entered landscape design very much by chance.

I had been torn between studying art in Paris in the years before the First World War and studying horticulture, but felt that horticulture was more likely to produce some returns, so went to Swanley. There I found a course in garden design being run by Miss Agar. As this seemed to combine my two choices, I changed to it after the first compulsory year of general gardening, and studied under her. I was among the leaders of a rebellion when she left, and her place was taken by a pupil of Thomas Mawson – who we felt knew less than Miss Agar had taught *us*.

Miss Colvin worked as Miss Agar's site assistant for a time on a war memorial in Wimbledon. Miss Colvin's mentor also advised the Conservators of Wimbledon Common, which had been damaged by army use during the 1914–18 War – an early instance of landscape design in the reclamation of derelict land!

By the late 1920s other Swanley students had also started practices in garden design, as had some from the RHS Gardens at Wisley and former pupils of Mawson, White, Percy Cane and various nursery firms. When the ex-Swanley students put the idea of forming a professional body to Thomas Mawson, the obvious leader for such an organization, he poured cold water on it. 'He thought that his own firm and that of Milner White were enough to deal with the British Isles and had no wish to encourage younger rivals,' suggests Miss Colvin. So the Swanley students did not pursue it. Others, however, did and in 1929 Richard Sudell and Stanley Hart placed their notice in the *Gardeners Chronicle*. The meeting took place. Miss Colvin remembers Sudell, Hart and

Marjorie Allen (later Lady Allen of Hurtwood) as taking part, and
that Percy Cane, an established garden consultant, 'hovered around
but did not make any comments or join the circle'. Mawson, she
is fairly certain, did not attend. 'Had he done so, he would have
been elected President.' After this, Sudell convened a meeting in
his own office in Gower Street, where they agreed to go ahead and
to invite Mawson to be President. Gilbert Jenkins, an architect/
landscape designer experienced in procedure, drew up a constitu-
tion which remained substantially unchanged until the incorporation of the Institute of Landscape Architects into the wider Landscape Institute in 1976. Geoffrey Jellicoe, Oliver Hill and Brenda
Colvin were among the half dozen others present at that Gower
Street meeting; and when a committee was set up to select other
members, it included Jenkins, Milner White, E. Prentice Mawson,
the President's son, and Marjorie Allen, with one of the co-authors
of the original convening notice, Stanley Hart, as Hon. Secretary.
Early members included Madeline Agar, who in a sense had started
it all, Oliver Hill, Geoffrey Jellicoe, Thomas Adams and Russell
Page. They made a nurseryman, Mr. J. Cheal, an Honorary
Member.

The influence of Adams on members of the fledgeling Institute
was considerable. It went further than simply influencing the founding members away from the too limiting title Garden Architects
initially preferred by Sudell and Hart. In 1931, the Institute provided the platform for Adams, who had been Founder President
of the Town Planning Institute eighteen years earlier, to deliver a
public lecture on the 'Meaning and scope of landscape architecture
and its relation to town planning'. 'My eyes were opened by
Thomas Adams,' says Brenda Colvin. 'I went to America on the
strength of that talk.' Adams gave her letters of introduction to
several American landscape architects and urged her to travel; and
since 'it was a period of slump, and my practice was at a standstill,
I sold my car and travelled to America on the proceeds'.

I learnt much through the help of Mr. Pond, then lecturer in landscape design
at Harvard, attending lectures and visiting many sites with his pupils – including
the Olmsted offices and some of their work. I was driven the length of the
Westchester Parkway from Boston to New York, where I met more landscape
architects. From there I went to Philadelphia and Washington, but had to give
up hopes of California and other centres as funds ran out.

Back in Britain, the 1930s were, according to Geoffrey Jellicoe,
'a period of consolidation by a very small number of practitioners

– enough only to form the council'. Thomas Mawson was largely a figurehead president who did not attend council meetings; but his successor, Edward White, was more active; his son, Milner White, became Hon. Secretary; and started the quarterly notes, which Brenda Colvin edited during his absence on war service. These eventually became the Association's journal, *Landscape Design*. Sudell, too, felt there was a need for more published information and discussion, and started a quarterly magazine *Landscape and Garden*. It was, says Jellicoe, 'at that time probably unique in the world, not excluding the USA or Scandinavia'. Thomas Mawson's son, Prentice Mawson, followed as President, after him came Jenkins; and then in 1937 came Dr. Thomas Adams, who had worked with Olmsted's office and came fresh from planning in New York and the Westchester Parkway. With his presidency the Institute blossomed into a body concerned with much wider matters than simply park and garden design. 'The foundations were being laid,' says Jellicoe, 'of the modern Landscape Institute.'

The 1930s, then, were a time of expanding ideas, though scarcely of expanding workloads. Brenda Colvin, returning from slump-ridden America to slump-ridden England, found a few jobs and 'by buying a secondhand car for £25, was able to limp along until times improved'. Almost all work was in garden design. The putting into practice of those wider notions of landscape design allied with planning would have to wait until another World War had blown away the cobwebs and created a new political and economic climate.

What sort of a body was that early Institute? Laurie Fricker, who as research fellow at the then Portsmouth College of Technology probed long and penetratingly into the Institute's early history, set out some of his findings in an article, *Forty Years A-Growing*, in the ILA journal for May 1969. Membership was by invitation and application. Aspiring members submitted drawings and photographs of their work and, if the committee considered these satisfactory, admitted them as associates. By 1933 the Institute had devised a syllabus of study; but there was still no question of intending members taking exams. Fricker suggests that it may have been 'easier to enter if one was already distinguished and therefore likely to reflect credit on the Institute than if one was unknown'. Apart from satisfying the committee that they were proficient in practice – on the basis of 'By their fruits ye shall know them' only – aspirants for membership seem only to have had to satisfy one other requirement. 'I am not,' they had to declare, 'engaged in the sale of anything connected with gardening, nor am I financially interested in any commercial gardening undertaking.' This brought bizarre replies from some aspiring members. Thus in June, 1939, in answer to a question about the nature of any business other than landscape architecture, applicant No. 55 replied, 'Professor of Town Planning, London University.' The same applicant, Sir Patrick Abercrombie, described his training as 'very various and strictly *un*academic'. His much younger colleague, William Holford, got in as a Fellow a year before him.

Whether the commercial gardening rule came in for any serious questioning is doubtful. It was, however, a significant step. The new profession of Landscape Architect was not only asserting the professional independence of the advice it would give the client. It was following the lead of architects in saying to members, 'You must not sell landscape as hardware or software – only as design, advice and supervision,' rather than saying to them what the engineering profession does: 'You can either use your professional skill as a consultant or as a contractor, but not both at the same time.'

The war years spelled lean times for the Institute, as for so many other voluntary and professional organizations denuded of personnel and resources. 'On the outbreak of war in 1939, landscape design as a profession virtually ceased to exist,' recalls Geoffrey Jellicoe, then President. He adds: 'In any case it had been little more than a stage army.' Jellicoe essentially kept it alive during the war; and under his generalship the 'stage army' began to look more and more convincing. Elected president in 1939, he continued to hold that office until Thomas Sharp succeeded him in 1949. Brenda Colvin testifies: 'But for his generous help during this period – including the use of his office and staff – the ILA could not have survived.' Yet it was during the war, as we have seen, that the foundations were laid of the huge postwar expansion in demand for landscape design as an essential ingredient of both town planning and architecture. Jellicoe says: 'The war gave great impetus to landscape, because the public grasped that building a better Britain implied building a better environment.'

The Institute by this time numbered many eminent people who had publicly spoken out for landscape and its better care and design. Besides Abercrombie, the council included John Forshaw, the LCC's planning officer. Their Greater London Plan not only set the pattern for conurbation planning the world over, but was a pioneer in giving landscape a place of importance in town planning, notably by its inclusion and extension of the great circuit of metropolitan green belt as an enforceable land use notation. The Institute also enlarged and enriched its membership by inviting to join its ranks such notable defenders and promoters of the concept of landscape as Clough Williams-Ellis, Christopher Hussey, Edwin Lutyens and John Dower (whose famous report later led to the establishment of our national parks).

These were great days for the Institute, but shoestring days. Jellicoe's secretary Mrs. Gwendolen Brown, 'heroically ran both myself and the Institute as a single office', he recalls – despite the destruction by a landmine of one set of premises in Holborn. The first priority at that time was to create prestige for landscape as an art and profession in its own right, and to broaden its publicly recognized scope from just garden design to something much more comprehensive. And the Institute had friends in high places. The Minister for Post-War Reconstruction, Lord Reith, was the ILA's first Honorary Fellow, on the Institute's council and indeed a regular attender, and Holford and Dame Evelyn Sharp were sympathetic allies in Whitehall. Reith had, indeed, been offered the ILA presidency, but declined it; so that Jellicoe, still supporting that office, recalls the persistent but pleasurable surprise of 'being called "Sir" by Lord Reith!'

Perhaps, though, as the thunderbolts crashed down on London, one of the gods was keeping a watchful, benevolent eye on the struggling Institute. Jellicoe remembers collar-studs being in short supply, so that on finding a shop with some in, he bought not one but a dozen. He thrust them into his overcoat pocket and forgot all about them until, in a taxi on the way to Whitehall for a meeting with the Parliamentary Secretary and the chairman of the Royal Fine Arts Commission – a meeting crucial to the profession's future – pop! his own collar burst suddenly open. The stud had broken. What was to be done? There he was, minutes only away from the Ministerial anteroom, in horrifying sartorial disarray, his collar falling helplessly apart. He could not with light heart or easy mind go in to lobby on behalf of a profession dedicated to visual decorum and good taste, with his shirt-front bursting out all over. In despair Jellicoe thrust his hand into his pocket and discovered the forgotten cache – not one collar-stud but a dozen. The day was saved; the ILA President's composure and appearance restored; the arguments put coolly and logically; the Minister duly impressed. Years later, at the end of his term of office, the ILA council presented him with a set of gold studs as a memento.

Despite the redeployment of landscapers with surveying skills to the siting of wartime factories and houses, and the departure, for instance, of Sylvia Crowe to serve with the Polish Red Cross, the Institute continued to flourish as an independent corporate body. When Jellicoe was sent to the USA on a mission for the Ministry of Works in 1942, it was as ILA President that he was hospitably received by chapters of the American Society of Landscape Architects 'in every city I visited from Boston to San Francisco'. Yet already the tide of war was turning; and the advent of the peace presented a Britain in which there were potentially plenty of jobs for landscape architects, but really not very many landscape architects to do them – and those who were available lacked what would today be regarded as an adequate training. 'There was,' says Jellicoe, 'no-one who could have passed the present LI examinations, and it was to fill that vacuum that the council gave education top priority.'

Important in this period, too, was an attempt to absorb the ILA into the Royal Institute of British Architects, as an only partly autonomous wing. Sensible, logical, economical, argued the idea's proponents. But others, notably Sylvia Crowe and Brenda Colvin, argued against it vociferously. They won the day; and in retrospect members who, like Jellicoe, were also architects became more and more convinced that that was right. After all, the two disciplines are very different. Architecture is finite; landscape organic and ever-changing.

Milestones in the early postwar years included the establishment of the first university course in landscape, at Reading under Frank Clark; and the convening in 1948 of an international conference which led to the establishment of an International Federation of Landscape Architects. The part played from the start by landscape architects in the new towns and the electricity industry we have already considered; the Festival of Britain in 1951 was also significant, with Peter Youngman, Peter Shepheard, Russell Page and Frank Clark all appointed to do designs. Lectureships funded by ICI at University College, London (Peter Youngman) and by the cement industry (Brian Hackett) at Durham seemed to underline the growing standing of the landscape profession; but, although both Youngman and Hackett were afterwards given chairs,

Plate 15
Parke Davis Pharmaceutical plant, Pontypool – Percy Thomas Partnership. Buildings sited in relation to existing trees to give a sense of imme-
diate maturity.

Bank of America Forecourt London, 1976 – Derek Lovejoy & Partners.
Plate 16

Coutts Bank London internal garden court, 1978 – Frederick Gibberd
& Partners. Tropical plants in central London using modern techniques.
Plate 17

New Ash Green, Kent, 1970 – Eric Lyons/Ivor Cunningham. High quality landscaping on a Span site.

Plate 18

Plate 19
Canberra, Australia. Model of Commonwealth Garden, 1964 – Sylvia Crowe.

Islamabad, Pakistan, 1964 – Derek Lovejoy & Partners. Detailing using locally made bricks around buildings in new capital city.
Plate 20

progress in the establishment of full-scale, properly funded undergraduate and postgraduate courses remained difficult and uncertain
of achievement for some years. The two immediately postwar
decades were a time of growth and achievement, but in which
slimness of resources – both the profession's numbers and the
Institute's resources – often seemed all too inadequate to grasp the
opportunities that in principle presented themselves. In its efforts
to establish itself as a recognized profession, the ILA moved steadily
towards entry limited to those who passed the required examinations. Though some courses (like the pioneering five year Reading
one) fell by the wayside, and others (like Peter Youngman's at
UCL) remained on the level of a landscape input into courses for
architects or planners, the contribution of universities and poly-
technics steadily increased so that no fewer than ten establishments
of higher education now offer undergraduate or postgraduate
courses in landscape architecture, with the great majority of
students using such courses as the launching pad for their assault on
the Institute's final Professional Practice Examinations.

We have seen from the experience of Cliff Tandy (who eventually resigned from government service in protest against non-
recognition of ILA membership as a professional qualification)
how important a stringent system of entry by examination might
be; and yet the Institute on more than one occasion resolved to
admit a new batch of members without this qualification. The
present Chairman of the Institute's Education Committee, Frank
Marshall, never actually found time to pass ILA finals and owes
his membership to the old category of licentiate: a device to
recognize that some practising professionals were amply qualified
by experience even if they lacked the requisite bits of paper.
Another admission en bloc brought in in 1956 such eminent names
as Gibberd and Casson. A professional body growing and evolving
is almost bound to experience such anomalies or paradoxes. After
all, of necessity most teachers in the early courses of the forties and
fifties could never have gone through the formal hoops they
required their students to leap through. The hoops, in their days as
students, had not existed. Like Professor Youngman, for example,
they searched out their own education, with a spell in a nursery
here, a spell in a practitioner's office there. Today sentiment in the
Institute, among younger members not least, favours increasingly
stringent entry requirements. This, of course, does not hurt the
most successful 'unqualified' landscapers like John Brookes, who

have plenty to do with their time without trying to pass exams they do not need to take. But some would argue that, on the contrary, it may on occasion make the Institute look marginally silly if it appears to have excluded some of the best known names in the business.

Be that as it may, numbers grew steadily. Lurching gaily into middle age, the ILA could record on its fortieth birthday a membership of over 900; by 1971 the total was 1,033; and by 1978 had reached the 1,500 mark. This may be compared with the RIBA's membership of more than 20,000; but even this comparison misleads, because out of, say, the 1975 total of 1,435 members, fully qualified members (fellows and associates) accounted for only 405 (28%); the rest were students. And this, in the aftermath of local government reorganization, led to great difficulties. The new local government units had mostly taken the point that they ought to employ landscape architects; but the supply of suitably qualified and experienced people was quite inadequate to meet the demand. So willy-nilly many councils took on either newly qualified associates with insufficient practising experience or else graduates and other students, for whom in theory at least they were to *provide* that experience. It became clear that the profession, even in its mid-forties, was suffering still from growing pains. Or, to put it differently, it lacked a solid 'middle management'; young associates were no sooner qualified than they found themselves shot into positions of authority. The growth of the profession and its potential workload have, of course, made for a young and lively set of practices, with people like Ellison and Clouston, when still in their thirties, taking a leading part in the Institute and heading private or public practices. But in the mid-seventies this generally desirable phenomenon of the advancement of youth clearly went a little too far and too fast.

Two events have greatly affected the character and direction of the profession and the Institute on approaching its fiftieth birthday. One, the growth of international consultancy, especially in the Middle East, we deal with in the next chapter. The other is the recent expansion of the Institute through the incorporation of the ILA (the professional body of landscape *architects*) into a widened Landscape Institute (which includes land scientists, such as ecologists and agronomists, and landscape managers). Numbers in these new classes are so far relatively small; and the change has been attended by some grumblings that entry qualifications are too restrictive; but the view has, probably sensibly, prevailed that stringent qualifications at the outset are a good fault. High standards once you set them are easier to maintain. Certainly the broadening of the Institute recognizes the increasing sophistication required of landscape practices, and amounts to a tacit acceptance of the warning spelled out most recently by Professor Weddle in his 1977 presidential address: that you cannot go on endlessly demanding of students that they learn more and more deeply about a wider and wider range of subjects. The doyens of the profession may look like Renaissance men and women; today's landscapists must specialize.

If education has flourished, and the profession can now boast a handful of professorships, landscape research has on the whole languished. The Landscape Research Group, founded in 1966, provides a forum to discuss research but scarcely a base from which to do it; and many experienced practitioners feel, with Frank Marshall, that too often when confronted with unfamiliar problems, they have no option but to 'start from square one' and discover for themselves; whereas there ought to be somewhere like a landscape equivalent of the Building Research Station, to which they could go for authoritative and up-to-date answers.

Chapter 14

THE BRITON ABROAD

British Influence on Landscape Design in Other Countries

It sometimes seems today that the economic survival of British landscape architects, as of British architects, depends on overseas commissions. Certainly the arrival on the profession's commercial horizon of potential clients from the Middle East with large oil revenues to spend – and with a craving after prestige projects which would demonstrate their nations' emergence from primitive to 'developed' status – coincided with economic recession at home in a way that has proved a godsend for both professions. Indeed as a member of one of the largest practices put it, the exporting of landscape design expertise was, until the 1950s, 'sparse and spasmodic'.

Landscape Architecture in English-speaking Countries

Nonetheless we have seen that the eighteenth-century 'English garden' exercised immense influence in many parts of the world, as did the English style of public park a century later. In the United States, for instance, both Washington and Jefferson reflected English tastes in the fashioning of their gardens. Andrew Jackson Downing was greatly influenced by Loudon and Repton, and enticed an Englishman, Calvert Vaux, to the United States in 1850. Frederick Olmsted's partnership with Vaux from 1857 onwards gave New York its Central Park; produced plans for Chicago, Buffalo, Montreal, San Francisco and Prospect Park, Brooklyn; and decisively shaped the development of public park design in the later nineteenth century. Olmsted's firm later designed university campuses and parkway systems. His general approach was affected by his conservationist principles – he was a leading proponent of the American national park system – and 'can be said to have created and defined the profession of landscape architect in America'. Indeed, before long some British landscape architects effected self-transplants to the then more hospitable American climate, and the influence, particularly in education, of Englishmen such as Christopher Tunnard as well as American-trained Britons like McHarg has been considerable. Crosscurrents of influence ran in two directions: the emigrating Britons brought individual talents and inspiration to the American scene; but they also responded to its wider horizons and liberating influence, as have scores of British landscape students who capped their basic training with such courses as the Masters programme at Harvard or the University of Pennsylvania.

In Australia, too, British ideas of landscape design and landscape planning have had a strong influence, as well as those from North America. Professor Denis Winston stresses that it took Australians some time to understand the very different nature of their new country's climate, with its extremes of burning heat, sudden frosts, and unpredictable floods. Cultivation of any kind remained a battle, and for many years left most people with little time or energy for garden or ornamental planting of the kind they remembered from 'home'.

All the same, when Australia was first settled it was still the eighteenth century, and some gentlemen settlers, with the help of convict labour, laid out their estates in the classical English manner. The influence of the plant exchangers is also important: Sir Joseph Banks was a keen proponent of the exchange of plant material between the two countries. The first large-scale landscape work, however, went into improving the surroundings of the governor's house in each state; and this has given Australia's principal cities the legacy of extensive botanical gardens and parks.

On the other hand, points out Winston, circumstances of history, geography and climate, and the very scale of Australia, inevitably made people aware of American practices and examples. Just as Australian lumberjacks use the American rather than the older English axe, so the names of Olmsted and McHarg are more familiar than those of Repton or Jellicoe. Thus it was that, when after Federation in 1901 the time came to design the capital city, the winning prize in the competition went to Walter Burley Griffin from Chicago, who was first and foremost a landscape architect with a keen eye for contours and for the siting of buildings in landscape. Canberra's site was in fact in a frost pocket; but, thanks to an experimental nursery established by the first Administrator in 1913, considerable planting has since been successfully carried out, thus ameliorating the climate.

The continuing work of the National Capital Development Corporation, with its landscape design section, distinguished overseas consultants (such as Crowe, Stephenson and Holford), Australian Forestry School, and College of Advanced Education's newly established Department of Landscape Design – all these have made Canberra a source of inspiration and expertise. A growing activity and enthusiasm for landscape design in Australia culminated in 1966 in the founding of the Australian Institute of Landscape Architects. Most states now have landscape schools, as well as the older schools of forestry and horticulture; most also have government departments dealing with the environment; and voluntary preservation and conservation societies as well as an increasingly successful National Trust (on similar lines to the English one) play their part in conserving Australia's heritage, including landscape. Winston adds:

A hopeful trend is the growing concern of federal, state and local authorities, as well as private firms and voluntary agencies, for good design and the employment of qualified landscape architects. The great highway programmes, airports, public housing schemes, new towns (often inspired by English examples), and mining and port settlements, mostly in inhospitable areas – all these have their landscape problems and opportunities, which are now generally well dealt with.

Local authorities have also been laying out or reclaiming plazas, forecourts, pedestrian malls and small open spaces. 'The art of landscape architecture,' concludes Winston, 'is alive and flourishing in Australia, and gives every indication of continuing to do so' (see Plate 19).

Allan Correy of the University of Sydney makes many of the same points. He stresses the way in which early immigrants, finding the Australian environment terrifying and strange, sought out of nostalgia for the home country to create their own English-style environments, around country homesteads and humble cottages alike. He points to the Joseph Banks link, and the 'great rivalry among members of the upper echelons of society to exhibit the latest varieties of plants, or to have their estates laid out in the English landscape manner'. The second half of the nineteenth century saw tremendous land exploitation for extensive grazing operations in marginal inland areas, and for industrial expansion in all major urban areas:

The land was seen always as a resource there for the taking, and few people tried to understand the environment or realise how different it was from the northern hemisphere. Farmers and gardeners alike continued to apply traditional English management techniques – often with heart-breaking results.

Correy, who was involved in the development of the Australian Federal capital, Canberra, makes the point that most planners and landscape architects employed there during the 1950s and 1960s were either British or Australians who had trained in Britain. In the early 1950s, however, a handful of Australians saw a need for trained landscape architects to work alongside the other professions involved in the planning field. No formal course in landscape architecture was available anywhere in Australia at that time, and naturally, these people turned again to Britain for inspiration. Several Australians who were already qualified in architecture or horticulture undertook postgraduate courses at British universities, then returned to practice; and for the next decade or so others followed, making what became almost a pilgrimage. Most of them studied with Brian Hackett at the University of Durham, then worked in Britain to gain practical experience and ILA member-ship before returning to Australia to 'begin the pioneering tasks of professional practice, establishing landscape courses, and educating the established professions and the public'. Correy continues:

These were difficult years. Australians have a reputation for distrusting academic qualifications at the best of times, and so a landscape profession has been slow to become established ... [The Australian Institute of Landscape Architects] unfortunately, in an effort to gain initial numerical strength, accepted into its ranks many non-trained members who had no real apprecia-tion of landscape in its wider context, and as a consequence in recent years there has been some conflict over the Institute's policy regarding conservation and environmental planning issues.

Because of similarities in the scales of the two countries, in recent years many Australians have turned to American landscape schools for their formal education in preference to British ones; but in 1973 two undergraduate landscape schools were established in Australia, with a third planned to open in 1980. A number of universities now also offer interdisciplinary programmes in environmental studies in response to a growing demand for wiser land use and environmental planning. Correy writes:

More and more Australians are becoming aware of the richness and unique-ness of their natural environments, and of the importance of their cultural landscapes. There is a need to identify, and then plan and manage, these valuable resources to ensure their continuance as dynamic environments both now and in the future. We urgently need a new breed of landscape architects, who have been trained to understand and appreciate fully the Australian landscape, and who can take their place as members of multi-disciplinary environmental planning teams.

During the difficult years of the 1950s and 1960s most Australians who qualified as landscape architects in Britain found it difficult to get suitable jobs on returning to Australia. Correy's own experience is a case in point.

I was 'on the dole' for several months before being employed, and even then, my employer could not understand why a landscape architect did not just sit down and design without wasting time gathering and analysing survey data. Many of my contemporaries had to make do with jobs as horticultural assistants or landscape draftsmen for many years, and private practice was frustratingly in competition with established nurserymen who offered design services free.

Stressing the influence of British and American landscape architecture on the profession in Australia, Rex Fairbrother of the Canberra College of Advanced Education argues that, because Britons and Americans hold key positions as practitioners and teachers, this 'foreign influence' is still spreading. He detects, however, 'a growing awareness, consciously cultivated by many of us, that the Australian landscape conditions (climate, soils, vegetation, land uses, scale, etc. – and perhaps especially the quality of the natural daylight) together with the very mixed racial society should generate a landscape style truly and uniquely Australian'.

From New Zealand A. L. Vasbenter comments that his country's landscape has evolved with 'very little, if any, influence from the British "ideal" of landscape'. As in Australia, early settlers assumed they were dealing with European conditions. They set about felling and burning the forests for agriculture, so that today only about 22% of the land remains in forest. Clearance led to rapid erosion in places, and New Zealand's rural landscape consequently has little of England's pastoral charm. Urban areas were laid out on a gridiron pattern, ignoring land form, though sometimes with green belts; and even 130 years have not broken down or humanized that grid; while smaller towns still have a 'frontier' appearance. Residential suburbs, with their detached, single-storey timber houses set typically in plots of five to the acre, are much closer to American than English models.

That is the backcloth against which New Zealand's landscape architects work. But the profession is small and young. The New Zealand Institute of Landscape Architects came into being only in 1973, and has at present just over 100 members. The country's only landscape course is at Lincoln College, started in 1969, and is run by Charlie Challenger, who received his training in landscape architecture at Newcastle. The landscape influences he passes on to his students necessarily to some extent reflect this. The two or three landscape architects practising in New Zealand before the Lincoln course started were, however, United States trained.

Vasbenter continues that, if the essence of the British approach is striving to retain 'the genius of the place', then many of the younger New Zealand landscape architects do understand and appreciate their country's *genius loci* and are 'feeling their way towards a truly indigenous landscape philosophy'. This appreciation helps less in urban landscapes, however, and in his opinion 'landscape architecture in New Zealand has a long way to go before a philosophy emerges to suit the life styles, climate and land form of urban areas'.

He considers that, by its very nature, the best landscape design in his country has been unobtrusive, using earth-shaping and native plant material to merge construction work into the scenery. He cites some state highways, hydro construction and work at Mount Cook Village; in the urban situation, some of the landscape design on Ilam University Campus and in school grounds.

Vasbenter is responsible for the environmental design section of the Ministry of Works and Development, where, although making much progress in providing landscape design services to the Ministry's various divisions, he and his colleagues still frequently encounter the attitude that landscape design is no more than a cosmetic to be applied after the real work has been done. He is trying to arouse professional and public interest in New Zealand's townscape heritage, which he says can easily be lost sight of if redevelopment is discussed primarily in terms of zoning requirements, plot ratios, and traffic flows.

From Toronto, Alan Graham of Prinsloo Graham Associates writes primarily of the situation in Ontario. He makes the point that the pioneering hardships of forest clearance are still less than a century away; the climate is harsh, with six month winters, ice storms, floods, hurricanes, caterpillar infestations, forest fires, and other hazards unfamiliar to us in Britain. 'The silhouette of the

LANDSCAPE BY DESIGN

"immemorial English elms" simply does not occur here,' he comments.

The scale of the country is quite different from England – continental vastness and very slow change from one kind of terrain to the next ... until recently gardening as it is understood in England has been the concern of a few rich people. Plant materials are extremely small in range even today – our catalogues are one-tenth of the size of Messrs. Hilliers. However, the last five years has seen an upsurge in interest: garden clubs founded; plant outlets and flower shops increasing dramatically in number; environmental assessment – all these sparked off by such national and provincial endeavours as Expo '67, the Montreal Olympic Games, the Toronto Zoo and Ontario Place in Toronto, and by 'the environment' as an issue.

Graham believes that the British landscape profession has had little or no influence either on education of landscape architects in Ontario or on the practice of the profession there. The main influence, he says, is America.

The reasons are, I believe, that Landscape schools (Universities of Toronto and Guelph) are less than 20 years old; many of the teachers were trained in such places as the Harvard Graduate School of Design; the landscape we have to deal with is American, as I tried to make clear above; our problem is to create a landscape ('... you should have seen it when God had it to himself'), rather than to conserve, preserve, enhance, fill in, complete landscapes as you have been doing for so long in England. Our problems are more like John Evelyn's in character.

From Johannesburg, Ann Sutton, of the Institute of Landscape Architects, Southern Africa, writes:

In South Africa the profession of Landscape Architecture is still relatively young, and the number of qualified professionals practising very few compared to Europe and the USA. The late Miss Joane Pim was mainly responsible for setting in motion events leading to the establishment and official recognition of the profession in South Africa. First trained as a draughtswoman in UK, Miss Pim became interested in horticulture and then landscape architecture. It was her determination that the gold mining industry should not scar the landscape as it has done everywhere else but that it should beautify it, and to this end the great wealth of the mines in the Orange Free State and the Transvaal have contributed to the planting of millions of trees and the landscaping of the mines themselves and their communities. To make this happen Joane Pim had to harness the might of the great Anglo-American Corporation and other bodies which gladly put their resources at her command. This enabled her to bring her ideas to fruition on a scale which has made her contribution to South Africa immortal.

Her influence on me was such that I went to England to take a 3-year course at Swanley Horticultural College in Kent, and later studied landscape architecture under Miss Brenda Colvin. On my return to South Africa Joane Pim encouraged me to start on my own as she did others, notably Roelf Botha, a

136

Pretoria architect, who obtained his MA in landscape architecture at Harvard in USA. He later was to become South Africa's first professor of landscape architecture at the University of Pretoria. It was in 1960 that Joane Pim, Roelf Botha, P. Leutscha and myself discussed the need for the formation of an institute. The Institute of Landscape Architects of Southern Africa came into being in May 1962 with Joane Pim as its first President.

South African landscape architects are now involved in ecological and landscape development projects all over the country – mainly public holiday resorts, new university campuses, nature and game reserves, new towns, marinas, mines, highways, water schemes and the new homelands as well as landscape reclamation and conservation schemes. With a steady stream of qualified professionals now being assured the Government, provincial and municipal authorities are being encouraged to create positions for landscape architects in their departments.

Last but most important, the Institute is in the process of researching for the training of black landscape architects and horticulturists, and hopefully, as its title suggests, will create an umbrella organization for the whole of Southern Africa which can only be to the greater benefit of the profession and the environment.

The problems of landscape design in parts of Africa nearer than South Africa to the Equator come out well from the experience of Michael Lancaster during the period 1958–61 when he was resident architect and landscape architect on the campus of Ibadan in Nigeria for Fry, Drew, Drake and Lasdun:

The temperature there rarely falls below 70 degrees F and is normally a good deal higher, the relative humidity drops below 70 per cent only for a few weeks during the dry season when it occasionally drops below 15 per cent. About April the rains begin and they gradually increase until in July and August the sun scarcely appears through a haze of cloud. The falls then become less and less frequent until they cease altogether about October, when the dry season really begins. Hot dry winds blow down from the Sahara; the air is full of dust, the grasses of the savannah dry up, the leaves fall and all the open land becomes parched. It is a time of beautiful and exotic blossoms.

Lancaster makes the point that the forests, protected by the shade of evergreen trees, remained humid; and at Ibadan they had the advantages of forest as well as cleared areas: 'Growth is extremely quick: for example it took only eight years to shade a road with rain trees.' The problem was to curb rather than to promote growth. To facilitate the necessary constant weeding, he divided off areas by herbs or paving, but 'even this was not entirely foolproof, since many of the plants used were regarded by the labourers as weeds'. During the season of rains there was too much water; during the dry season planting needed constant watering and there was always a shortage of water. 'But,' concludes Lancaster, 'perhaps the greatest difficulty of all was to gain the confidence and respect of those on the staff of the university, both Africans and Europeans, for what we were trying to achieve.' Landscape architect readers will have heard that sentiment before, and rather nearer home.

Lancaster went on from Nigeria to serve as Colombo Plan adviser for the new Pakistan capital Islamabad (Derek Lovejoy & Partners); to landscape a motorway service station near Brussels; and to do the landscape design for a new university in Iran, a naval base in Libya, and (with Brian Clouston & Partners) new Residence gardens for the Sultan of Muscat.

British Consultancy Overseas

Derek Lovejoy & Partners were among the first British landscape architects to throw themselves into international consultancy on a large scale. One of the DLP partners writes:

The exportation of landscape architectural expertise was, until the 50s, sparse and spasmodic. It was not until the 60s that consultants, due to periodic recessions in the United Kingdom, sought work overseas and were excited by the varied nature of the work in differing climates and cultures. Working in places like the Indian sub-continent, the middle East and Africa, presented challenges and a need to adopt new techniques and methodologies for achieving satisfactory landscape standards in sometimes appalling circumstances.

In Islamabad there were enormous consultancy problems, such as trying to convince the Pakistan Government and the Capital Development Authority of the need for comprehensiveness on landscape design, and the skills necessary for professional input and on site implementation. It was necessary to study the religious, cultural and historic development of the country, in order that the designs were in sympathy with natural and Islamic aspirations; many consultants have failed in this respect. The lack of local technical expertise at professional level and scarcity of skilled and semi-skilled on site labour presented acute problems; for example, contract drawings for landscape of motorways could be presented only in the form of photographs of the motorway taken at 100-metre intervals, with corresponding sketches from that point of the suggested completed landscape treatment. The consultancy lasted until the Indian–Pakistan conflict and by that time some 5,000 landscape drawings had been prepared, which were sufficient to enable Pakistan eventually to progress further with the development of the new capital city for many years to come (see Plate 20).

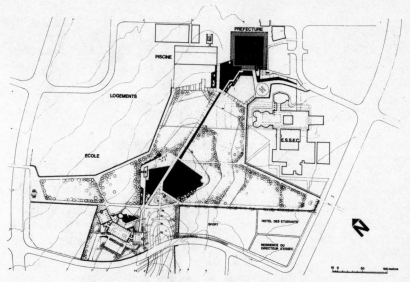

Plan of Cergy-Pontoise Central Park near Paris, 1970. Derek Lovejoy & Partners.

As a result of the landscape treatment of the Government and Presidential area of Islamabad, DLP were appointed environmental consultants for Dodoma, the new capital city of Tanzania; and here many of the early problems experienced in Islamabad repeated themselves. Work on this new city has now commenced and already the old town of Dodoma, on which the new city is being grafted, is in an advanced state of rehabilitation. DLP is currently working on developments for the British Government in the new capital cities of Brazil and Malawi. But it has also, more surprisingly, won two major commissions in France: landscaping in the French new town of Cergy-Pointoise, twenty-four miles from Paris, including a 10-hectare town park extended from the Préfecture at the heart of the town to the looping line of the River Oise; and La Courneuve, a huge new regional park for Parisians, covering an area of some 300 hectares with a total budget of (at 1974 prices) £24m. The existing landscape at La Courneuve was flat and un-inspiring, crossed by a railway and a new motorway, and with some distinctly ugly development about it. The designers led by John Whalley of DLP's Manchester office, have accordingly sought to create an inward-looking landscape by forest-scale planting and ground modelling, the largest feature of which is a

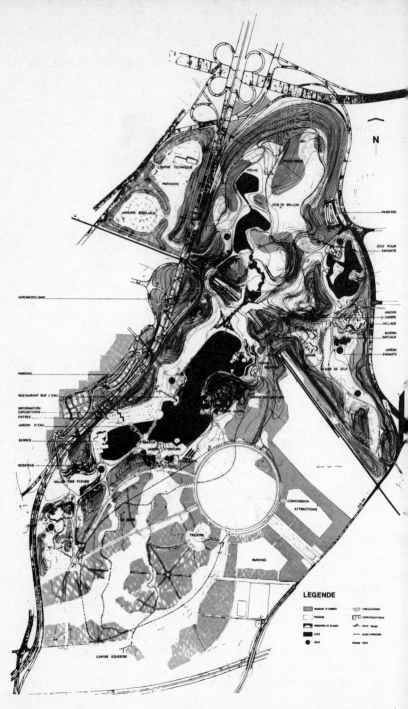

Park at La Courneuve near Paris, 1972. Derek Lovejoy & Partners. Use of extensive earth shaping relating to motorways and new lakes.

25-m (180-foot) high manmade hill – built with the spoil from excavations for new buildings and underground car parks in Paris, which arrived at the rate of 1,200 lorry loads a day. La Courneuve includes a £2m tropical house, exhibition halls, lakes, a sailing club, a zoo, a farm, amusements and water garden, restaurants and refreshment kiosks, swimming pool and solarium, skating rinks, arboretum, ski slopes, and cross country cycle tracks. Traffic-free, it is served by a monorail. The park has been described as the biggest open space project to be carried out in Paris since the days of Baron Hausseman.

Several features are remarkable about Cergy-Pontoise and La Courneuve: first, that the French, with their tradition of formal landscape, should have, as a result of an international competition, commissioned a British firm to design such important projects. Secondly, as the DLP team discovered with surprise, the government agencies concerned set about carrying both schemes into effect quite rapidly and with the minimum of bureaucratic encumbrance – this in contrast to the practice's competition successes for Newcastle Town Moor and Everton Park, Liverpool, where the clients have never actually translated the winning designs into reality.

A British practice on a rather smaller scale operating extensively abroad is that of Robert and Marina Adams, who have worked in Saudi Arabia, Bahrain, Gibraltar and Cyprus, as well as in Greece, which is Marina Adams's native land. The practice has offices in both London and Athens, and has undertaken a wide variety of work ranging from military bases, hospitals and schools to hotels, archaeological sites, private gardens and landscape planning. One project of which they are particularly proud was a landscape master plan for the greater Athens region – a project instigated by the Ministry of Public Works and directed by the Athens Master Plan Office. The landscape study dealt in particular with the topography, geology, climate and vegetation of the region as well as the quality, character and use of open space – woodlands, cultivated areas, urban squares, urban and rural roads and parks, etc. The landscape proposals referred not only to conservation but to the development of open space as well. 'The study,' they add, 'has never been implemented but, nonetheless, it provided our office with invaluable experience and a good knowledge of Attica.'

The Adamses recall that, when the practice started in 1967 the

Sief Palace, Kuwait. Brian Clouston & Partners.

availability of indigenous plants was very poor. They are, however, being grown in nurseries today and private clients more
readily accept planting proposals when native species are predominantly used.

The State, local authorities, the National Tourist Organization and other public
departments are now under continuous pressure and are beginning, albeit resent-
fully, to accept our point of view, and it seems likely that our policy of using
predominantly indigenous vegetation might be accepted to the extent that the
state nurseries may soon be producing the plant material so urgently needed.

They list their disappointments as including the continuing re-
fusal of the Greek government to recognize the profession of landscape architect; the state Archaeological Services' prejudice against
any proposals to improve pedestrian access – which would simul-

taneously limit damage to the archaeological monuments, to planting in suitable locations, and to the removal of plants which are
damaging the monuments themselves; the lack of awareness of the
local populations that the Greek landscape is gradually being
destroyed around the cities, towns and villages, along the coasts
and the main highways – so forcing people searching for nature
further and further out into a sensitive and precarious landscape
that is unable to cope with the impact of increasing crowds
because there are no measures to accommodate the people and
safeguard the landscape; and the general absence of planning
policies, and the continuous almost random expansion of industry,
in particular the extractive, with little or no respect for environmental values.

John Ford, who for many years lived and worked in the Middle

Courtyard planting, Kuwait. Brian Clouston & Partners.

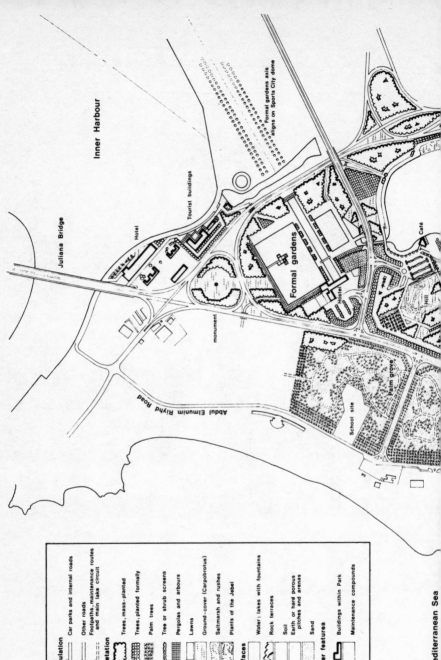

Inner Harbour

Juliana Bridge

Hotel

Tourist buildings

monument

Abdul Elmunim Riyhd Road

Formal gardens

Hostel

Café

Hill

Formal gardens axis
aligns on Sports City dome

School site

Palm grove

Mediterranean Sea

Circulation
Car parks and internal roads
Other roads
Footpaths, maintenance routes
and main lake circuit

Vegetation
Trees, mass-planted
Trees, planted formally
Palm trees
Tree or shrub screens
Pergolas and arbours
Lawns
Ground-cover (Carpobrotus)
Saltmarsh and rushes
Plants of the Jebel

Surfaces
Water: lakes with fountains
Rock terraces
Soil
Earth or hard porous
pitches and arenas
Sand

Other features
Buildings within Park
Maintenance compounds

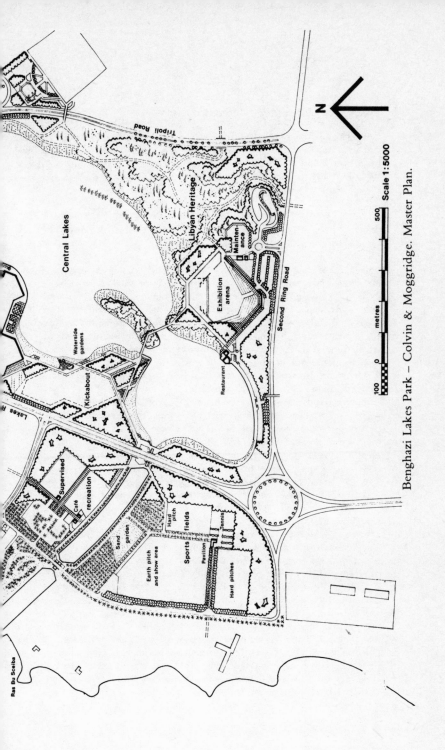

Central Lakes

Waterside gardens

Kickabout

Libyan Heritage

Mainten-ance

Exhibition arena

Restaurant

Tripoli Road

Second Ring Road

Lakes R

Supervised recreation

Café

Sand garden

Hard pitch

Sports fields

Tennis

Pavilion

Earth pitch and show area

Hard pitches

Ras Bu Sceiba

N

0   metres   500
100   Scale 1:5000

Benghazi Lakes Park – Colvin & Moggridge. Master Plan.

147

East, makes the following observation from his experience of the practice of landscape architecture there:

> In most Middle Eastern countries a practice with one principal landscape architect and a management and drawing office 'backup', totalling from 3 to 9 people, needs to collaborate with a large engineering firm for one of the bigger projects for at least part of the time. Otherwise it may not survive the vagaries of so unpredictable a market.

Ford's commissions varied in type and scope from gardens of prestige residences, country parks and large-scale housing schemes, to beautification of streets and of holy areas.

> Values here are almost meaningless, for, apart from relative exchange rates, one can often find extreme extravagance required for smaller jobs, but almost miserly 'penny-pinching' requirements in the public sector, in the scramble for bids.... Achievements tend to be restricted to the smaller projects or on those projects where one is called in to improve an already on going scheme requiring less dogmatic controls, which ensures a quicker implementation and thereby job satisfaction.... [Disappointments] can be largely associated with either fickle changes or the lack of implementation after the initial euphoria and clamour for demand; also from the fundamental lack of caring or understanding and appreciation of maintenance requirements.
>
> [Future trends] will inevitably be, as it is worldwide, geared towards the more practical and economically viable schemes. The initial rush towards the twenty-first-century fantasia is becoming tailored to the sociological, environmental and intelligible sphere of the cultures concerned, while a growing interest is being shown in the use of indigenous plants and materials as understanding and appreciation spreads by means of education....
>
> While I lived and travelled in the region, it was very evident, and not least noticed by the local people themselves, that most of the overseas consultants' advice almost carried a plastic veneer – a quick rush in, flash the beads and depart, whereas they required more of a willingness to come to terms with their problems – and there are many – not least of which is the use of water for schemes other than domestic supply. During my time there, I was also able to spend some time with one of the local Universities on their botanical field trips (this being one of my personal philosophies – get to know the people. It proved more difficult in this part of the world due to their closed family structure, than most I have met overseas.) It was definitely evident that while their senior staff had mostly been educated abroad, there was a growing awareness towards their surroundings by the students themselves, and like their colleagues the world over they would question the relevance and values of the things they encountered both on the academic side and in their environmental surroundings. It is, therefore, these people who will become the next generation of discriminating clients requiring workable schemes but founded on their own cultural values and not arbitrarily imposed from outside.

Chapter 15

LOOKING AHEAD

An Exercise in Collective Crystal-gazing into the Future of Landscape and the Landscape Profession

This final chapter attempts to express the results of a collective crystal-gazing exercise which took place partly at a gathering at the Arts Club in the Spring of 1978, partly through subsequent correspondence. An early question was: how far forward should we attempt to look? With an Institute fifty years old, a span of a further fifty years had obvious attractions. The target formally adopted for the exercise was thirty-five years, as representing 'the working lifetime of younger members'. But in practice almost none of the contributing futurologists focused on anything like thirty-five years hence. As one of those 'younger members', Jenny Cox, put it: 'The future depends on so many unforeseeable factors. I have difficulty in seeing two weeks in advance – the present is always so time- and energy-consuming.'

Readers will, however, I hope find our tentative conclusions in some degree both helpful and stimulating. The ground covered in our discussions we may roughly subsume under three headings: (1) the future scope and nature of the profession's work; (2) the need for a more effective dialogue with, and influence over, society's attitudes and decisions as they affect landscape; and (3) how practices, the Institute, and professional education should be organized to cope with (1) and (2).

First, then, the future scope and nature of the profession's work. It should be said here that the expansion of the Institute of Landscape Architects under its new title of Landscape Institute to include landscape scientists and managers is still recent enough for many landscape *designers* to talk and think instinctively as if 'the profession' still meant 'the profession of landscape architect'. Numbers of members in the new categories are still relatively small, though it seems that their quality and contribution to such a debate as this is out of proportion to mere numbers. They form a solid base from which many of the hopes expressed for a larger and more influential role can be realized. That said, there remains a degree of ambiguity or ambivalence in many of the contributions to this discussion which stems from landscape architects still talking *as landscape architects*, and not as members of an integrated landscape profession.

We can start by accepting that the scope in our society for the exercise of all the skills of the landscape profession – design, scientific and managerial – has increased, is increasing and, short of some unimagined setback, will continue to increase. We can detect several reasons for this. First, the two decades of full-blooded development from the mid-fifties to the mid-seventies have included so many things done badly in environmental terms by architects and engineers and their public and private clients that public and official opinion is now more wary and selective. It is receptive both to the reasoned argument that says: 'You should not put that development quite in that place because it will cause X, Y and Z kinds of environmental damage,' and to the experienced professional voice which shows how much better the job could be done.

Second, many people see the conservation lobby not as a spent force, but as a movement about to get its second wind. As arguments about scarce resources and ecological interdependence sink in, so more and more of our society's decision-takers will act upon them. If this occurs, then what one member of the Arts Club discussion group, Jenny Cox, sees as an increasing conservationist society is likely to take altogether greater heed of, and make greater use of, a profession offering both creative skills of design and a deep and expert understanding of nature and how to care for it.

If we look first at the designer – the landscape architect, which is the role that most members of the Institute were trained for – some comments of Dame Sylvia Crowe seem illuminating and to the point. Landscape architects, she says, have two basic roles: (*a*) the design of habitats for all species; and (*b*) the transmutation of landscape into art. Role (*a*) requires considerable knowledge of, and feeling for, the natural world; role (*b*) requires a high degree of creativity. One landscape architect may carry out both roles, but will probably incline more to the one than the other. Both require ability to design, to synthesise a varied range of information, and a basic knowledge of the materials of landscape. But even where the skills needed for both (*a*) and (*b*) combine in one person, in any given project either pure creative design or the organic, recessive function will have precedence.

What kinds of design jobs do we see exercising the profession in the years to come? One view is that there will continue to be a steady build-up both of quantity and quality in some fields of rural landscape design – country parks, the integrating of recreational provision with conserved landscapes and rich wildlife habitats; and – if the Countryside Commission's experimental New Agricultural Landscapes projects fulfil their early promise – in adding some visual richness and distinction, as well as ecological reservoirs, to the open and relatively empty spaces of efficient agro-industry. Against a background of more fundamental debates about sources of energy, rural conservation, and consuming or conserving patterns of society, the profession will continue to fulfil an honourable role by using its skills of siting and design to soften the impact of artefacts in the rural landscape and to integrate them visually and to some extent ecologically. Here we can expect to see the landscaper's influence on overall design continuing to increase, with architects and engineers calling in the profession earlier, according it a bigger say, and in individual cases accepting that the landscape consultant is best equipped to view a project as a whole and coordinate it. But, more than this, we may well see the increasing exercise of a new professional independence and power, with a chosen consultant on occasion saying to his client, in effect: 'I will go into the witness box and demonstrate how this scheme, if given permission, can be designed to do the minimum damage to the landscape; but if counsel for the objectors asks me if I believe it should be happening here, I shall be bound to say No.' This is part of true professionalism. You cannot do it very often, but you do not need to. This kind of professional objectivity has an 'iceberg' effect on big public and corporate clients, who know they need leading landscape consultants' testimony to get their proposals through, and may therefore be expected to plan them increasingly with that in mind, and to call in the landscape profession earlier and to more effect.

So much for the countryside. A swifter growth point could well be urban landscapes. The great field of past and present activity here is new towns; the profession is conscious that official emphasis is now switching to the inner city; and this is seen by some members as *the* great opportunity. Some disquiet and uncertainty exists, however. The attractions of the large, key inner area landscape scheme are numerous. Of course, it means big money for the consultants concerned; but it also offers the opportunity to transform for the better the lives of thousands of people, not just (as with country parks) on their odd Sundays out in the country, but for most of their waking hours, day in and day out. So repair and upgrading of urban environments is a clear growth area for landscapists. As Arts Club debate participant Michael Ellison put it, 'Landscape design has more to offer than practically all the other professions put together. It produces results quicker and cheaper, and can transform suburban and urban environments within six to eight weeks.' Why then the doubts? Partly, it seems, because the inner city is a more 'political' situation, which landscapers are not always too confident about handling; partly because it requires very much closer integration with rehabilitation work being done by others. The future here may therefore require the landscape profession on occasion to move into a leading or co-ordinating role simply in order to safeguard the framework in which its own product can be effective; or to supply the landscape ingredient as members of an interdisciplinary team covering, for instance, housing improvement and traffic measures as well as gardens, playgrounds, parks and general environmental treatment. Where landscape has a strong voice in a truly multi-discipline office, this can have what we may call a 'multiplier effect' on the quality of environmental improvements. But if its voice is weak, then (as Professor Weddle's 1978 presidential address warned) the danger of such 'quasi-consultancies' comes if (say) an architectural or engineering practice uses employment of landscapers as window-dressing – 'the landscape architect works at the No. 5 level, never meets the committee or client, visits the site infrequently, and is expected to provide a cosmetic service only'. If that happens, the client is misled and the landscape profession devalued.

It is a fair assumption, too, that the present growth of overseas work will continue – though, most of those involved would hope, without quite the hectic pace of some commissions generated by Middle East oil revenues. The ardent hope of the profession here must be that a sound grasp of local ecologies and aesthetic and social traditions will enable the British landscape architect abroad to avoid the criticism made of some Western architects working in this region – that (albeit with the acquiescence or even encouragement of their clients) they are foisting upon peoples with their own valuable cultures an alien pattern that responds neither to their social nor to their functional needs. Perhaps here, as in the British 'urban repair' situation, the landscape architect's ability to produce what Ian Laurie calls 'a social environment with a warm, unpretentious aesthetic appeal' will prove to be one of the keys to success.

Another role which the landscape profession clearly sees itself as increasingly fulfilling is in town and (especially) country planning. This will happen at two levels: strategic landscape planning, and the landscape aspects of development control. Each level has both a defensive and a creative element. Thus, at the strategic level the landscaper is seen as exerting a stronger and more beneficial influence on the landscape content of plan-making. Development of 'New Agricultural Landscapes' will depend not only on consultant managers and designers, but on what Professor Weddle calls 'imaginative use of landscape architects in country planning work'. Members present at the Arts Club discussion strongly doubted whether we yet possess in this country a planning framework which takes sufficient account of landscape factors; the landscape content of structure plans is claimed to be patchy and uneven.

At the development control level, which largely concerns district rather than county councils, potential for growth of influence would seem to be even greater. The Arts Club discussion expressed concern that many newly qualified landscape architects recruited by local authorities in or soon after the 1974 reorganization had (and still have) too little practical experience; and Professor Weddle made the point in his 1978 presidential address that 'as yet we have too little new landscape on the ground' to show for the build-up of teams in public offices. He was of course speaking rather of actual design of landscapes than of landscape advice on development proposals; but it is arguable that, at the development control level, the soundest advice is likely to come from the landscape architect with varied, full-blooded design experience behind him.

Professor Weddle took encouragement from a recent symposium on landscape and development control mounted by the Institute, at which it was the town planners present who argued strongly for a bigger landscape input into development control. 'If we have sold ourselves to the planners in this way, we have already cracked a very tough nut,' he commented; and went on to suggest that, not only should planning authorities more often require planners to submit landscaping schemes, but that they should get in first by preparing design briefs for particular locations to guide those submissions in the right directions. So there seems, all in all, great scope for the landscape profession to play a very much larger and more effective role in town and country planning, both defensively as expert conservationists and creatively. The one proviso being widely expressed concerns experience and practical status. If a bigger landscape presence in planning is to be effective, it must be based on adequate experience providing advice of high quality tendered at the right level – not 'No. 5' in the hierarchy, in his first job after graduation and with little on-the-ground experience, offering dubious advice to No. 4, which is then anyway watered down and misinterpreted by the time it reaches the real decision makers. The point should also be stressed that *designers* have no monopoly on the landscape advice tendered to local authorities. Research for the 1976 expansion of the Institute revealed that, even then, local authorities employed some ninety landscape conservation officers from non-design disciplines to whom the Landscape Institute has now opened its doors. Their specialist, on-the-ground advice will often, it may be argued, go deeper and wider than the advice a landscape architect alone can offer.

Our second topic concerns the need for a more effective dialogue with, and influence over, society's attitude and decisions as they affect landscape. The profession, it is generally accepted, now works in 'an increasingly sympathetic climate' (Professor Weddle), the quality of its output has improved greatly, and there is now enough of it about for it to have clicked with opinion-formers and decision-makers at least that 'landscape' means more than roses, York stone terraces or decorative planting, designed by head-in-the-clouds aesthetes, and convenient for axing if cuts have to be made in the overall budget.

And yet widely-held misconceptions still abound. When it comes to the crunch, the lay public still regards the work of the profession as an extra decoration or adornment, applied after the event, and expendable in a way that bricks and mortar, roads and drains are not. And they become indignant if what they see as inessential goes ahead and their more concrete, seemingly more urgent, needs have to wait. This is true of slum-dwellers who see trees and grass going into their back yards, but baths and boilers inexplicably delayed; it is true of new town dwellers at Milton Keynes who ask the Development Corporation's landscape men how they can justify spending a million pounds on trees when a start has yet to be made on the new city's promised hospital. People notice tangible deficiencies; they are only slowly realizing that poor environments can, in an intangible way, breed ills in society which ultimately cost it just as dear.

Should the landscape profession take to itself the role of environmental conscience of society? The question was posed, but scarcely answered. Professor Weddle, in his presidential address, argued:

It is now likely that social and technical pressures much greater than we could exert will come from other professionals, special interest groups and the public [in defence of the landscape] ... if this is the case, we should focus our energies and expertise and our own involvement on the solution of the landscape problem, making sure that we are engaged professionally to advise the developer.

As a piece of general advice on sensible tactics when manpower and time are limited, that will surely commend itself to the profession. And yet, willy-nilly, many of them are likely to become involved in lobbying conservationist causes and the like. For there are times when not to stand up and be counted, not to set the alarm bells ringing, not only tears at the conscience but makes laymen think that all professionals are fence-sitters and time-servers.

However, that does not strike people as being the main issue here. Instead, members seemed to be asking themselves: how does the profession sell itself – to the client and to the public? And though not doubting the need for the first, some people seriously questioned whether the profession could, or needed to, sell itself to the public. Attitudes here ranged from, 'Yes, we ought to – but how?' to a deflating, 'Good wine needs no bush.' To which the reply must surely be: good wine needs no bush in a country of wine drinkers. But in places where the population has subsisted for several generations exclusively on small beer, good wine needs much more promotion than merely hanging out a sign. More precisely, the magazine- and book-reading, televiewing public is already showing a burgeoning interest in landscape. We need to seize on this and make them aware of landscape *design* – of landscape design as a 1970s activity which can satisfy at once their yearnings for repose in nature, and actual, urgent social needs. It can be, they will see, a great healer and synthesiser.

How to do it? Well, use more and better publicity, more and better public relations; so that a wider public knows what landscape architects really are and what they are doing. But foster also better client relations, particularly in the public sector. The testimony of Michael Ellison, with his experience not only of the Property Services Agency, but as both local authority employee and, on the other side of the fence, elected member and planning committee chairman – carries great weight.

Landscape architects are on the whole very naive about politics and will shy away from it – which is foolish. They ought to understand the benefits of harnessing political energy, and demonstrate clearly what landscape design can do for ordinary people. The profession is still basically addressing itself to an eighteenth-century private client. Today the important client is the public client; and we need to get the popular image of landscape design modified. If you level with these people about what you are trying to do, then you can get all that political energy behind you. I would like to see the innocence of the Institute abandoned. I'd like to see something more specific and more realistic.

The landscape profession of the next fifty years, then, should it seems be more outward-going in selling landscape design (design, several people insisted, not designers), and cannier and more purposeful in mobilizing decision-makers and political muscle behind them.

What kind of profession should it be? What kinds of professionals, put through what educational hoops? What kinds of practices? What sort of an Institute? As to the first question, Crowe and Weddle point the way. Even within the basic discipline of landscape design, they are both suggesting, there needs to be specialization according to particular interest and aptitude. Thus Professor Weddle:

The profession must be objective in defining what it wants of new graduates: the range of duties, skills, activities – first-class, third-row drawing office draughtsmen or plantsmen, skilled negotiators with clients and administrators, research workers or teachers, imaginative designers and planners, senior environmentalists in public or private offices by the age of 35, men and women ready to retrain for second careers by the age of 45? And, please, it is no use asking for a blend of all these, as there are just not enough supermen and superwomen to go round.

Professor Weddle suggests good technical underpinning to a basically broader, more flexible education – with the possibility of specialist options of one kind or another. Unlike some other educationists, he believes both postgraduate and undergraduate courses have their value, but comments unfavourably on mediocre architecture graduates who come looking to a landscape course as an alternative soft career option. 'It is an architectural arrogance that only architects can become landscape designers!' (Could we, incidentally, look forward in about the year 2009 or 2019 to the profession getting rid of that misleading tag 'architect' and calling themselves landscape designers or, simply and more unifyingly, 'landscapists'?)

One point which came over very strongly from the Arts Club discussion concerned the need for sounder and more varied experience. Contractor Tony Brophy's plea for a compulsory six-month period with landscape contractors and/or nurserymen early in any landscape course met with general agreement; and Jenny Cox argued strongly that existing courses mostly overemphasized aspects like construction design but left the graduate weak on ecology and horticulture. Perhaps then, the thirty-year-old landscape designer of the future will be, say, a geographer who spent a year in a nursery before his postgraduate landscape course, and six months with a contractor during his second year; who worked in a multidisciplinary office after graduation; and is now going on to join a six-man professional landscape team in a medium-size district council, doing both design and planning brief work. His arrival is awaited with eagerness, because one senior member of the team has been seconded for a year to lecture at a university in the Middle East; and another member of this highly valued and influential council department has been given the go-ahead for a three month sabbatical looking at new landscape methods in the States, conditional on the new recruit arriving in post.

What of practices? More large, interdisciplinary offices are clearly needed; and more men and women with a firmer grasp not only of contract management (a weakness lamented as all too common by contractor Brophy) but a clearer, firmer, more businesslike handling of client, contractor and other professionals. Big practices will surely flourish, if only because the best of them are able to provide a comprehensive, well-managed service. As Brian Clouston over-modestly put it, 'All I do is provide opportunities for other landscape designers to work and gain experience – that, in part, is the function of a large office.' But everyone at that Arts Club discussion saw small, specialist practices also flourishing, either through force of personality and creative design skill or by sure and respected grasp of a particular specialization. The days of dilletantism, with the assumption that every landscape architect can try his hand at any kind of landscape job, are over – as witness Professor Weddle (1978 presidential address again) on the possibility of landscape advice being offered to farmers as part of the agricultural advisory service: 'I hope that not all landscape architects will consider themselves already qualified for this sensitive area of operations.' Nonetheless, a growth of public sector employment will eventually provide more of a firm understanding of the nature and needs of local landscapes, as well as some points of design excellence and expertise in Whitehall and state agencies. But here we must look, if the pudding is not to become lumpish, to the increasing and enlightened use of consultants as well as staff designers, and a very much freer and more frequent interchange of professionals between public and private offices, and between both and the world of landscape education.

The Institute of the future? Well, it will clearly be a much more equal partnership than at present between designers and non-designers – this is why one looks to the acceptance of some such neutral term as 'landscapist' to describe all professionals in the field. It should, one hopes, be more outward-going, with perhaps some sort of supporters club, non-professional contribution to carry forward on a more populist basis the intentions behind the old 'subscribing membership'. And delegation to chapters will have shaken down into an arrangement which, far from weakening the centre (which seems to some members at present to be the case), leaves the Institute nationally to concentrate on those tasks of organization, standard-setting, negotiation, lobbying and – yes – promotion which can only be done at the centre.

As a final coda to this book, may a mere layman looking at the profession from outside (but having listened to many insiders) venture to offer an arbitrary six-point check list for the future? If he may, it runs rather like this:

1. more attention to the framework of ideas – both aesthetic/philosophical and practical/political within which specific skills are exercised;
2. more diversity of approach: solutions to suit particular problems or places rather than design clichés;
3. aim to get the landscape profession in earlier and out later –

the earlier the involvement, the better the design; the longer the aftercare commitment, the more likely the design will stick;

4. more practical experience in the early days of professional training, more refresher courses for older professionals;

5. much freer, more frequent movement between different kinds of practice: public and private, small and large, specialist and multidisciplinary, and between practice and teaching;

6. more two-way rapport with the public. They are today increasingly the ultimate client. The profession knows that landscape design is today a humane and *necessary* art; a wider public still needs to be convinced.

BIBLIOGRAPHY

Ackers, C. P. *Practical British Forestry* (Oxford: Oxford University Press).

Adams, R. and M. *Dry Lands* (London: Architectural Press, 1978).

Appleyard and Lynch, K. *The View From the Road* (Boston: M.I.T. Press, 1964).

Arvill, R. *Man and Environment; Crisis and the Strategy of Choice* (Reprint Books, 1967).

Ashworth, W. *The Genesis of Modern British Town Planning* (London: Routledge and Kegan Paul, 1954).

Bagger, B. *Nature as a Designer* (London: Frederick Warne and Co. Ltd., 1967).

Barber, D. (ed.). *Farming and Wildlife: a Study in Compromise* (R.S.P.B., 1970).

Bauer, L. D. *Soil Physics* (Chapman and Hall).

Bean, W. J. *Trees and Shrubs Hardy in the British Isles* (several volumes) (London: John Murray, 1970).

Beazley, E. *Designed for Recreation* (London: Faber and Faber, 1969).

—. *Design and Detail of the Space Between Buildings* (London: Architectural Press).

—. *Designed to Live In* (London: George Allen and Unwin).

Bedall, J. L. *Colour in Hedges* (London: Faber and Faber).

—. *Hedges for Farm and Garden* (London: Faber and Faber).

Beranek, L. L. (ed.). *Noise Reduction* (New York: McGraw-Hill, 1967).

Best, R. H. and Coppock, J. T. *The Changing Use of Land in Britain* (London: Faber and Faber, 1962).

Best, R. H. and Rogers, A. W. *The Urban Countryside* (London: Faber and Faber, 1973).

Bowler, V. and Hillier, R. M. *The Encyclopaedia of Gardening* (London: Marshall Cavendish, 1975).

Brett, L. *Landscape in Distress* (London: Architectural Press).

British Trust for Conservation Volunteers. *Hedging* (1975).

Bugler, J. *Polluting Britain* (London: Penguin Books Ltd. 1972).

Bush, R. *The National Parks of the Country of Wales* (London: John Dent and Sons, 1973).

Caborn, J. M. *Shelter Belts and Windbreaks* (London: Faber and Faber, 1965).

—. *Shelter Belts and Microclimate* (Edinburgh: HMSO, 1957).

Chadwick, G. F. *The Park and the Town: Public Landscape in the Nineteenth and Twentieth Centuries* (London: Architectural Press, 1966).

—. *The Works of Sir Joseph Paxton* (London: Architectural Press, 1961).

Chermayeff, S. and Alexander, C. *Community and Privacy* (New York: Doubleday and Co. Inc., 1963).

Cherry, G. *The Evolution of British Town Planning* (London: Leonard Hill, 1974).

Clark, K. *Art into Landscape* (London: Penguin Books Ltd., 1949).

Clouston, B. (ed.). *Landscape Design with Plants* (London: Heinemann, 1977).

Colvin, B. *Trees for Town and Country* (London: L. Humphries, 1972).

—. *Land and Landscape* (London: John Murray, Council of Europe, 1970).

BIBLIOGRAPHY

Council of Europe. *Freshwater* (Nature and Environment Series) (Strasbourg: Council of Europe).

Countryside Commission. *Upland Management Experiment* (HMSO, 1974).

Crowe, S. *Tomorrow's Landscape* (Architectural Press).

—. *The Landscape of Power* (Architectural Press).

—. *The Landscape of Roads* (Architectural Press).

—. *Garden Design* (London: Country Life Ltd., 1958).

—. *Forestry in the Landscape* (London: HMSO, 1966).

Cullen, G. *Townscape* (London: Architectural Press, 1961).

Denman, D. R. and others. *Commons and Village Greens* (G.B.: Leach Hill Books, 1967).

Dep't. of Education & Science. *Playing Fields and Hard Surface Areas* (Building Bulletin 28. London: HMSO, 1966).

Dep't. of the Environment. *Housing Development Notes II. Landscape of New Housing* (London: HMSO, 1973–4).

Dep't. of the Environment/Property Services Agency. *Design with Trees* (London: HMSO, 1974).

Dep't of the Environment. *Report of the National Parks Policies Review Committee (Sandford Report)* (London: HMSO, 1974).

Devon Trust for Nature Conservation. *Wildlife Conservation and Woodland Management* (Supplement to Journal Devon Trust for Nat. Cons. 1970).

Duffey, E. and Morris, M. G. and others. *Grassland Ecology and Wildlife Management* (London: Chapman and Hall, 1974).

Dumbleton, M. J. and West, G. *Preliminary Zones of Information for Site Investigations in Britain* (T.R.R.L. Lahmaty Rest. 403 – Transport and Road Research Laboratory, Crowthorne UK, 1976).

Eckbo, G. *Urban Landscape Design* (U.S.A.: McGraw-Hill, 1964).

Edlin, H. L. *Guide to Tree Planting and Cultivation* (London: Collins, 1979).

—. *Know your Broadleaves* Forestry Commission Booklet No. 20 (London: HMSO, 1968).

Estall, R. C. and Buchanan R. D. *Industrial Activity and Economic Geography* (London: Hutchinson University Library, 1966).

Everard, J. E. *Fertilisers in the Establishment of Conifers in Wales* (London: HMSO, 1974).

Fairbrother, N. *New Lives New Landscapes* (London: Architectural Press, 1971).

—. *The Nature of Landscape Design* (London: Architectural Press, 1974).

FAO/UNESCO. *Irrigation, Drainage and Salinity* (London: Hutchinson, 1960, 1973).

Geddes, P. *Cities in Evolution* (London: Benn, 1969).

Geiger. *The Climate Near the Ground* (Boston: Harvard University Press, 1950).

Graham, M. *Soil and Sense* (London: Faber and Faber).

Grillo, P. J. *Form, Function and Design* (New York: Dover, 1960).

Grime, J. P. and Lloyd, P. S. *An Ecological Area of Grassland Plants* (London: Edward Arnold, 1973).

Hackett, B. *Landscape Development of Steep Slopes* (Newcastle: Oriel Press, University of Newcastle upon Tyne, 1972).

—. *Landscape Planning* (Newcastle: Oriel Press, 1971).

Hadfield, M. *The English Landscape Garden* (Aylesbury: Shire Publications, 1977).

Halprin, L. *Cities* (Boston: M.I.T. Press, 1972).

BIBLIOGRAPHY

Hartwright, T. U. *Planting Trees and Shrubs in Gravel Workings* (London: Sand and Gravel Association).

Haywood, S. M. *Quarries and the Landscape* (London: The British Quarry and Slag Federation, 1974).

Heal, H. G. *Conservation Aspects of Amenity Planting* (Unpublished paper, 1969).

Heap, D. *An Outline of Planning Law* (London: Sweet and Maxwell, 1973).

Hebblethwaite, R. L. *Landscape Maintenance* (CEGB, 1967).

Helliwell, D. R. *A Methodology for the Assessment of Priorities and Values in Nature Conservation.* Marlewood Research and Development Paper No. 28 (The Nature Conservancy Council, 1971).

Hillier and Son. *Hillier's Manual of Trees and Shrubs* (Newton Abbot: David and Charles, 1973).

Hills, E. S. (ed.). *Arid Lands: a Geographical Appraisal* (London: Eyre Methuen, 1966).

Hilton, K. J. *Lower Swansea Valley Project* (London: Longmans Green, 1967).

Holliman, J. *Consumer's Guide to the Protection of the Environment* (London: Pan Books, 1971).

Hookway, R. J. S. *The Management of Britain's Rural Land* (Countryside Commission, 1967).

Hoskins, W. G. *The Making of the English Landscape* (London: Pelican Books, 1970).

Howard, E. *Garden Cities of Towns.* (London: Faber and Faber, 1946).

Hudson, N. *Soil Conservation* (London: B. T. Batsford Ltd., 1971).

Hunt, J. D. and Willis, P. *The Genius of the Place* (London: Elen Books, 1975).

Hunt, P. (ed.). *The Shell Gardens Book* (London: Phoenix House in Association with George Rainbird, 1964).

Hutnik, R.J. and Davis, G. (eds.). *Ecology and Reclamation of Devastated Land* Vols. 1 & 2 (London: Gordon and Breach, 1973.

Hyams, E. *A History of Gardens and Gardening* (London: J. M. Dent and Sons, 1971).

—. *Capability Brown and Humphry Repton* (London: J. M. Dent and Sons, 1971).

Jellicoe, G. *Studies in Landscape Design* (Oxford: Oxford University Press, 1960, 1966, 1970).

Jellicoe, Sir G. and S. *The Landscape of Man* (London: Thames & Hudson, 1975).

Johnson, H. *The International Book of Trees* (London: Mitchell Beazley, 1973).

Jones, M. J. *Minerals and the Environment* (London: Hutchinson, 1975).

Keenleyside, C. B. *Farming, Landscape and Recreation* (Countryside Commission, 1971).

Kellet, J. R. *The Impact of Railways on Victorian Cities* (London: Routledge and Kegan Paul, 1969).

Klein, R. (ed.). *How to Build Walks, Walls and Patio Floors* (California: Lane Books, 1973).

Klingender, F. D. *Art and the Industrial Revolution* (London: Evelyn Adams and Mackay, 1968).

Lambert, J. *Adventure Playground* (London: Penguin Books Ltd., 1974).

Land Use Consultants. *Opencast Coal – A Tool for Landscape Renewal* (London: National Coal Board, 1967).

BIBLIOGRAPHY

Lovejoy, D. (ed.). *Land Use and Landscape Planning* (Aylesbury: Leonard Hill, 1973).

Lynch, K. *The Image of the City* (Boston: M.I.T. Press, 1960).

—. *Site Planning* (Boston: M.I.T. Press).

Mabey, R. *The Unofficial Countryside* (London: Collins, 1973).

Machin, T. T. and Worthington E. B. *Life in Lakes and Rivers* (London: Collins, 1951).

Macmillan, H. F. *Tropical Planting and Gardening* (London: Macmillan, 1972).

Maddox, J. *The Doomsday Syndrome* (London: Macmillan, 1972).

Manley, C. *Climate and the British Scene* (London: Collins, 1952).

McHarg, I. L. *Design with Nature* (New York: The Natural History Press, 1969).

Meteorological Office. *Tables of Surface Windspeed and Direction of the United Kingdom* (London, HMSO, 1968).

Ministry of Agriculture. *Shelter Belts for Farmland.* Leaflet No. 15 (Min. of Agriculture, Fisheries and Food, HMSO).

Mitchell, A. *A Field Guide to the Trees of Britain and Northern Europe* (London: Collins, 1974).

Morling, R. J. *Trees* (London: Estates Gazette Limited, 1963).

Munson, A. E. *Construction Design for Landscape Architects* (U.S.A.: McGraw-Hill, 1974).

Odum, E. P. *Ecology* (New York: Holt Rinehart and Winston, 1963).

Olgyay, V. *Design with Climate* (Oxford: Oxford University Press, 1963).

Opie, I. P. *Children's Gardens in Street and Playground* (London: Oxford University Press, 1970).

Oxenham, J. R. *Reclaiming Derelict Land* (London: Faber and Faber, 1966).

Papanek, V. *Design for the Real World. Making to Measure* (London: Thames and Hudson, 1972).

Paturi, F. *Nature, Mother of Invention* (London: Thames and Hudson, 1976).

Pfannschmidt, E. E. *Fountains and Springs* (London: Harrap, 1968).

Reader's Digest. *Encyclopaedia of Garden Plants and Flowers* (London: Reader's Digest Assoc., 1973).

Russell, E. J. *The World of the Soil* (London: Collins, 1957).

—. *Soil Conditions and Plant Growth* (London: Longmans Green, 1961).

Sharp, T. *English Panorama* (London: Architectural Press).

Simmonds, J. O. *Landscape Architecture* (Illiffe).

St. Bodfan Gruffydd, J. *Protecting Historic Landscapes* (Landscape Institute, 1977).

Steele, R. C. *Wildlife Conservation in Woodlands* (London: HMSO, 1972).

Straub, H. *A History of Civil Engineering* (London: Leonard Hill, 1952).

Tandy, C. R. V. (ed.). *Handbook of Urban Landscape* (London: Architectural Press, 1972).

—. *Landscape of Industry* (London: Leonard Hill Books, 1975).

Tansley, A. G. *Britain's Green Mantle* (London: George Allen and Unwin, 1968).

—. *Introduction to Plant Ecology* (London: George Allen and Unwin).

—. *The British Isles and Their Vegetation* (London: Cambridge University Press, 1939).

Temple, J. *Mining – An International Industry* (London: Benn, 1972).

Tunnard, C. *Gardens in the Modern Landscape* (London: Architectural Press, 1938).

Turrill, W. B. *British Plant Life* (London: Collins, 1962).

BIBLIOGRAPHY

Trueman, A. E. *Geology and Scenery* (London: Penguin Books, 1973).

Tschebotarioff, G. P. *Soil Mechanics, Foundations and Earth Structures* (New York: McGraw-Hill, 1973).

Wallwork, K. L. *Derelict Land* (Newton Abbot: David and Charles, 1974).

Warren, A. and Goldsmith, F. B. *Conservation in Practice* (Chichester: John Wiley and Sons, 1974).

Webster, C. C. *The Effects of Air Pollution on Plants and Soil* (London: Agricultural Research Council, 1967).

Weddle, A. E. *Techniques of Landscape Architecture* (London: Heinemann, 1967).

Weller, J. *Modern Agricultural and Rural Planning* (two vols.) (London: Architectural Press, 1967).

Westmacott, R. and Worthington, T. *New Agricultural Landscapes* (Countryside Commission, 1974).

Whitaker, B. and Brown, K. *Parks for People* (London: Sealey Service and Co., 1971).

White, L. L. *Aspects of Form* (London: Lund Humphries, 1968).

Williams-Ellis, C. *Britain and the Beast* (London: J. M. Dent and Sons Limited).

—. *England and the Octopus* (London).

Willis, P. (ed.). *Futor Hortensis* (Edinburgh: Elysium Press Limited, 1974).

Wood, A. B. *Terrace and Courtyard Gardens* (Collingridge).

Wraers, B. and Vipond, S. *Irrigation: Design and Practice* (London: B. T. Batsford, 1974).

Wye College, Kent. *Aspects of Landscape Ecology and Maintenance* (1972).

—. *Tree Growth in the Landscape* (1974).

Zion, R. L. *Trees for Architecture and Landscape* (New York: Van Nostrand Reinhold Company, 1968).

LIST OF SUBSCRIBERS

Ian Allan B.A., Ross Anderson, Martin Andrews, J. R. Anthony, G. V. Armitage, Askam Bryan College Library, Mrs. W. L. Banks, S. A. Barden, K. R. Bartram, Barbara Batts, Heather Blackett, Blakedown Gulf Limited, Rachel Berger, Jeffrey Bernard, Louis Edward Bond, Charles Bosanquet, Judith Brace, Veronica Brewer, Brian Clouston and Partners, British Architectural Library, British Association of Landscape Industries, Richard Brooker, Arthur Broom, Diana D. Broughton, Michael J. Brown, Susan Brown, Karen Buckley, Building Design Partnership, BWD (Landscapes) Limited, William J. Cairns, Crawford W. Campbell, Richard Avery Canovan, Robert Carson, Richard Cass, Cedric Linsey Partnership, Philip E. Chadwick, M. J. Chapman, Patrick J. Charlton, R. V. Cheeseborough, Douglas Childs, Hugh Clamp, John Clark, Norman Clark, Ralph O. Cobham, Timothy Cochrane, Geoffrey A. Collens, Colvin and Moggridge, Julian Cooper, Allan Correy, Countryside Commission for Scotland, Robert Critchley, Dame Sylvia Crowe, Crowther of Chigwell, J. A. Cunning, Ivor Cunningham, Anne Dalley, J. A. Darbyshire, Graham Darrah, Anna H. Davis, Patrick Davis, Graham Davy, Dr. M. P. Denne, Rt. Hon. Viscount Devonport, Pashaura Dhillon, I. R. Dillen, Alan Duckworth, Gregory Dunstan, David John Dutton, James P. Eardley, Peter M. Emberson, Penny Evans, Exbury Gardens Limited, C. E. Fair, Geoffrey Farnell, V. A. Fishleigh, John A. Ford, Mrs. Margaret A. Forster, Robert H. Foster, R. Frank Marshall for Milner White and Partners, Frosts Landscape Construction Limited, Miss Marjorie Fryer, T. D. V. Gale, Anne Valerie Garton (Garden Designer), Sir Frederick Gibberd, Andrew G. Gilg, Christine I. Grant, S. C. Green, Roger Greenwood, Harlene B. Griffiths and Roger B. L. Griffiths, Roger H. Griffiths, A. B. Grove, R. Gulati, Professor Brian Hackett, Nicholas W. Hall, Alan Hart, S. D. Hart, J. Harte, Miss Kate Hawkins, J. R. Hayes and Sons, Mrs. Sheila Haywood, Michael R. Hodges, Peter Hodgson, James Hodson, Ann-Sofi Hogborg, Robert Holden, Kathryne Holland, John Holliday, Horticultural Trades Association, Gordon Howe, Robert Huddleston, Hugh Watson Partnership, John Hulton, Edward Hutchinson, Sheila Jackman, David Jacques, Preben Jakobsen, Robert Johnston, Gordon Jones, Ronald and Sheila Jones, Colin and Susan Jubb, Terence Kearley, G. S. Kemp, Elizabeth A. Kendrick, K. Knowles, Fossa Knut, Leo Kramer, Peter Lancaster, Ian C. Laurie, Learning Resources, Brighton Polytechnic, David Lee, Maurice Lee, David G. Lever, Sydney Litherland, Georgina Livingston, John E. Lodge, D. M. Longbottom, J. M. Lonsdale, P. J. Lyons, I. D. M. MacGregor, Martin Madders, Susan Panter Marshall, John M. McCauley, John Medhurst, Medway and Maidstone College of Technology Library, Stuart L. Mellor, J. Meredith, E. J. M. Miller, Gordon J. L. Molellan, Victoria R. Molyneux, Geraldine C. Moon, John R. Morgan, Susan J. Mort, Diarmuid Mulrenan, Ian Murdock, Keith Murray, National Capital Development Commission, John and Ann Nevett, Barry Newland, Andrew Nichols, North Tyneside,

LIST OF SUBSCRIBERS

Alex Novell, H. Oakman, Michael Ogden, Ove Fossa, Christopher Palmer, A. Dugard Pasley, Robert Paton, Kevin Patrick, Gordon Patterson, Maurice E. Pickering, Madeleine Pickthorne, Wendy Powell, David E. Randall, Reading University Library, Reavell and Cahill, Redditch Development Corporation, Stuart M. Reid, Simon Rendel, Lyndon J. Rickards, Ridley Nickolls Partnership, W. Ross, Sir Gordon Russell, Jeremy William Sacha, Douglas Sampson, Joe Samworth, Harold Sanders, Scottish Development Agency, Scottish Special Housing Association, Frank Shaw, D. M. Singleton, Jenefer Slater, Alan W. Smith, Anthony Smith, Benjamin J. W. Smith, Douglas H. Smith and St. John P. Stimson, M. C. Smith, Neil Smith, Brian and Susan Snell, Michael C. Spickett, Strathclyde Regional Council, Christopher H. Stratton, Peter Styles, David Summersgill, Daniel Sutherland, Cliff Tandy, Gillian Teasdale, Telford Development Corporation, The Lady Evershed, The Library, Leeds Polytechnic, Catherine E. Thomas, Dewi Wynne Thomas, Wyn Thomas, John H. W. Thompson, Marian R. Thompson, Steven Thompson, Mark Turnball, University of Edinburgh Department of Architecture, University of York Institute of Advanced Architectural Studies, James Usher, Paul Vining, Ian Walker, G. B. Walkiden, Richard Webb, Stephen Wells, Ian White, Robert Whitelegg, D. Wilbie-Chalk, William Gillespie and Partners, Miss S. Williams, Dr. Graham Wills, Norman H. Wilson, Susan R. Wilson, Gordon Wither, Wyn Thomas and Partners, Colin Mallow Young, Peter Youngman, Professor Yuen-Chen Yu.

INDEX

INDEX

INDEX

INDEX

INDEX